1989:

WHAT HAPPENS WHEN A KILLER RETURNS FOR REVENGE

JAMES SMITH

Charleston, SC
www.PalmettoPublishing.com

1989

First Edition

Paperback ISBN: 9781649907035
eBook ISBN: 9781649906069
Hardcover ISBN: 9781649901422

DEDICATION

TO MY WIFE LYNNETTA, THANK you for your love, support, and encouraging words throughout this process, it means the world to me. To my daughters, Nicole and Blythe, thank you for being daddy's motivation. Thank you to all my family and friends who supported me through this process.

CHAPTER 1

As NICOLE JONES OPENED the door, the smell of fresh lilies greeted her. She was instantly taken back to her childhood in Blinton, Georgia. She could feel the grass in between her toes and the breeze blowing against her as she ran through the fields, as her father chased her. It was part of their daily routine. Every day at 6 o'clock, before it got dark, they would go outside and play, the only requirement being she needed to finish her homework first. She always did! She spent every free moment she had from the time she got the assignment working on them. She made sure she was finished before he got home so they could play together.

Her favorite activity was playing chase with her father; she could hear his voice breaking with laughter: "You can't catch me!" While he was a lot faster than her, somehow, she always managed to catch him. After every game, before heading into the house, they would lay in the field, looking up at the stars talking about their day and the future. Their discussion often centered on life and how she should never let anyone stop her from achieving her goals. She treasured those moments because it was time, he made for her every day, time they got to spend alone and just have fun together, no distractions. At that moment she could feel a tear running down her cheek.

As she wiped away the tears, she could hear "A Change is Gonna Come" by Sam Cooke in the background. Hearing this brought a smile to her face as her father was a big Sam Cooke fan and would often sing his songs on the porch after dinner. She would often attempt to sneak out and watch him, but he always managed to see her. Instead of telling her to get ready for bed, he would wave her over and they would sing together, looking out into the night. She thought her father had the best voice in the world. She would later learn that her father first got his passion for singing in the choir as a child and it was where he learned to perfect his voice.

These memories brought her a great sense of joy and pain. She was happy she had those memories, but sad and angry because that was all she had of her father. He was taken from her, something that still drove her to this day. She refused to let his memory be in vain, so she worked hard to make sure she followed his advice. She set goals and worked like hell to make sure she made them a reality. She dedicated herself to being successful and reaching the goals she had set in order to honor his memory. She was now a senior partner at Jones, Jones, & Keyes. However, the road to get to this point was hard and one with many sacrifices.

She spent countless hours studying in school, making sure she was as prepared as possible. She eschewed parties, friends, and family to some extent to make sure she didn't fail. She knew she needed to make time for other people and activities, but she couldn't bring herself to do it. Anytime the thought crossed her mind, she felt as if she was not only cheating herself but all those people who had helped motivate her as well, she wasn't just doing this for herself, she was doing it for them as well. So, she kept her head down and studied. Her hard work paid off, not only was she Valedictorian in College, but in law school as well.

After graduating law school and passing the Bar, she immediately began working as a public defender in the District Attorney's office. She had other offers that provided her with more prestige and money, however she felt that working as a public defender would help in her in the long run. Additionally, Nicole was doing something she enjoyed, helping those who would otherwise be swallowed by the system. The District Attorneys, at both the local and state level, tried to get her to switch over and become a prosecutor not just because they were tired of losing cases to her, but because they saw how talented she was. However, this was not the path she wanted to take. She felt a calling to helping those less fortunate. She knew first-hand the consequences of a loved one being failed by the system.

However, there reached a point when Nicole realized she was not going to be able to accomplish all that she wanted unless she took a different path. This was a difficult decision for her to make; one that was met with skepticism. She was leaving something she loved doing, to go do something she despised. She left to join Wallace & Bennet, the largest law firm in the Southeast, which dealt mainly in corporate law, a far cry from what she loved about law and what made her become a lawyer in the first place. But it was something she knew she had to do in order to accomplish all the goals she had set for herself.

In order to get her own firm dedicated to helping those less fortunate, she realized she needed the money to finance her goal. To serve as a reminder and to hold herself accountable, she drew up a contract she signed outlining her plan and goals and identifying at what point she was to leave to start her own firm, which she had framed and placed on her desk so she would not lose sight of the bigger picture.

The day Nicole accepted the position she told herself this was temporary. She was going to work harder and longer than anyone in the firm. She would dedicate all her time and efforts into making her dream come true. This sacrifice extended to her personal life as well. She lost friends, boyfriends, and the relationship with most of her family became strained, as she devoted all her efforts into achieving her goals. The first couple of years she could count on one hand the nights where she got more than three hours of sleep. She worked twice as hard as everyone else. The managing partners appreciated this hard work and saw it as a major reason for their growth. They couldn't understand her dedication to the firm, but they loved the results. However, in her mind this wasn't dedication to the firm, this was dedication to her reaching her goals.

At that moment, Nicole snapped out of her dream and began to smile as she saw the lilies in front of her with a card and gifts beside them. She slowly opened the card and read the message:

Baby the day we met I never expected that I met the person who I would grow to call my best friend. You are truly an amazing woman and I am lucky to have you in my life. I ask myself everyday how did I get so lucky to have met you. Every day with you is day that feels like I am living a dream, because I have you. I know how important today was for you and everything that you put into making it happen. You deserve this. This is just a little token of how much I love and appreciate you.

As she looked at the lilies, she couldn't help but ask herself with a smile on her face: "Did he buy every lily in town?"

As she read the note a second time, she saw a P.S at the bottom that said: Follow the petals. Just then she looked down and saw the lily petals on the floor. Before she could follow the petals, she had to open her gift. The first thing she noticed was a Butani diamond chandelier necklace with matching earrings. She couldn't contain the excitement as she looked at the pieces, holding them up to her face in the mirror, admiring how beautiful they were. As she looked down in the box, she saw a black piece of clothing.

She pulled it out only to realize it was a black Christian Dior evening gown, with a pair of silver Louboutin heels. She couldn't believe it, but she thought, where am I going to wear this. This is when she noticed an envelope inside the box, once she opened it, she couldn't believe what was inside. Inside were two tickets to New York City and two tickets to see *Hamilton*. She was ecstatic; she had wanted to see the play, but didn't think she would get a chance. She couldn't believe he was able to get tickets.

After standing there in astonishment for a few minutes, she decided she had to see what else the night had in store, so she decided to follow the petals. They lead her to the bathroom door, were a note was attached saying: Open the door and take a moment to relax, you deserve it. No phones are allowed, place them on the table outside the door. She did what she was instructed to, before opening the door. Once she opened the door, the impossible happened, the night got even better. Inside the bathroom there were candles lit, with roses leading to the tub, a bottle of 2009 Sequoia Grove Cambium, and chocolate-covered fruit, which had already been filled with bubbles and lily petals. She also found the source of the music, as she heard Sam Cooke continue to play.

As Nicole soaked in the tub, she everything she had accomplished hit her. She could feel herself beginning to cry. She was so overcome with emotion she could not contain herself. After a lifetime of working to get to this point, she had finally reached one of her goals. She could picture her dad working long hours to provide for his family, then her mom doing whatever she had to, to make sure she had everything she needed as kid, once after her father's death. The sacrifices and help the rest of her family made and gave to help her. She was truly blessed and the best example of the saying "it takes a village to raise a child." She couldn't have made it to this point without their help. But she was not finished yet, there were still something she had to finish before she could truly move forward and to honor her father's memory.

After sitting in the tub for what seemed like a few minutes, but was in reality was an hour, she decided it was time to get out and go see her husband. As she grabbed the towel to dry off, she noticed underneath towel was a black Annushka Guipure and lace chemise, with a matching lace kimono. Underneath it was a note saying "I picked up myself a little something, for being such an awesome husband. I figured you wouldn't mind." This made her laugh and reminded her of one of the many reasons she loved him: his sense of humor. After getting dressed, she walked outside the bathroom and saw a trail of petals leading up the stairs. Remembering her directions from earlier she followed them.

As she walked up the stairs her anticipation grew, she wanted to see her husband talk about everything that happened today, how happy she was, how proud her father would be of her, and more importantly how much she loved him. As she approached the door, she could hear Anita Baker playing in the background and she could smell Crème Brulee French toast, two of her favorites.

As she opened the door to the bedroom, she saw her husband lying in bed. She thought to herself; just like him to fall sleep. As she started walking closer to the bed, she started to remove her robe and thinking about how magical the night had been so far and how good it would feel to be wrapped in her husband's arms. But as she got closer to the bed, she realized something was wrong. She rushed to the bed and frantically began saying, "Marcus, Marcus? Wake up, honey!"

But he didn't move or speak, and she knew something was wrong. She began to get nervous and panicked. She was screaming for him to wake up, as she shook him frantically now. She then realized he was gone; she couldn't move or speak. She just stood there; she didn't even notice the police had arrived.

"Step away from the body and put your hands up!"

All she could do is stand there, paralyzed in the moment. The officers repeated themselves: "Freeze! Put your hands up! Step away from the body!" Still she didn't move, she couldn't take her eyes off of her husband, lying there lifeless. She had slipped into shock; she couldn't process what was going on. Even as the officers placed their hands on her, pushing her against the wall as they placed handcuffs on her, as they read her Miranda Rights. As they led her down the stairs, she knew they were talking to her, but she couldn't make out what they were saying, everything was in a blur.

Walking out the front door of their home, all she could see was her husband lying there dead. She didn't notice the multiple police cars that had arrived, as well as the crowd that had begun to form. Those in the crowd whispered and looked at each other in shock as they questioned each other as to what just happened, no one knew. The last they saw of her, she was being put into the back of a patrol car, guilty of something they thought, but not knowing what it exactly was.

As she was being placed in the car, she overheard the officers telling another officer they had gotten an anonymous call about a fight at this address and when they got here, they found her standing over the body. Hearing that caused her sadness turn to anger, as she realized she was set up.

CHAPTER 2

SERGEANT MIKE ALLEN HAD heard the call come in over the radio and had no idea what to expect or what happened to people he considered family. Sergeant Allen had been on the force twenty years and he loved every day of it, except for today. Driving up to the home, all he could do was think the worst. He heard the call come in over the radio; "Officer's respond to 122 Grace Lane in response to reports of possible domestic disturbance." He knew the address; in fact, he had spent many days there with his partner and his wife. He tried calling them both, but had gotten no answer, and that only made his anxiety grow.

Sgt. Allen and Detective Jones had been partners for the past seven years. During that time, they had been there for the most important and also the saddest part of each other's lives. Sgt. Allen had been there the night Marcus met his wife, Nicole. He remembered thinking how much he didn't like her in the beginning, but over time he grew to see how truly special she was; now she was more of a sister to him than his own sisters. He was there when they got married and they were there for the birth of both his children. They were also there for him when his family died tragically in a house fire. A tragedy for which he blamed himself.

They were supposed to be out of town on vacation, but they delayed it a day, because he had received a phone call from an informant about an ongoing case. When he left, he didn't realize that would be the last time he would see his family alive. He could picture his wife and two kids sitting on the couch as he walked out the door, telling them he loved them all, as he walked out the door. They were not upset, because they knew how important they were to him, because he usually put them ahead of the job. So anytime there was an emergency they understood. His wife had said they could leave tomorrow. However, they didn't know it at the time, tomorrow would be too late.

The cause of the fire was an electrical short in the basement. Mike's family was asleep when the fire started; they never had a chance. What was left of their bodies was found in the master bedroom. It looked like they were all in bed together. The months after their death were the hardest time of his life. Every day was a struggle and there wasn't a day that went by where he didn't think about killing himself. But through it all, Marcus and Nicole were there to help him get through it. He did not know what he did to deserve friends like them, because he was a miserable SOB to be around during that time. They were there for him every day, even those days he didn't want them to be.

If it wasn't for their constant love and support, he wouldn't be here today. In fact, Nicole had come over one day and literally saved his life. He was about to kill himself; he had his service pistol in his hand, pressed against his head, saying a prayer before he pulled the trigger. However, before he finished the prayer, Nicole walked in and saw him. She called his name and he swore it sounded like his wife. Mike turned around and saw her. The look in her eyes, made him realize that he that he had people in his life who cared about him and he didn't want to let them down. They both sat and talked for hours that day, not about what he was about to do, but about life and how much his family would want him to be strong. In fact, they never mentioned it again and she never told Marcus about it. It was a secret between family.

As he stopped his car, he saw the large crowd that had gathered out front, as well as the police cars and ambulance. His heart almost stopped in that instant, he had no idea what he was about to see, so he began to prepare himself for the worst. Mike pushed his way through the crowd, not acknowledging a neighbor who called out his name. He was on a mission. As he approached the door, he was stopped by Officer McCarthy, who said, "I am sorry sir, but I am going to need you to step outside, you are not allowed to be in here."

In that moment, Sergeant Allen didn't have time to deal with this, so he pushed the officer out of the way and made his way into the home and up the stairs. As he made his way up the stairs, he recognized a familiar flash ahead and his heart sank. As he approached the door, nothing could prepare him for what he was about to see. There was his partner lying in bed, lifeless. It took every ounce of restraint he had not to throw everyone out of the room and go wake up his partner. He couldn't be dead; they had to have messed something up. However, he knew in his heart that he was gone. In that instant he heard a familiar voice calling him to the hallway, but he didn't move, he couldn't leave his friend there like that.

He then turned around and recognized a familiar face, Detective Bryan Johnson, affectionally known as Hercules or Herc for short. Hercules was the nickname he was given when he first joined the force. He was 6'6, a solid 280, and everyone suspected he was as strong as Hercules. Sgt. Allen was no small man himself; he was 6'2 and 220 lbs, however he paled in comparison.

"What happened? Where is Nicole?" were the first questions he could ask.

"We do not know yet, we are still trying to figure it out. Someone made a phone call saying they heard screams coming from inside the house. The first two officers on the scene found the door open, they searched the house and found a female suspect beside the bed, who they then took into custody. It was Nicole." Sensing what Sgt. Allen was about to say, he raised his hand and stated, "I know it has already been taken care of, I made a phone call and told them to not treat her like a suspect, instead like one of our own. She is being taken to the station right now."

"I don't understand how anyone could do something like this. Marcus never hurt anyone or had a bad word to say about anyone," stated a still visibly-shaken Sgt. Allen.

"I know that is why we will find out who did this. They killed one of ours, so this bastard better enjoy tonight, because it will be his last night of peace. We will find him!" declared Detective Hercules.

"I need to go back in and see his body one last time."

"That isn't a good idea; let forensics do what they need to do. Go be with Nicole!"

"I will but first I need to do this!"

Realizing there was no way he was going to be able to stop him from going in, Detective Hercules relented and let him go back in. Once inside, Sgt. Allen went into detective mode; he started looking around for clues, careful not to disturb the crime scene and mess anything up. The only thought in his head was he had to make this right, not only for his partner, but for his "sister" as well. As he got closer to his friend's body, Mike felt his body get weak and had to catch himself for a second. But he knew had to do it. As he approached the body, he couldn't help but think; "why Marcus!"

As he approached the body, he couldn't stop thinking how it looked like Marcus was sleeping. He half expected him to wake up and say what the hell are you all doing in my home. But he realized that was only just a dream and it wasn't to be. As he looked over his friend's body, he didn't see anything that stood out, initially. However, that changed as he lifted the cover off his friend's body, he saw something that immediately sent a chill down his body. There lying on his friend's stomach was piece of paper with a penny on top of it. He hadn't seen this in over twenty years and the fact he was seeing it now was a big a shock as when he saw it the first time.

As he reached down to grab the paper, he could hear the forensic tech in the background asking what he was doing. He didn't care he had to see what the note said, he had to confirm if what he was seeing was real. As he opened the paper, there it was written in plain English:

A Penny For Your Thoughts: What Happens to A Man Who Awakens a Ghost?

He couldn't help but read it over and over it again, hoping that it would change the words on the paper somehow. As he stood there paralyzed in the moment, unable to speak, and not even aware of his surroundings at this point, a hand was placed on his shoulder that instantly caused him to flinch and reach for his service weapon.

"Calm down, Sergeant Allen, what the fuck is wrong with you," exclaimed an exasperated Detective Johnson.

Realizing where he was and what he had done, he couldn't do anything except leave the room. He had to get out the house and get some air; he felt as if he was about to pass out. As he walked out the bedroom door, down the hall, down the stairs, and out the back door all he could think was what is going on. Not only was his friend murdered, but the killer was a ghost, long forgotten. As he stood in the backyard all he could think of Nicole and how he was going to have to explain this to her.

As he stood there, he heard footsteps and as he turned around, he saw Detective Johnson walking up to him. "I am sorry man, I have no excuse for what happened upstairs," he said to the Detective as he approached him.

"What the fuck, man!"

At this point Sgt. Allen realized he had to explain everything to his fellow officer. As he looked up at him, he said "I apologize again and I can explain. Do you remember the Penny Murder?"

"I remember reading about it, but it was way before my time. What does that have to do with what happened upstairs, he is dead?" a confused Detective Johnson asked.

"Yes, he is, this is why what I saw upstairs is all the more confusing and upsetting. On Marcus's body was a penny and note."

"Ok, so you found a penny and note. The Penny could have just been a coincidence and the original Penny Murderer didn't leave notes."

"Actually, he did; the note was a detail we left out of the original murders, because we didn't want to release all of the information to the public. He would always start the note out with phrase "A Penny For Your Thoughts," which was always followed up with another statement. At this point he realized he still had the note in his hand. This is when he handed it to Detective Johnson and said, "Just like this!"

As Detective Johnson looked at the note, he was confused. "If the original suspect is dead and no one knew about the note, then how did both end up on Marcus?"

"I don't know, but I am going to find out, because someone is trying to mess with us. That is the only explanation, because the person who was responsible for the original murders is dead. Whoever did this has access to information that was only known by a few individuals and a lot of them are dead or physically unable to do this."

They both stood there in the dark for a few more moments. They finally realized it was time to go back inside. As they did, they did so in silence, neither one knowing what to say. As they walked back inside and back into the bedroom, they saw the coroner, Adam Anderson. He had been the coroner for the past five years and was quite good at his job. He had to be, because if not he would not have lasted five minutes. He was quite abrasive and what some people would describe as socially awkward. In fact, the running joke was that if he wasn't a coroner, then he would have been a serial killer.

"So, what can you tell us right now," asked Sgt. Allen.

"Not much right now, but looking at his body and basing it off body temperature and the lack of rigor mortis, I put the time of death around 5 p.m. That is all I can say right now. There is no obvious sign of struggle or cause of death.I will have to wait to get the toxicology report and do further examination before I can give you a definitive time of death."

At this point Sgt. Allen realized he had gotten as much information as he could and know it was time to go find his friend, comfort her, and tell her everything he knew so far. Before he walked out the door, he looked at both Adam and Herc and told them to keep him updated on any changes.

As he walked out the door into all of the lights and people, he looked back one last time at his friends' home and realized things would never be the same.

CHAPTER 3

"The moment I met you was the greatest day of my life. Every day with you since that day has been better than the last. You continue to amaze me each and every day. I would pinch myself to see if this real or a dream, but I am afraid I would wake up to find it was all a dream. Your love has been the greatest gift I have ever received. I treasure you and everything you do. If God would have asked me to describe what my perfect woman was, I could not have come close to describing you. I guess it's a good thing he didn't ask me, because I would have messed it up," words spoken to her by her husband on their wedding day.

At that very moment flashes of her husband's lifeless body came into her head, interrupting the memory of the best day of her life. She could still see everything from that moment as if she was still in the room. She could feel her throat close and it was difficult to speak; her airway began to constrict as she struggled to breathe. It felt as if her heart was going to beat out of her chest as her heart rate increased to a level she could only surmise was to the level of someone before they had a heart attack. She tried to move, but her body refused to cooperate with her mind. She was paralyzed with sorrow, anger, and guilt. She didn't know what to do to overcome it. She felt her heart sink, as she felt truly alone for the first time, since her father was murdered.

She felt herself falling into a depression similar to the one she fell into when she lost her father. She could feel tears forming in her eyes as the pain began to overwhelm her. But before she could reach that dark place, she felt a calming presence come over her, returning her voice, ability to breathe, and her ability to move again. Her heart rate slowed to a normal level. She was sure it was her father taking care of her, as he had done so often in the past. What was once sorrow, was now replaced by anger and the promise that the person responsible for his death would be punished.

As the patrol car pulled into the station, she began thinking this is what this feels like. Being a lawyer and the wife of a cop, she had heard stories of the experience from both sides, but in that moment, she realized it was as bad as her clients had described it to her. Her emotions ranged from anger to frustration, sadness, and embarrassment. She was having a hard time processing her emotions but pulling up to the 21st precinct only made things worse. This had been her husband's second home and the fact that she would be walking through the doors in handcuffs was a moment she was not ready for.

"Ma'am, I need for you to get out of the car," the young officer said to her. "Ma'am, I need for you to get out of the car," he repeated a second time after Nicole failed to move after his first set of orders. Looking up at the doors to the precinct, she could feel the tears welling up in her eyes, but she told herself you will not walk into this building and let them see you crying. She knew most of the people in the building, some who would be concerned for her, but most would be happy to see her in cuffs. Her tenaciousness as lawyer had not won her many friends within the department. It was these people whom she didn't want to give the satisfaction of seeing her at her weakest, most vulnerable state.

Walking into the precinct, she kept her head and eyes to the front. She didn't look anywhere but at what was directly in front of her. She could hear the whispers in the background, but she refused to acknowledge them or let them know they affected her.

"It is about time she got arrested," whispered one officer.

"Do you know why she got arrested," said another officer.

"I don't care why! She and her uppity, anti-police rhetoric has made it harder for us to do our job."

Nicole was the farthest from anti-police; she was married to a cop, for God's sake. He was just upset because of her efforts to hold officers accountable when they messed up. Long ago were the days where officers could take shortcuts or live with the belief they were above the law. She loved the police and was grateful for everything they did for the community. However, she didn't believe that entitled them to a free pass to do what they pleased in the name of justice.

"Nicole, what happened? Are you ok?" asked Detective Mary Wagner, who was affectionally referred to as Wags. Wags was one of the few officers she considered a friend in the precinct. People didn't understand how they could be friends, they both came from different walks of life and believed in different things. However, their friendship was built on mutual respect and the fact they could learn from each other. They could have a strong discussion about something and the next minute they are going to lunch, laughing with each other. If they could make it past their first argument, there was no argument that could tear their friendship apart.

The first time they met, Wags was a witness for the prosecution and Nicole was the attorney for the defense. They engaged in what was one of the most contentious exchanges between a lawyer and a witness most people in that courtroom had ever seen. However, in a moment that would have made most people enemies, it brought about mutual respect between the two. They both only wanted to see justice served and to both of them that meant seeing the person responsible for committing the crime was convicted.

"You bastards!" Wags shouted at the officers as she covered Nicole in her jacket. It was in that moment she realized she still had on the lingerie her husband had bought her. She was so out of it, she forgot what she had on. In that moment, she became enraged. They could have at least given me a jacket, I bet they all got a kick out of seeing me dressed like this, she thought. She did not let her anger show as she continued to walk stoically. While she was grateful for the jacket, she couldn't look at Wags, she could only manage to say thank you, barely above a whisper. She felt embarrassed in that moment. She knew Wags would understand. After being given the jacket by Wats she was led into booking. As the officer removed the handcuffs, she felt a sigh of relief as she could move her arms. The moment was short-lived, as the officer began the booking process.

"Name!.................Name!" repeated officer Nathan Daniels, who oversaw booking her.

"You know my name, you short, pudgy-faced bastard!" she thought to herself. But she realized this was part of the process/game she would have to put up with tonight or until at least someone realized what the hell was going on. "Nicole Tamara Jones, born on January 31, 1979. I am 5'9, weight 185," as she began to answer the other questions before he could ask.

"Don't be a smart ass!" was the officer's response. Come on, follow me time to take your glamor shots. As she stepped up to take her mug shots, she thought to herself, "these will end up on the internet and be the first thing shown on the morning news." She could already picture the headline "Prominent local attorney murders her husband in cold blood." As she stood there, she didn't care what she looked like. She was a beautiful woman by anyone's standards, but not at this moment. She looked like she had been hit with the ugly stick in that moment. But her looks were the furthest thing from her mind.

After he was finished taking the mug shots, he led her over to the cage where she was instructed to remove all personal items from her person. She thought I don't have anything of value on me. However, at that moment as she rubbed her hands together, she realized that wasn't entirely true. She had on her wedding ring. In that very moment, she could picture her husband at their annual Christmas party attempting to sing the Temptation's version of "Silent Night." Attempting, but failing horribly to hit all the notes, just the way the Temptation's did.

"Ma'am, you do not have to give me that. You can keep it." The officer said through the cage. She didn't recognize the officer but was great full for his act of kindness. As she was being led to the fingerprinting area, she heard a familiar voice.

"Where is she! Where is Nicole? Nicole! Nicole! Someone better tell me where she is or there will be hell to pay!"

It was her partner Alan Keyes. Where she was the quiet type, Alan was the exact opposite. To those who didn't know him, he was loud, abrasive, or simply put, an ass. But the man she knew was the exact opposite. He was one of the kindest and most loyal people you could ever meet. Was he loud, yes, but he was also a loving family man. She came to realize over time, most the time he was loud, it was strategic. Unlike her, he didn't grow up wanting to be a lawyer. He had dreams of playing in the NFL. He was pretty good; he was an All American in high school and he made the All-American team as a freshman quarterback at the University of Georgia. However, the summer after his freshman year he was involved in a horrible car accident.

He was hit one night after a party by a drunk driver and that ended his hopes of playing in the NFL. However, he didn't look back on that night with anger or regret; he instead saw it as a blessing. She couldn't understand his optimism, but she respected that about him. It was after the trial for the person who hit him that his dream of becoming a lawyer was born. The trial was a train wreck and the person who hit him was acquitted. He didn't blame the person who hit him or they lawyer, they took advantage of the system and made it work to their advantage.

"Someone tell that lunatic to shut the hell up!" shouted detective Umpa Lumpa.

Just as he said that Alan walked through the door and his demeanor changed instantly. Gone was the abrasive, smart ass officer. He was replaced by someone who appeared to be afraid of his own shadow.

"You....... you..........you..........ca.......nt......... be......hee...heee.......here!" he stammered.

What Alan did next was the reason some people called him an ass. Alan walked to the officer and bent over and said, "I am sorry from up here, it sounded like you were telling me what I can and cannot do. I know that can't be true, so I had to come down here to make sure what I heard was correct. Alan was 6'6 and all muscle, and while his football career had ended, he still kept himself in tremendous shape.

"How can I help you?" said the terrified officer now.

"Me, you can't help me! But you can help yourself! You have my client here in your custody. So, what you are going to do is release her to me, before I have you arrested, and some prisoner takes advantage of your height. Are you going to just stand there with your mouth open, like you are special or are you going to talk?" Alan said as only he could.

Just then the officer was granted a lifeline as Captain Lucas Brown walked in. "Officer Daniels, release her and go to my office and wait for me!" the Captain told his now-petrified officer. Captain Brown was a friend to both

Nicole and Marcus. He was considered a fast-tracker, as he had made Captain faster than anyone had ever done so in the state. Both Nicole and her husband respected him and thought he was a good cop who was stuck in a tough position. He was placed in the toughest precinct over people who had a hard time accepting the fact he was in charge. However, he didn't let any of that stop him, as he made the necessary changes to improve his precinct and gain the respect of the people under him.

"I am sorry Nicole! I got here as fast as I could. Alan, still the same wonderful person as always," said the Captain to his two friends.

"Well when your officers decide they want to take out personal vendettas and not follow common sense, then this is the me you get."

"Thank you both!" was the only words she could muster out as she felt herself go dark. The events of the day had finally caught up to her. When she awoke, she was in the back of Alan's car with her head on the lap of his wife, Patricia.

"What happened?" she asked still groggy.

"You fainted." She heard Alan say from the front. "We are taking you to the hospital just to make sure you are ok and then tomorrow I am going to finish my discussion with the Brown."

"I don't need to go to the hospital, I just need to lay down and leave the officer's alone," was her response.

"No, you are going to the hospital. We are going to make sure you are okay," he responded.

"No, I do not want to or need to go, I just need to lay down."

Just as he was about to respond, he felt his wife's hand touch his shoulder. He knew what that meant. "Fine, but you are coming back to our place. There will be no arguments on the subject, because if you do, I will take you to the hospital." She didn't have the energy to respond and she also knew that if she did, he was crazy enough that he would take her to the hospital.

The Keyes lived in Whispering Oaks, the nicest and most expensive area in the city. But when the husband is a partner in one of the largest firms in the southeast and his wife is a world-famous neurosurgeon, you can afford to live wherever you like. Their home may not have been the biggest, but it was on the hill overlooking all the other homes. This is why they picked the house, they could have picked a bigger one, but they wanted that one because it sent a message. They knew most of the people didn't want them to move there, because they didn't match the make-up of the community. They remember the stares and the whispers when they were house hunting, those only made them more interested and determined to buy a home in the area. However, over time those ill feelings on both sides, disappeared.

Walking through the door of the Keyes' house gave her a sort of comfort she needed at this moment. It was good to be with people she cared for and who cared for her.

"This is your room. Everything you need is here and in the bathroom. If you need anything let me know." Alan said.

"She knows, now get out so she can get some rest." Patricia said. While Alan may have run things outside of his house, he knew who ran things at home. Patricia and Alan were high school sweethearts who have been inseparable since the day they met in the 9th grade. She was the main reason he was able to get past the pain of losing any chance he had of playing professionally. She was the one who helped him see he could do so much more with his life instead of just throwing a football, so in the greater scheme, while this was a setback, it was more so a door opening showing him how much greater he could be. He looked at her and everything she had been through and saw the strongest woman he had ever met before in his life.

"I love him, but why does he always like to try to play like he is someone's overprotective daddy." Patricia said.

"I don't know why, but I thought Officer White was going to break down crying when he saw him," Nicole said.

They both started laughing at the picture of Alan, bent over talking to the officer and how it looked like he was about to cry. At that moment, Nicole started crying. "What am I supposed to do, I don't know what I will do without him," she said as tears poured down her face.

"I can only imagine the pain you are going through right now. But you know me and Alan are here for you. Whatever you need, you know we got you. You are family and we will help you get through this," Patricia said as she also began to cry.

"I know you will, thank you."

"I need for you to try to get some rest. You have been through a lot and tomorrow will be another long day, so you need to get some rest or else you will not make it," her friend told her.

As Patricia got up, she gave her friend a hug and told her good night. As the door closed, the reality of the situation hit her once again. Being in the room alone, all she could do was look up at the ceiling and try to picture how her life would be now, but she never could, because she kept flashing back to how her life use to be. All she could see was her husband's smiling face. She spent most of the night awake, unable to sleep.

CHAPTER 4

As SERGEANT ALLEN MADE his way back to the station, he could not do anything but sit in his vehicle and try to come to grips with what he had seen. The Penny Murderer was responsible for 12 deaths in the 80s and 90s. Initially, there was no known connection or motive behind the killings. The only thing that tied them together was the note. The note would always start off "Penny For Your Thoughts:" and would be followed by mysterious statement. The victims were both men and women, multiple different ethnicities, and ranged in age from 26 to 56.

It was learned that Samuel Johnson, law school student, was connected to three of the victims; Maureen Trudeau, Laura Johnson, and Timothy Brown. He was seen arguing with both Maureen Trudeau and Laura Johnson shortly before they were murdered. He claimed he was having an affair with both of the ladies and the arguments stemmed from the fact he was breaking things off with them, because he didn't want to lose his family. No one confirmed his story, in fact everyone who knew the two women stated they would have never had an affair with him, and it was more than likely that he was obsessed with them. Both Mrs. Trudeau and Mrs. Johnson were white women in their mid-30s who married into and grew up in powerful families.

Mrs. Trudeau was married to Johnathan Trudeau, who at the time was the Assistant District Attorney, and her father was Joseph Winchester, who owned over half the city. Mrs. Johnson was married to Victor White, the son of Judge Phillip White. Their deaths brought added scrutiny and pressure to close as a result. Timothy Brown did not have the family connections of Mrs. Trudeau and Mrs. Johnson; he was a college student who grew up in a middle-class neighborhood. However, his death was where connections were established to Samuel Johnson. They had gotten into a fight shortly before Mr. Brown's death. Witnesses stated Mr. Johnson punched Mr. Brown unprovoked. Johnson stated the fight started because Brown had been stealing his work and he had grown tired of it. The note left on his body was what made Mr. Johnson a suspect. The note said "A Penny For Your Thoughts; what happens when you decide to cheat your way to the top?"

While Timothy Brown was the starting point for the investigation, four other people were killed before Samuel Johnson was charged with 12 murders. Prosecutors argued he killed Jennifer Thomas, likely because he refused his advances. The note found with her body said; "A Penny For Your Thoughts; What Happens When You Think You Are Better Than A Man?"

It was argued this was part of his pattern, that he would kill women who refused his advances. It was argued he killed the men because of jealousy. They all had achieved things in life he never had. He was tried, convicted, and sentenced to death by the electric chair, a sentence that was not ultimately carried out. Samuel Johnson was killed in prison shortly after the trial. Sgt. Allen was there to watch him die. Samuel Johnson never admitted to what he did, even at the sentencing, he proclaimed his innocence. This only made Sgt. Allen even madder. He was furious the family never got closure.

The Penny Murder was the first murder he had ever worked as a detective. While the first victim was Jennifer Thomas, who was killed in 1989, the first one he responded to was Daniel Morehouse. Daniel Morehouse was the the sixth victim, who was a twenty-year-old college student. He was found in his dorm room, in 1991, with a note reading; A Penny For Your Thoughts; What Happens When You Take Something That Doesn't Belong to You.

As he drove back to the 21st, all he could do was think about his friend laying there dead, flashing back to images of some of the "original" victims. He just drove in a trance trying to figure out who would do something like this. Who would awaken this ghost? He could not bring himself to any other conclusion other than this had to be a copycat, because the Penny Murderer was tried, convicted, and subsequently got the punishment he deserved.

As Allen arrived back at the station, a sense of embarrassment and anger with himself took over him. He had gotten lost in the moment of everything and totally forgotten about his friend. He realized she must be going through hell right now. As he pulled into the parking lot, he didn't take the time to find an open spot; he created his own. He was in such a hurry to get out of the car, he turned the car keys to the off position without putting the car in park. He didn't even care to take the time to do so; he had to go find his friend. As he got out of his car, he didn't remember closing the door. As he made it into the precinct, he immediately went to Captain Brown's office.

Captain Lucas Brown had been on the force for 10 years. He was from the area and as a result he knew everyone in the city. He grew up in the Murphy Projects, the toughest and most deadly neighborhood in the city. In fact, this is why he decided to become a cop. He had seen the crime first-hand and the impact it had on the community as well as how some officers treated people in the neighborhood. He told himself he would be different and he would bring about the change that was sorely needed. He could have been anything he wanted. He had his Master's in Psychology and was in the process of working on his Ph.D.

As Allen approached the door to the Captain's office, before he could open it, Officer Daniels opened the door and walked out. He had the look on his face officers usually had once they did something to get on the Captain's bad side. It wasn't that he yelled, it was the fact they had did something to disappoint him. Although he was younger than a lot of the officers, he still had everyone's respect and everyone would run through a burning building for him. As he walked past, he figured he would find out what happened, but at that moment he had more important things to address.

As he opened the door and began to speak, it was like the Captain could read his mind. "She is gone already; Alan and Patricia took her home. She was doing well under the circumstances. I do not think it has fully hit her yet, but luckily, she had people who can be there for her. Because you know how stubborn she is."

"Thank Goodness!" stated a relieved Sgt. Allen. "I will call her tomorrow to see how she is doing."

"I have no idea of who would want to do something like this to Marcus. He had no enemies and he always treated people with respect and did the right thing," stated the Captain.

While Marcus Jones wasn't from the area, you couldn't tell by how he interacted with the community and how much everyone loved him. He made sure to interact with everyone and not just when they were in trouble. It took him some time to gain the communities' trust, but he eventually earned it. In this sense, he reminded the Captain of himself.

As he looked at the Captain, Sgt. Allen's voice got lower and he had this look of extreme sadness and confusion on his face. "There is something else I need to tell you."

At that moment the District Attorney Harry Wallace walked into the office. Prior to working in the District Attorney's Office, he had been a decorated police officer. In fact, his last case was the Penny Murder with his partner Sgt. Allen. Over the course of his career, he had earned the reputation of being a no-nonsense attorney whose only goal was to get a conviction at any costs and if the person was actually guilty, then that was icing on the cake. You couldn't tell by looking at them that the two of them used to be partners. They both had this level of disdain for each other leading to tension so thick you could cut it with a knife anytime they were in the same room together. This time was no different.

"Where is she?" he asked as he walked through the door.

"I really need to put a sign on my door, outlining steps people must take when they enter my office. The first step will be to at least say: hi, how are you doing," was the Captain's response.

"I don't have time for your games tonight. I asked you a question. Where is she?"

"You can ask all the questions you want, but the last time I checked I do not work for you, so you will treat not only office, but me with the respect I deserve. If not, you can walk out of not only this office, but this building as well. Now if you are referring to Mrs. Jones, she is not here," responded the Captain in a stern voice.

"Where is she?"

"I let her go home!'

"Who gave you the authority to release her? She needs to be here answering questions. You will get her back here tonight," a noticeably angry D.A. Wallace responded.

"The only thing I will be doing tonight, is going home to my beautiful wife, getting in bed with her, making sweet love, and then going to sleep." He added the last part just to get under the skin of the D.A. The D.A.'s son had dated her previously and had fallen hard for her, as had the rest of his family, the D.A. included. However, she didn't feel the same way. She had met the future Captain shortly after she had broken up with him and they were married a few months later.

"She will be back tomorrow. There is no reason to keep her here tonight; she is not going anywhere."

"Who gave you permission to send her home?"

"I decided to send her home, because as the Captain of the 21st Precinct I have the power to do so. There is nothing we could have gotten tonight that we won't get from her tomorrow. She is not going anywhere; I am sure of that. I doubt there is anyone who is more invested in finding out who killed her husband than she is."

"I will be speaking to the Police Chief about this."

"You do that, but you will have to do it from somewhere else. I am going to need you to get out of my office, because I need to handle some police business that doesn't concern you. Good night!" After hearing that, D.A. Wallace paused for a second, trying to process what he had just heard, before ultimately walking out the office and the building, rather angrily.

"I do not know how you managed to work with him! Was he always this unbearable?"

"More so! But I have something more important to talk to you about."

"What is going on? You are scaring me, Sergeant!"

"It is about Marcus's death; there are more details about his death that are sure to cause some problems."

"I have a dead cop, there isn't anything that can add any additional stress than that!"

"Someone is attempting to awaken ghosts from the past." As Sgt. Allen began to speak, the Captain had a puzzled, yet concerned look on his face, as he mouthed the words ghosts.

"Yes ghosts. There was a note and a penny on the body!"

After hearing those words, the Captain instantly found himself in a place of shock. He was not on the force at the time of the original murders, but being from the area, he remembered the fear and panic that were rampant during the city until the murderer was captured. The Penny Murderer was like the boogeyman. He was the monster in the stories, parents told their kids to keep them from getting in trouble, the monster kids told their friends when they wanted to scare them or show how tough they were.

From 1989 to 1992 the Penny Murderer killed twelve people using different types of poison. The victims were all white and consisted of seven women and five men. It was believed he committed more than those twelve, but it was not confirmed. During those three years and up until the time Samuel Johnson was tried and convicted, people in the city lived in fear. During and after the trial there were a series of protests and the town almost exploded as people who thought he was innocent clashed with those who thought he was guilty. It took a year for things to die down, but even after that, things were never really the same. A level of skepticism formed in the town on both sides, that wouldn't go away. There were those who questioned the legal system and then there were those who questioned the motives of the ones protesting.

A level of fear also came over the Captain. What if the wrong person was convicted? There was always a concern with some in the community that the wrong person was put in jail. He remembered what happened to the city and how it was almost ripped apart the first time. He immediately started thinking about the worst-case scenario. He was going to not only have to worry about solving this case, but also the possibility the city could be ripped apart.

They both sat there in silence for a second, thinking about what this meant. Sgt. Allen was trying to figure out who could have done this evil thing. Not only did they kill his friend, but they did so by bringing back a ghost that everyone had forgotten about. There was no doubt in his mind this was a copycat and not the original killer because he was buried in an unmarked grave behind the prison.

Finally, Captain Brown broke the silence. "This is what we have to do; we can't let this get out, yet. We have to make sure we cover all of our bases and make sure we handle this the right way. I will leave you on the case because you have experience working it. But I will be assigning you a partner, to alleviate any potential concerns. Before you say you do not need a partner you can either take the partner or you will not be on the case. I will work on a contingency plan. Because if and when news leaks there will be protests."

"Given that I have no choice, I guess I have a new partner," stated a dejected Sgt. Allen.

"I will talk to the Chief, but from this moment on you will run point and will keep me apprised of everything that goes on with this case. There cannot be any surprises, and everything has to be done above board. Damn!"

"What is it," asked Sgt. Allen.

"Wasn't D.A. Wallace your partner during the investigation of the original Penny Murders?"

In that moment they both realized things just got a little more complicated. The D.A. was notorious for attempting to insert himself into investigations. It was the same when he was a Detective; he thought he was above everything then and could do whatever he wanted. The only reason he got away with it was because he was good at his job. But now they both could only imagine the level of involvement he would attempt to have in this case. He had championed his involvement in the original case and still continued to do so.

"Go get some rest Sergeant; and that is an order. This is probably the last night you will have the opportunity until this is over. Hopefully, this sick bastard doesn't kill anymore, and this was just a one-time thing."

CHAPTER 5

"WHY ARE YOU DOING this to me," Melissa Landry said while crying uncontrollably. She wondered how she got in this situation: tied up in her living room, begging for her life to a masked intruder.

"Sins of the father and daughter," retorted a voice she did not recognize.

Melissa Landry was a lawyer, mother of four, wife of Arthur Landry, a successful business owner, and the daughter of the former Dr. Josiah Wilson, who had died 10 years earlier. She had plans to relax tonight, enjoying one of the rare nights when her kids were not home. Her husband was out of town on a business trip. She was used to his trips, so she didn't mind. In fact she was glad everyone was gone beause she needed some "me" time. She had planned on relaxing for the night, taking a nice bath using Ambrosial Ofuro Shizumi Bath Salts and drinking some 1945 Chateau Mouton Rothschild. Her husband was going to pissed, but she didn't care, in fact the reason she was drinking it was to piss him off. She never heard the intruder behind her. When she woke up, she found herself tied to the chair in front of this "monster."

"Wha.....What does that mean, you bastard?"

The intruder didn't say anything, they just kept doing what they were doing, as if she was not in the room.

In that moment all she could do was think about her kids and how they would have to grow up without her. She thought about the birthdays, parties, all of their first moments, the weddings, and the birth of grandkids. "I don't want to die! My kids!" she could barely muster out through the crying.

In that moment she thought she had gotten through to them. In that moment, the intruder looked at her and placed the knife they were holding down. Through the tears she managed to say thank you, multiple times.

The intruder walked over to her, placing their fingers on her lips. They then untied her hands from behind her back. The intruder then walked over to the table, examined the bottle of wine and poured two glasses and then walked back over to Melissa, handing one to her and keeping one for themselves. "Let's talk," the intruder said.

In that moment Melissa was relieved, saying thank you repeatedly as she drank the wine. In that moment she didn't know if it was because of the quality of the wine or the fact she wasn't going to die, but she thought to herself this was the best wine she had ever tasted.

"How does it feel to be an accessory to murder?"

Melissa paused for a few moments, not really understanding the question. Accessory to murder she thought. She hadn't been a part of anyone's death and had no idea of what the killer was talking about.

"Mrs. Landry do not try my patience, answer the question please."

"I don't know what you are talking about, I haven't done anything that has led to someone dying," she cried.

The intruder just sat there for a second, studying Mrs. Landry. Mrs. Landry looked confused trying to figure out what was going, trying to think of ways to get this person to see they have they wrong person. The intruder stood up and reached inside their pocket, startling Mrs. Landry. They pulled out a newspaper clipping, it was the obituary section. Mrs. Landry was confused as to why were they showing her this. Then it hit her, she saw a name she recognized, as she looked up at the intruder, who was shaking their head.

Mrs. Landry tried to speak, but she couldn't. She started to feel funny, her vision was getting blurry, her throat became scratchy, she found it hard to talk, all she could get out was gasps. She had no idea what has happening, until she looked at the intruder, who was now standing and walking towards her. As they got closer to her, they bent back down and whispered "now you remember!" Those were the last words she ever heard.

Sgt. Allen sat at his table, staring at the bottle of Bourbon in front of him, trying to resist the urge to drink. The last time he had drunk was seven years ago when he had almost killed himself. In fact, the bottle had been in his house since then. After everything that happened that day, the death of his friend, and the reemergence of long-forgotten ghosts, he had no idea how he would cope with everything that happened. He remembered how he felt when he drank so long ago. He wanted something that would help him to feel numb; he didn't want to feel anything anymore. He thought that was the only way he could get through this. He kept thinking about Nicole finding her husband, his friend and partner, lying there in the bed with the note and penny on his body. He couldn't stop the visions from appearing in his head. He couldn't hold the emotion in as tears began falling down his face. In that moment, he missed his wife more than anything, she was always the one that could help see the light. How he needed that right now. He was truly lost.

As he picked up the bottle to pour a glass, his phone started ringing. "Sergeant Mike Allen," he said as he answered the phone. It was dispatch, they were calling him to tell him a body was found. He was just about to tell them to call another detective, but what he heard next, sent chills down his spine and made him realize his nightmare was just beginning. A body of middle-aged white woman was found in the alley. He instantly forgot about the drink and grabbed his jacket, badge, and gun and ran out to his car. He was in such a hurry he didn't pay any attention to the address.

On his way to the scene a multitude of thoughts race through head: how did this happen? Did he arrest the wrong guy? How could he have been so wrong? He shook all those doubts away and came to his original conclusion this was a copycat, because the real killer was dead; he died in prison twenty-seven years ago. As he drove to the scene, he got the feeling of déjà vu. As he pulled up to the scene and walked through the evidence tape. As he got closer to the alley a strange sensation come over him. As he made his way to the alley, what he saw next almost made him pass out. He got weak in the knees and felt lightheaded.

It was like he was transported back in time. There was the body of middle-aged Caucasian woman, lying as if she were in bed; she was laying on a pillow, with a blanket covering her, as if she was sleeping. It was the same scene he saw almost thirty years ago, she looked eerily similar to a previous victim, Maureen Trudeau. Out the corner of eye he could see Adam Anderson, so he walked up to him.

"Two times in one night, if we keep meeting like this, I may start thinking you like me," Anderson said.

Sgt. Allen didn't have time for his antics, and he didn't even ask or wait for the coroner to tell him what happened. He already knew. "Middle-aged Caucasian woman, no signs of a struggle or trauma, she has been dead for approximately a day now. She was killed somewhere else and moved here, likely sometime tonight, when all of the attention was on the homicide of Marcus. When you get her back to the lab, test her for poison, more specifically Batrachotoxin."

The coroner looked puzzled. "Trust me, test for the poison and you will find that I am correct." In that moment it hit him where he was. He was on the corner of 110th and Steven Street, the same place the body of Maureen Trudeau was found. To confirm his suspicions, he walked closer to her body to see what was under the blanket. As he lifted the blanket, he saw she was wearing a nightgown, and as he lifted it a little further, what he saw next paused him in his tracks.

"Well you can't say she didn't have taste. That is a Gucci Lace and Silk lingerie dress," stated the coroner."

While it was troubling that he knew what she had on, that is not what had caught his attention. He bent down to a knee, carefully placing the blanket to the side, to show the penny on top of a note. He reached into his pocket and put on a glove, picked up the note to see what was written on it: "Penny for your thoughts: What happens when your "father" covers up the taking of an innocent life and you do nothing to stop it?'

In that moment, he wanted to crawl into a dark corner and drink himself to sleep. Why was someone doing this? In that moment he felt sick to his stomach. He knew who the victim was; it was Melissa Landry, the daughter-in-law of the former Governor; George Landry. In this moment of realization, he jumped back, startled, in shock, unable to process what was going on. The only thing that snapped him out of it was someone placing a hand on his shoulder. He turned around and saw it was the Detective Hercules. He saw his mouth moving, but in that moment, he couldn't hear anything he was saying, he was in shock.

He was finally able to snap out of it. In that moment he jumped up, not even acknowledging the Detective. He ran to his car, needing to be alone. He had no idea how to process this. Who would be doing this? He was more than sure the person was a copycat, looking to punish those associated with the original trial, but why? There was no miscarriage of justice, the right person was convicted, there was no cover-up, he said to himself. In that moment another thought hit him; his partner was dead because of him. His actions all those years ago had led to his death.

"It can't be," he whispered to himself.

Just then there was a knock on his door. It was an officer he didn't recognize; he didn't have time for this. He opened the door and told the officer excuse me, I have somewhere I need to be, and rushed past him. As he made his way back up to the alley, he found the coroner.

"You need to test Marcus for poison."

The coroner looked at him puzzled, not really sure what to make of what he was saying, especially given the fact he just gave a specific poison to test the newest victim for. "What poison should I test him for, Batrachotoxin?"

"Yes!"

In that moment the coroner was both confused and nervous. He had never seen Sgt. Allen like this, not only that he was going to provide him a list of poisons. "Sergeant, what is going on?"

"I don't have time to answer any questions right now, but I will stop by tomorrow and provide you with information."

As Sgt. Allen turned around to walk away, he saw the same officer who was at his car. "Excuse me, officer, I am not sure what it is that you want, but I'm in the middle of something important and do not have time to entertain anyone!"

The officer looked puzzled and taken aback. Holding out his hand to shake, he stated "I am Detective Justin Howard."

Not letting the young officer finished his introduction, he interrupted "I am not sure who you are and quite frankly, in this moment, I do not care who you are. Now if you will excuse me, I have something I need to do."

"Not to be rude, but you need to be concerned who I am. I am your new partner. We were supposed to meet tomorrow, but I heard your name on the radio, so I decided to come here and introduce myself tonight."

Detective Howard had been on the force for seven years and a detective for the last two. He was considered an excellent cop by all standards. Ever since he was a little kid, he had dreamed of nothing more than being a cop, catching the bad guys. While it is a dream of a lot of kids, unlike most kids his dream didn't change. In fact, his desire only got stronger the older he got, especially after his sister was killed. Everything he did in life had been in preparation for being a cop and ultimately a detective. He told his family and anyone who would listen he was going to be a cop and clean up the neighborhood.

Sgt. Allen didn't have time for this, but he also knew he had to entertain him, or else he risked being pulled off the case. He couldn't believe the Captain would assign this officer to work with him. He wasn't ready for what was about to happen. He told himself he would entertain the "kid" tonight, and when he called the Captain later tonight, he would address it with him.

"So, what do we have here?" asked Detective Howard.

"Excuse me, I have to go make a phone call to the Captain and catch him up to speed with what is going on right now. We can finish this conversation tomorrow." He had no intention of sharing any information with this officer. In fact, he was pretty confident after he talked to the Captain, he would be getting a new partner of his choosing.

As he got back to his car, he called the Captain to let him know what was going on and to tell him, whatever it was, it had only begun.

CHAPTER 6

As SHE LAY IN the bed, her mind began to race; trying to figure out how she got here. The pain she felt when she saw her husband's body, that had kept her up all night, was still there, tearing at her. She laid there, the bed soaked in tears, unable to come to grips with her new reality. She saw Marcus when she closed her eyes; she saw him when she opened them. That night she wished for just a moment of where she could feel normal, but she realized she would never feel "normal" again. Just then she began to doze off, which was welcomed, as she had spent the entire night awake.

As she felt herself drifting away, she heard a familiar voice from outside the door. "Knock, knock!" said the child's voice.

As tired as she was and as much as she wanted to sleep, the sound of her god daughter's voice brought a smile to her face. Lindsey was 5 years old and full of energy, but she loved her god mommy, or Mommy Nicole as she had called her since she first began talking. In fact, Nicole would argue with Patricia playfully that the first time she said mommy, she was talking about her.

"Who's there," she replied.

"Orange," Lindsey replied shouting.

"Orange who?"

"Or'ange you glad it's me and not the boogey man," Lindsey shouted back as she began to laugh at her own joke. This was one of their routines, they would tell each other some of the corniest jokes. Oftentimes the only people who got them were the two of them.

"Are you going to come or are you going to stay outside and keep the boogey man out?"

"Mommy Nicole! You know I can't open the door!"

"Well I guess you are going to stay outside to keep out the boogey man," she said as she began making her way to the door. She opened the door just before Lindsey could respond. "Hello, is anyone out here? I know I heard someone, but I guess they got tired of waiting," she said with a smile on her face. At that moment, she could feel someone tugging on her shirt, trying to get her attention. "Oh hey, there you are I thought you left." At that moment, she picked up the little girl and both gave each other a big hug and lots of kisses. She then carried her to the bed, where they began to tell each other the silliest jokes you could imagine. This moment was therapeutic as during this time, she was able to have fun with someone and not think about the painful events from the night before.

"What are you two doing, "Patricia asked as she stood in the doorway looking at the two of the playing in bed. In that moment, after everything her friend had been through the night before and everything that lay ahead of her, it pained her to interrupt their moment. She understood her friend would smile less and less over the coming days, and possibly the only one who would be able to make her smile was in the bed with her. She knew how much the two of them loved each other and it made her happy. She realized some mothers would be jealous of their relationship, but not her. She was thankful there was someone who loved her daughter and she could count on just in case something happened to her or Alan. But in this moment her friend needed her, so she told herself she would do whatever she could to make things less painful for her friend.

"We are playing," replied Lindsay, her voice filled with laughter.

"Well it is time to get up, both of you. Especially you, Ms. Keyes." She would refer to her daughter as miss, because she and Alan liked to joke she was five going on thirty. They would often joke she was the parent and they were the children. "Up, up! Time to get up so you can eat breakfast and get ready for school," she replied.

"But mommy, I want to stay with Mommy Nicole and play," was the response she received.

In that instant, there was no need for words, Patricia looked at Lindsay with that all-too-familiar look. The one where Lindsay knew that her mom was serious and not joking. As she got up, she whispered in Nicole's ear "I have to go, mommy is being mean!" The problem with that is a whisper for Lindsay was normal volume for everyone else, so her mother heard every word, which brought a smile to both Patricia's and Nicole's faces. As Lindsay got up, she began to walk away at the pace of snail with her head down in an attempt to hopefully change her mother's mind, or to at least make her feel bad. "1, 2.........," and before Patricia could get to three, Lindsay was out of the room.

"Aww, she looked so sad. Does she have to go to school," asked Nicole, who was now making a sad face as well.

"She'll be alright. All she is going to do is go running to her father and give him that sad face and he will give her whatever she wants just so he doesn't have to see her sad. How are you doing this morning? Would you like some breakfast?"

"No thank you, I'm ok. I think I am just going to jump in the shower and get dressed."

"Both Alan and I will be going to the station with you this morning."

Nicole didn't bother saying that wasn't necessary, because she didn't have the energy and the outcome would have been the same even if she did. She and Patricia had grown close over the years to the point where people just assumed they were sisters. However, if those people would have been around when they first met, they would be shocked they hadn't killed each other by now. Their relationship in the beginning was tumultuous. She would actually feel bad for Alan, because she knew he was in the middle and he tried his best to get them to at least be sociable. It took some time, but they finally did, but neither one of them knew why they didn't like the other or why the other didn't like them, they just knew they didn't like each other. They would laugh today about how much they hated each other and didn't know why.

The feeling of the water hitting her body was therapeutic. She instantly felt a moment of calmness she had not felt since the day before. However, the feeling didn't last long, as thoughts of her husband began to force their way into her head. The thought of seeing his body lying there was powerful and hit her to her core. The pain was sudden and almost knocked her off her feet, and she stumbled momentarily, having to using the shower wall to brace herself. She could feel tears running down her face, as she began to wonder how she would possibly make it through this. Her best friend was gone, and it was her fault.

Just then she could hear Patricia knocking on the door asking if she was okay. She couldn't find the words to answer. She was so overcome with emotion, it took every ounce of energy she had to stand up.

As Patricia knocked on the door, she realized her friend probably didn't want to be bothered right now. However, she still had to check to make sure she was okay. She had no idea of how hard this was; all she could do was to attempt to place herself in her shoes, but that was too hard. She just wanted her to know that she was there for her if she needed anything. Realizing she was not going to get an answer, she reminded her friend she was there if she needed anything.

She stayed in the shower for 30 more minutes, not able to bring herself to leave. It was the first place she was able to be alone and not have to worry about seeing anyone else. She appreciated her friend's help, but she needed to be alone to try to process everything that happened the night before. It was in the shower that she realized she would have to plan his funeral. In that moment of realization, it was like she was reliving the moments of the previous night all over again. She was going to have to bury the love of her life.

As she walked up into the kitchen, she saw her friends at the table finishing their breakfast and listening to Lindsay tell them about a girl from her class who had got in trouble the previous day.

"I am going to send you a copy of the water bill for all the water you used," Alan said as he saw her walking inside the kitchen.

She mustered what she hoped was a smile, but she wasn't too sure what face she made. Alan realizing his joke had missed the mark, felt a sharp pain in his leg. He looked down to see the source of his pain. He caught a glimpse of wife's hand leaving his leg and at that moment looked up and saw a familiar look. The one his wife usually gave him when he had said or done something wrong.

"Would you like some breakfast?" he asked as Nicole sat down at the table.

"No, I am ok," she replied as she sat down.

"Ok, we are finishing up here. Lindsay go brush your teeth and get your book bag, then come back to the table," Patricia said. As Lindsay walked out Patricia said, "Whenever you are ready to leave, we will head out. We will drop Lindsay off at school and then we will go to the station. Alan as already called in this morning and talked to all of the clients you both were scheduled to meet with today and rescheduled all of the meetings."

As they got in the car, she was thankful her little friend was in the car with them. She always enjoyed the time they spent together, but she enjoyed it even more now. She wasn't able to focus on the events on the previous night. Instead she was told the story she had missed this morning about Kayla getting in trouble in class and how Lindsay was a good girl and never got in trouble at school.

"Time to finish your story Lindsay; you are at school," Alan said looking back at the two of them.

Lindsay finished her story and got out of the car and walked towards the door. But before she could make it to the door of the school, she realized she had forgotten to do something, so she ran back towards the car. Luckily Patricia was paying attention and was able to tell Alan to stop the car. Lindsay opened the door and reached over and gave Nicole a hug and kiss and whispered, "I am sorry about Uncle Marcus, but he is heaven now, so don't be sad." Hearing this little angel say those words to her made her feel better and she didn't want to let her go, but she knew had to.

"Thank you so much, I love you," she responded back. Now Lindsay was ready for school. As she walked back toward the school, she saw one of her friends and they held hands and walked inside the building together.

The rest of the trip was made mostly in silence. Both Alan and Patricia tried to engage Nicole in conversation, but each attempt was met with a half-hearted attempt at an answer, so they decided it was best to not push the issue. They realized their friend probably had other things on her mind more important than what they were trying to talk to her about.

Nicole appreciated her friends' attempts at conversation, but she just wanted to be alone in her thoughts in order to prepare herself for what was about to happen. She didn't know if she was ready to relive the events from the previous day. It was one thing to think about them, but the thought of having to go over the details of seeing her husband dead was something she didn't know if she could handle. She was debating if she wanted to have a lawyer present, not because she had anything to hide, but just so her friend could be in. However, she decided against that. She knew that he and more than likely Patricia would be watching and the thought of them there watching provided her a source of comfort and helped prepare her for the interview.

Pulling up to the police station, thoughts of the night before began to creep back into her mind. She could feel the hands of the officers leading her into the station, everyone in the station looking at her, some feeling sorry for her, some feeling sorry for her husband, and others enjoying seeing her led through the station like some criminal, especially that ompa lompa. She began to get angry remembering the events at the station the night before. She gathered her composure, as she told herself they would not see her that vulnerable and get to take delight in seeing her broken again. She was going to go in with her head up and not let anyone see how truly broken she was right now.

The sound of a door closing and opening woke her up from thoughts, as Patricia opened her door. As they walked to the door, Patricia whispered "We are here with you." Hearing those words gave her additional strength she didn't realize she had. She could feel the stares from people like knives piercing her skin. As she looked out the corner of her eyes, she could see people whispering and could feel she was the center of their conversations. Let them talk, she thought.

"Nicole," she heard a familiar voice call out her name as she walked through the precinct. She looked up and saw the captain and he motioned for them to come to his office. As they walked into his office, they saw him putting a folded blanket and pillow into the closet in his office. As he turned around, she could get a closer look at his face and could tell she was not the only one who didn't get any sleep last night.

"Good morning everyone!" Thank you all for coming, I wish it was under different circumstances," stated the captain as he tried to muster the energy to talk. He may have gotten two hours of sleep last night. The deaths of Marcus Jones and Melissa Landry by a copycat had sent shockwaves through the department and city leadership.

"May I offer you all some coffee," before Nicole could say anything, the captain finished his statement: "and hot chocolate for you, Nicole? It has milk and two marshmallows like you like."

Patricia and Alan politely declined, but Nicole was happy to accept. She took the hot chocolate and instantly felt a calmness. Even in those hot and muggy Georgia summers she still enjoyed a nice cup of hot chocolate. It is something her and her father would do together, and something she continued to do even after his death.

"Please, everyone take a seat! Excuse the mess, this turned into my bedroom last night."

"Is everything okay?" a concerned Nicole asked.

"That is why I wanted you to come into my office first. I don't know of any other way to say this, other than to be direct."

"Thank you, I appreciate that."

"There was another murder last night." Nicole was puzzled for a moment as to why he would be telling her about another murder last night, especially under the circumstances. But as he continued his reasoning became clear.

"Melissa Landry, the daughter-in-law of George Landry, a former Governor of the state, was found in an alley last night. We believe it was the same person that killed Marcus."

Hearing those words created more questions. How were her husband and the newest victim connected?

"Who would want to kill them both?" she found herself saying out loud.

"I know this hard, but there is more."

"More? How could there possibly be more?" she responded as she felt the hand of her friend grasp hers.

"Both your husband and Marcus were killed by someone copying the signature of the Penny Murderer. There was a penny and note found on both Marcus's and Mrs. Landry's body."

Hearing those words sent a shock down her spine. She recognized the case. Hell anyone who had been in the town longer than a day knew about the case.

"What did the note say? I want to see it!"

"Nicole you know I can't show it to right now or tell you what it said. I promise I will make sure you find out what it said, just not right now."

"Is Nicole safe? Are you going to provide her with a security detail just in case this crazy bastard comes after her?" demanded a concerned and angry Patricia.

"Yes, we will provide her with a security detail to make sure she is okay, but from what I understand about the previous case, he never attacked in the same place more than once, so we do not think this version of the killer will come back."

Trying to take everything in was hard for Nicole. Not only was her husband dead, but he was killed by a serial killer. For some reason. Marcus never hurt a fly; he was loved by everyone.

Captain Brown could not bear to tell her the reason why it was believed Marcus was targeted. He knew it would eventually come out, and he would make sure she was told before it did. But in this moment seeing the pain in her eyes, he couldn't be the one to cause any more at that moment. He didn't know if she could take any more.

This was the last part of the conversation Nicole remembered hearing as she got lost in thoughts about everything that had transpired over the course of day. How did it get to this point? How could she erase everything that happened and start all over again, going back to before her husband's death? She wanted so much to just go lock herself in the closet and escape everything.

CHAPTER 7

As Sgt. Allen drove in the car, it was all over the radio that Melissa Landry, daughter-in-law of the former Governor, had been found dead in alley. Thankfully, no other details about her death had gotten out yet. He figured it would only be a matter of time before they did, and it would only make things worse. The death of his friend and fellow officer was treated as mere footnote, with no mention of it, except as footnote to the morning news.

He decided he had enough of the news. Allen needed to time to process the death of his friend and everything that and the re-emergence of a ghost. He was up all night going through old case files trying to see if there was something he missed. He ended the morning with the same belief he started with; the original killer was in fact Samuel Johnson and whoever did this was a copycat.

But he had no leads. He tried identifying potential suspects, first starting with family members. However, that search wasn't successful; Johnson did not have any kids and his wife died shortly after he was arrested. With his wife being dead, there was no one else to talk to to see if they could provide any additional information. He didn't have any friends in school; there was no one close to him that he could identify that would be responsible for this.

With everything going on he still had not had a chance to speak with Nicole yet, and for that he felt horrible. Allebn wanted to be there for her, like she had been for him. But he also wanted to be there for his friend. He thought by actively working this case he would be helping both of them. He told himself he would talk to Nicole today. As he pulled up to the station, he started to prepare himself for the madhouse he was about to walk into and not only that, he had a new partner. His conversation with the Captain didn't go as he had hoped, but from what the Captain told him and what information he found out about Detective Howard on his own, he came to the conclusion he may be useful. But he would still be wary of what information he shared.

Just as he was about pull into the precinct, he received a phone call; it was Captain Brown. "Hey Captain, I am about to pull into the parking lot and will be in your office shortly."

"Change of plans, I need for you to go to Melissa Landry's home. Her husband got back this morning and will be expecting you and Detective Howard. Detective Howard will meet you at the Sunset Bar and you both can go to the home from there. After you leave, call me and let me know what happens. I have to go to a meeting with the Chief."

With that the Captain was gone. The drive to the Landry's home gave him extra time to think about everything. The only thing it didn't do was give him time to talk with Detective Howard to let him know to just sit there and not say anything. The Landrys lived in the city of Sunset Hill; population of 100. The city was founded 60 years ago, when some of the wealthy white citizens decided they did not want to be overrun by colored people. In response, a select few individuals petitioned Governor George Landry and the state legislature at the time to expedite the process and to relax the rules of incorporating a city. The process took only a month, compared to the normal time frame of a year.

The city was nestled in between a mountain range and the Atlantic Ocean; the rest of the city was enclosed by a wall. There were only two roads into the city. There used to be a gate restricting access, however as times changed the city had to open its access to everyone else. The city sat on over 500 acres and was considered one of the richest in America. The city had two championship golf courses, 28 Har-tru tennis courts, pickleball, squash, croquet, two gas station, a shopping center, and many more social and recreational activities.

The homes were spread out all across the city, mountainside, ocean front, and traditional land; each sitting on at least ten acres. Residents of the city included lawyers, doctors, successful business owners, and politicians, including former Governor George Landry. The Landry's' home sat on approximately 50 acres, nestled in the back corner of the city. The home was next to the former Governor's home. They were considered the two best locations in the city and it was widely speculated they were given to the Governor for his help in helping establish the city.

As Sgt. Allen drove through the city, he thought to himself how it had changed over the years. Not only in the way the town looked now, but also because several black families lived in the city now. He thought about how that not only must have pissed off the founders of the city, some of whom either were still alive or had family who still lived there. As he got closer to the home, he could hear the crashing of the waves and smell the fresh ocean air. In the distance he could see the homes of both the Governor and his son.

About a mile from the Landry estate was the Sunset Bar. As he turned in the parking lot there was Detective Howard, standing beside his car looking out at the ocean. Detective Howard was 5'8 and approximately 215 lbs. He was not overweight; you could tell from his appearance that he kept himself in shape. As he pulled up beside his car, Detective Howard turned and waved at him. Sgt. Allen figured this was a good time to get out and talk to him before they went to speak with Mr. Landry; they were going to be partners whether he liked it or not, so he had to make sure they both were on the same page, because there will be a lot more scrutiny on this case as opposed to other cases.

As he got out of his car and walk towards Detective Howard, they both said good morning and exchanged pleasantries. After which, Sgt. Allen felt it was the right time for him to be the bigger man.

"Detective, I apologize about last night. I was dealing with a lot, but that is still not an excuse for me to treat you the way I did."

"No worries, Sergeant, I totally understand. That is water under the bridge. Let's work together to catch this bastard before anyone else gets killed."

"I appreciate that. When we get to the home, let me take the lead. I know these people and I am from here. They are big on trust and unfortunately they do not know you, so they do not trust you."

"I understand and I'll follow your lead. I think it would be best if we ride together in your car."

With that, they both got inside of Sgt. Allen's car and headed to the Landry estate. As they made their way to their destination, Detective Howard couldn't help but comment about the town, the homes, and finally the Landry Estate.

"Damn, this is nice. I never thought I would see something like this up close and personal. We don't have homes like this where I am from," Detective Howard said in shock as to what he was seeing.

"Try not to drool too much when we get inside. Now how about we go in here and talk to the family."

As they walked to the front door, Detective Howard couldn't help but think how grand this house was. This would be his first time to the Landry Estate. He had been to the Governor's home before, but this home hadn't been built at the time. He remembered talking to the Governor and Arthur about the home and how they told him how grand the home was going to be and all of the stuff they had planned for it. He could see they spared no expense and their descriptions at the time didn't do it any justice. As they rang the doorbell, they both looked at each other. While no words were spoken, they both communicated to each non-verbally that it was game time.

Shortly after the doorbell rang, the door opened there was the Landry's butler. Just as they were about to speak, the butler told them there was no need, he knew who they were, and that both Mr. Landry and the Governor were in the backyard waiting for them. As they walked through the door the butler handed them shoe booties to put on. As they walked through the home, they realized why: the floors were made from Brazilian Cherry. The rest of the house was made of similar expensive materials.

As the butler led them outside, they could see figures sitting at a table in the distance and what appeared to be kids running along the beach playing. As they got closer, they could see it was Mr. Landry and the Governor.

"Good morning, gentleman, it has been a while since we have seen each other, and I wish it were under different circumstances. This is Detective Howard," stated Sgt. Allen.

"Let's cut through the bullshit, what are you doing to find the killer of my wife!" was the reply from an angry Mr. Landry.

"Mr. Landry we can appreciate your sense of urgency and the level of pain not only you, but your family must be experiencing, and I can assure you we are working as fast as we can to solve your wife's murder."

"If that were true you wouldn't be here, you would be out trying to solve the murder."

"We have people working on it, but we need to ask you a few questions to help us in our investigation."

The Governor, sensing things were about to get out of hand, placed his hand on his son's shoulder, calming him down and then said, "Please forgive my son, he is going through a lot right now and doesn't understand how this works. So please ask whatever questions you need to ask, and he will answer them." As he was speaking, he looked his son as if to tell him to calm down and answer the questions.

After the Governor spoke, his son didn't say a word, he just simply looked over at the two officers and nodded; this gave them the okay to ask what needed to be asked.

"Let's start with where you were last night and whether you know of anyone who would want to hurt your wife," asked Sgt. Allen.

"I was out of town on business and no, I do not know of anyone who would want to hurt her. She was loved by everyone; there was no one who didn't like her."

"What about her father; has she ever said anything about anyone being upset with her about something her father might have done?"

"No, why do you ask?"

"I am sorry we cannot disclose any more information that is part of an ongoing investigation."

With that last statement, the Governor rose up and decried "Bullshit! You will tell us what the hell is going on or else I will make some phone calls and the both of you will be out of a job before you make it back to your cars."

In that moment Detective Howard interjected "I am sorry sir, I understand both of your concerns, but this policy so……"

Before Detective Howard could finish his statement, the Governor shouted, "Look here boy, I don't care about your policy this my goddamn daughter and you will answer the question."

"Boy, who…"

Sensing the situation was about to spiral further out of control, Sgt. Allen stood up from his chair, cutting off Detective Howard, and asked the Landry's to excuse them for a second. "Look, I understand your frustration, but I think it is best if you go back to the car and let me handle the rest of the questioning."

"No, I will stay here. I will not let him dictate to me how I act or how I will conduct this investigation, and furthermore I am not his boy and he will not talk to me like we are back on a plantation."

"I understand your frustration, but let me handle this, I know these people, I know how they operate and more importantly, I know who they actually know. You can stay, but if you do not let me handle this, being fired will be the least of our worries."

Detective Howard heard what Sgt. Allen said, but simply turned his back and walked back to the table and sat down, not acknowledging anyone.

Sgt. Allen breathed a sigh of relief and turned around and came back to the table and began telling the Governor and Mr. Landry about the events from the previous night and how they believed it was a copycat that was perpetuating these crimes. Lastly, he told them what the note said, "Penny for your thoughts; what happens when your "father" covers up the taking of an innocent life and you do nothing to stop it?"

The contents of the note put both the Governor and his son in a state of shock; there was nothing that her father had ever done wrong, in fact not only was he well-respected by the state, but members of the community loved him. He offered free check-ups to everyone in the community and oftentimes he would treat people he knew were unable to pay him. That is why at his funeral there were people from every race and background, and even from outside of the state. He was that beloved. It sent shockwaves because they knew in their heart she was killed because someone had a problem with something the Governor had done.

"I am pretty sure she was not killed for something her father did, but for something I did. I have never heard anyone say a word negative word about him. If she was in fact killed for something her father did. But why is someone copying this monster? The real killer was brought to justice," stated the Governor.

Hearing him say that brought a sigh of relief to both Detective Howard and Sgt. Allen as the working theory was currently that she was killed for something her father-in-law did, a fact they believe to be true based not only on the fact that her father was a well-respected doctor but more importantly that her father-in-law was hated by many. Additionally, the fact the father in the note was put in quotation marks made them believe the father was not her actual father, but someone who was a father figure to her. It seemed like forever, but in reality, it was only a couple of minutes before someone spoke.

Mr. Landry then asked the question that was on everyone's mind, but the officers had yet to ask, "What does the death of Melissa have to do with the death of a police officer, whom she never met and didn't have any of the same friends?"

"That part we do not know and are trying to figure out what is the link that caused the both of them to be killed. They both were killed by the same person, but it could be that they didn't know each other, but are linked some other way. Governor we will need a list of anyone who has threatened you over the past 10 years."

"I will have someone send over a list to the precinct."

"I have one more question," stated Detective Howard. He didn't even wait to be acknowledged, he went ahead and asked, "Did you play a role in the initial Penny Murder investigation?"

The sound of that question angered the Governor; who was this boy to ask him questions? He still hadn't learned his lesson from earlier. Realizing this was a good time to end the conversation, Sgt. Allen said to the Landrys: "Thank you for your time, we will keep you updated on the status of the investigation and if you think of anything else please let us know." As Sgt. Allen stood up to leave, he could see Detective Howard was not only not happy with his question not being answered, but he was angry with his partner as well. But he didn't care; he told him to follow his lead. It was obvious he and his partner were going to have to have a conversation.

As they got up to leave, the Governor asked Sgt. Allen to stay behind for a second. This request caught both of the officers off guard, but Sgt. Allen looked at Detective Howard and told him to go ahead, he would catch up. As Detective Howard walked away and saw the three of them talking.

About 15 minutes after Detective Howard made it to the car, Sgt. Allen walked up.

"What was that about," he asked as Sgt. Allen unlocked the doors and got inside.

"It was nothing; they just wanted to convey to me how important it was that we solve this case."

Once they got in the car, it was obvious neither one of them was happy with the other. Sgt. Allen didn't even want to speak with him, so he called the Captain to tell him what all they had just learned. Detective Howard just sat in the car thinking about everything that just happened, trying to process everything he had just learned from their conversation with the Landry's. As they pulled up to the parking lot so he could get his car, the only words spoken were I will see you at the office. As Sgt. Allen drove away, Detective Howard knew he was on the outside looking in for this investigation and no matter how much he wanted this partnership to work, he realized the chances of that happening were slim. He looked at Sgt. Allen drive away and simply shook his head in disgust.

"Remember the promise you made twenty years ago. If you do not, I promise you will regret it," the angry former Governor had stated.

"I remember and nothing will happen to you or me; no one knows about what any of us did and I will make sure it stays that way," replied Sgt. Allen.

"Are you sure about that? You better keep your partner in check before someone has to teach him some manners," threatened an angry Mr. Landry.

Sgt. Allen's phone rang waking him up from his daydream about his most recent conversation with the Governor and his son from the day before. As he picked up the phone, he realized it was the Captain.

"Good morning Captain! What's going on?"

"I need for you to come in ASAP! There has been a development in the investigation. Detective Howard is already here in my office."

New development, he thought. What could that possibly mean? "I am on my way!" As he grabbed his coat to leave, he thought out loud, "What is Detective Howard doing in the Captain's office already and without me?" Were they talking about the case or was Detective Howard complaining about the meeting with the Landrys? He told himself he would figure out what was going on in due time and he would have another conversation with Detective Howard about the partnership.

On the way to the precinct he figured it would be a good time to check on Nicole to see how she was doing. He had finally spoken to her last night; it wasn't a long conversation, just long enough for him to see how she was doing and let her know he was there for her and he would find out who did this.

CHAPTER 8

NICOLE WAS LYING IN bed; she had not been to sleep. How could she; she had lost her best friend, the love of her life, she couldn't go home, and on top of that she had no idea when she would get his body so she could have a funeral for him. The plan was for her to go and pick out a casket for her husband; she may not be able to pick a date, but she could at least do that. She decided to do it today, because the longer she waited the harder it would get. In that moment her phone rang, it was Mike. She appreciated him calling her, but right now she didn't feel like talking to him right now, so she just let it go to voicemail.

Then she heard a knock on the door; "Good morning, sleepy head," she could hear Alan say from the other side of the door. "Come on in," was her reply.

"How are you doing this morning? Would you like some breakfast? I am making my famous avocado and egg bake and pancakes?"

Hearing the paring of avocado and eggs caused Nicole's nose to turn up. She had never thought to try the two before and she told herself this morning wouldn't be the morning she tried it either. Sensing her hesitation in trying it, Alan made attempted to persuade her that it was actually good, and that she would enjoy it. Just then she could see Patricia behind him, nodding her head in approval and giving her the thumbs up. Seeing that and the sad look on his face, she thought to herself she needed to eat and after everything they had done for her, she could at least try his breakfast, that he seemed so proud to make.

"I will be more than happy to try it," she said.

Hearing her say that brought a gigantic smile to her face, as he told her breakfast would be ready by the time, she got she dressed and with that he closed the door and she was back alone. She told herself she needed to get up and after battling with herself she finally moved. As she got undressed and got in the shower, she dreamed of the moments when she and Marcus would take a shower together; how he would put his hands on her body, holding her, caressing her, she could feel his breath against her neck. In that moment she broke down crying; "Damn you Marcus! You were not supposed to leave me, not this soon, not ever," she cried out. In that moment she made a promise to not only herself, but to Marcus as well, she would do everything she could to find out who did this to him and she would not let this defeat her. She was not only going to live for herself, but she was going to live for Marcus as well, because that is what he would have wanted.

As Nicole walked towards the kitchen, the smell of breakfast hit her. "I guess Alan was right, at least it smells good," she thought to herself. "Something smells," she said as she walked into the kitchen.

"Glad you could join us! Welcome to Café Le Keyes! Have a seat and prepare to have your world changed forever," Alan said excitedly.

"Please excuse him, I think he fell and bumped his head this morning. He is even more abnormal than usual," responded Patricia.

As she sat down at the table, she looked at the two of them in the kitchen together and it made her think of Marcus and how on Saturdays they would do this very same thing: cook together in the kitchen. While she was sad she would no longer be able to do this again with Marcus, she was happy they had each other. Seeing them happy and smiling made her happy.

"Where is my girl at?" asked Nicole.

"She is with her grandparents this weekend; but she left you something. She made me promise to give it to you when you woke up or she wasn't going to leave," responded Patricia. Just Patricia pulled a rose and something else from the counter and brought it to her. "She wanted you to have this and for me to tell you that she loves you."

"Yeah that rose is on loan, she pulled it from my yard. I am going to need it back so I can reunite it with the rest of its friends," said a joking Alan.

Seeing this brought a smile to Nicole's face, as she smelled the rose and began to read the card: "I am sorry about Uncle Marcus. I am sure he still loves you from heaven. I love you and if it makes you feel any better, you can have anyone of my stuffed animals, except Mr. and Mrs. Poopsy, and Ms. Giggles." That last line made her laugh.

"That child of ours," responded Patricia.

"Alright, honey take a seat," Alan said as he began to bring the food to the table.

"Where did you come up with this recipe?" asked Nicole.

"He googled it," Patricia responded quickly not giving Alan a chance to answer.

"It doesn't matter where I got it from. It only matters that I took the original recipe and improved it."

With that they all sat down to enjoy breakfast. With everything that happened, it felt good to be around people she loved and loved her. As she sat down to eat breakfast she began to think about how the moment when they both decided it was time to leave Wallace and Bennet. It was five years after they had both started. She had decided it was time to step out on a limb and make her dream a reality.

It wasn't the most ideal time to do so, but she realized it was time to start focusing on her and building her firm, instead of continuing to build someone else's. So, she decided to step out on a leap of faith and her friend Alan Keyes took that step with her. They both started at the firm at the same time and had similar aspirations, so they made a deal that when one was ready to leave the other would join them. When she made the decision, it was time for her to leave, surprisingly Alan didn't hesitate to leave with her. In fact, she was surprised when she told him she was leaving, he already had his letter of resignation typed and ready to give to the firm. She would later learn he typed it the same night they made the agreement.

It was something she was grateful for. His confidence in her gave her even more confidence in herself. Alan would always tell her he didn't hesitate because he would have been a fool if he didn't join her, because she was the most talented lawyer he had ever seen. Today, other than the day they started their firm, was the most important day in their firm's history. Today her firm had expanded its practice to not just include corporate law, but to take pro bono cases as well. Previously, every lawyer at the firm had to take one pro bono case a month; that was non-negotiable.

She had turned away several prominent lawyers who refused to accept this clause, but it was not hard for her to do. She had finally reached the point to where she could do things her way and she was done compromising. She viewed it as their loss. With this new expansion, she had an entire department that was dedicated to taking pro bono cases in order to provide a defense to those who deserved one but couldn't afford a defense. However, the requirement to take one pro bono case a month was still in effect.

They sat down and enjoyed breakfast, Nicole listened to Alan's off the wall stories and jokes that made absolutely no sense. She could see why they loved each other so much: they both could be themselves. In that moment she could feel a tear running down her check, as she wiped away before they could see it. Sensing more were about to follow she excused herself from the table. As she was walking away, she heard Patricia asked if she still wanted to go out today. Her reply was a quick yes, as she walked into the room and closed the door behind her. She climbed on to the bed and put a pillow to her face, as the tears starting streaming down her face.

After lying in bed for what felt like an eternity, but was only a couple of hours, Nicole decided it was time to get up. She decided it was time to start making good on her promise from earlier. She grabbed her purse and left her room. As she was walking out the room, she found her friends in their library.

"Excuse me!" she started as she walked through the door. "First I would like to apologize for earlier."

"No, there is no need," both of her friends said at the same time, as they shook their heads and walked towards her.

"I appreciate that. Would it be possible if I borrowed one of your cars; there is something that I need to do. I am not in the right mind to go looking for a......," her voice trailed off, as she couldn't bring herself to say the word casket.

"Are you sure you are okay?" asked Alan. He already knew the answer to the question before he asked it, but he just wanted to make sure.

"Yes, I am," she responded back.

Realizing her friend needed some time to be alone and process things, Patricia readily said yes. As she handed her friend the keys, she whispered to her "I love you and if you need anything let us know." With that Nicole got inside the car and drove away. As she drove away, she felt a sense of relief come over her that she hadn't felt since all of this happened. It felt nice to be able to let her emotions go without drawing the attention of someone else. Although her friends meant well, it felt good to be by herself. As she was driving, she started trying to formulate some semblance of a plan to bring her husband's killer to justice.

After coming up with rough ideas, she knew where she needed to go first, so turned on the radio and drove towards the city. She was so deep in thought she didn't even realize she had made it to her destination. As she got out of the car and looked at her house, it looked different than it had before. Before when she saw it, it was a place of happiness and love, now looking at in that moment, it brought feelings of anger and sadness. She wasn't supposed to be here, but she didn't care, this was her home, she had every right to be here. As she walked to the door, there was a do not enter sign on the door, she almost ripped it off, but she thought better of it. She then realized there was a problem: she didn't have her keys. "I am off to a good a start!" she said to herself as she stood next to the door.

She then laughed, remembering she did have a key. There was a key on Patricia's key chain. They had given her one just in case something ever happened. As she unlocked the door and was about to open the door, she braced herself, having no idea of what emotions would overcome her once she walked inside. She paused for a second, almost locking the door and turning around. But she told herself she needed to do this, not just for Marcus, but for herself as well. As she walked through the door, she was hit by a smell that almost knocked her off her feet. It was the smell of dead flowers. The smell and sight of the flowers brought tears to her eyes and her knees got weak.

She forced herself to keep walking. As she walked through the house, she thought to herself everything was the same as the last night she was in the house. "Damn you Marcus!" She said as she continued to walk through the house. She couldn't but think it had to have been someone who knew him, because no way anyone could have snuck in and did this to him. But who would want to harm him? She started running through a list of people in her head, but she told herself this was crazy, no one that knew him would want him dead. As she continued walking, she had made it to her destination, the bedroom.

Before she opened the door, a sense of dread overcame her. This room use to be the place of so much joy, happiness, and pleasure, but now all she felt was pain and anguish as she was about to open the door. Opening the door and walking through it brought a sense of nothing; she felt numb as she walked in; there were no tears, no anger, no smiles, just numbness. She looked over at the bed and all she could see was her husband laying in the bed, lifeless. She didn't even notice she had started walking, and by the time she did she was on her husband's side of the bed, touching his pillow, imagining she was rubbing his head.

She didn't know what overcame her, the next thing she knew she was lying in the bed, holding his pillow tight to her body with tears streaming down her face. Lying there she was reminded of what she had and what she lost. Lying there in that moment, she knew she couldn't get lost in her sorrow, so she decided to try to focus on finding out what happened to her husband. Lying there, she started questioning if her husband really went through all the effort of planning the night or if it had been part of a sick game by the killer. "He had to have planned it, there were too many personal details that only he knew and no one else." She reached over in the nightstand and grabbed a pen and notebook.

She started to write down all the questions that were coming to her mind; making a checklist. She thought of all the questions she needed that would get her the answers she craved. The first question was one she thought she would never have about her husband: "Does Marcus have secrets?" Writing it sent a twinge down her spine; she was ashamed of herself for writing it, but she knew that in order to find out what happened she had to operate under the premise that there was something about her husband that she didn't know.

"Bang!"

"What was that?" She thought to herself. It sounded like it came from downstairs, but what or who could that be. She immediately got up and went to the bottom of the closet and opened the safe hidden underneath the floorboard. It was still there. She grabbed her Springfield 1911 EMP 9mm and slowly made her way to the steps, in a slow crouch like her husband had taught her. As she was walking slowly down the stairs, there was a rattling noise that scared her and almost made her fall down the stairs. She was able to catch herself, but in doing so the handle of her gun hit the railing on the steps.

"Shit!" She whispered to herself. Just then it sounded like someone was opening the backdoor. "Damnmit!" She ran down the steps and to the kitchen, just in time to see the backdoor close. "Who could that have been?" Things were starting to get crazy, why had someone just been in her house and what the hell was going on? She realized there must have been something her husband didn't tell her. Why else would someone be in their house going through their things looking for something? She turned on lights to see what the person could have possibly been looking for. She walked into her husband's office, which was off to the side of the kitchen. Once she walked in, it was a mess.

"Who was it and what could they have been looking for," she thought out loud. She walked to his desk and began to look at the papers that were now spread across his desk. In that moment she became frustrated and sat down in his desk. "What the hell is going on?" She thought to herself. As she looked up, something caught her attention. In the office was a painting of the two of them, but it looked like something was behind it. To the side of the painting appeared to be a brown folder. She got up and walked over to the painting, lifting it up and finding a folder.

What is this? she thought. She opened the folder and it was bank account information with a series of payments dating back years. Then she saw a name that she recognized at the bottom written in ink, circled with a question mark and she froze instantly.

"What the fuck!"

CHAPTER 9

As SGT. ALLEN PULLED into the station, he had no idea not only of what the Captain wanted with him on a Saturday, but also what was his partner doing talking to the Captain without him. Before he went inside, he wanted to try to call Nicole one more time. Straight to voicemail! Walking into the precinct still felt different, as he walked through the door, he looked to left and saw both his and Marcus's office and for a second, he thought he saw him sitting at his desk working. "Good morning, Sergeant," he heard a voice say waking him from his daydream. It was Adam Anderson, the coroner.

"I need to see you this morning, I got the results back for both Marcus and Mrs. Landry and I think you will find the information from them to be interesting."

"I have to go see the Captain first, but I will come by and see you immediately after I see him." As he walked towards the Captain's office, he wondered what he meant.

Walking into the Captain's office, he saw was the Captain and Detective Howard sitting at the table talking to each other, like they were long-lost friends. They didn't even notice him when he first came in.

"Good morning, I see you started the party without me!" He said as he walked to the table.

They both responded back good morning and he had a seat. "So, what is the new development you mentioned over the phone?"

"I will let Detective Howard explain it to you, since he is the one who found it."

"So last night on the way home, I got to thinking about the two cases and how they could possibly be linked. So, I decided to go back to Marcus's house last night, just to look around."

"What, you went back to the crime scene last night by yourself?" asked a shocked Sgt. Allen.

"He called me first and I told him it was okay," responded the Captain.

"I tried calling you, but I didn't get an answer. I even left a voicemail letting you know what I was doing and left one after I was done for you to call me." As Detective Howard started talking, Sgt. Allen pulled out his phone to see if what he said was true. As clicked on the voice mail app, he saw that there were two voicemails from Detective Howard. He read them and Howard was right; he did leave voicemails. He didn't even realize he missed the calls.

"As I was looking through the house, I happened to go upon a piece of paper that was in some notes about the original Penny case. On the note, the words parking ticket was written with the date April 23rd, 1989, and all the words were circled," stated Detective Howard.

Sgt. Allen didn't even need to hear the next part as he said the words "The date Laura Johnson was killed."

"That's right. So not only was Detective Jones looking into the original Penny case, but he found a potential lead that may have cast some doubt about the guilt of Samuel Johnson. If the note about the parking ticket is actually a lead for the case, this is significant because Samuel Johnson didn't have a car. It would also cast some doubt not only on the murder of Laura Johnson, but the other eleven victims as well."

"Let me stop you," Sgt. Allen interjected forcefully. "I was a part of the investigation and there is no doubt the right person was tried and convicted. Just because you found a note about a parking ticket on the day of the murder, that doesn't change anything. We had witnesses, evidence…."

Before he could finish his statement, Detective Howard replied, "and a judge who tried the case who should not have been allowed to." One of the biggest arguments by those who thought Samuel Johnson was innocent and was a victim of the system was that the judge of the trial was Abraham White, the father of Laura Johnson's husband.

"Here we go with that argument again. Was it good, optics-wise, that Judge White was the judge of record? No. But he didn't let the death of his daughter-in-law cloud his judgement. His behavior was above reproach."

"Of course, you would say that!"

"What does that mean?"

"Okay, that's enough, let's get back on track here. We are all on the same team here. We all want justice for Marcus and Mrs. Landry, as well as to prevent this sick bastard from killing again. A goal we will not accomplish if we sit here and argue amongst ourselves. Adam finished both the autopsies and got the toxicology results back. So, I need the both of you to go see him and find out what he has. Keep me updated."

Sgt. Allen had been around the Captain long enough to know when to keep going and when to stop and this was a time to stop and do what he asked. Sgt. Allen got up and made eye contact with Detective Howard to let him know it was time to get out before things got bad. As they were walking out the door the Captain said in a calm voice "Whatever you two have going on between the two of you, work that shit out!"

"I guess we pissed him off," said Detective Howard.

"Yes, you did," Sgt. Allen said with a laugh. His attempt to lighten the mood between the two of them. "I have a question; let's operate under the premise Samuel Johnson was innocent. Why after all these years would the killer come back after they had gotten away with it originally?"

"That is the million-dollar question, for which I do not have an answer," a disheartened Detective Howard said.

The morgue was in the basement of the precinct. It had been updated over the years, but it still felt they were inside a bunker. It felt like it was 25 degrees cooler down there. It was so cold; they both could see their breaths. "Adam likes it cold down here, I see," stated Detective Howard.

"Yes, he does. He does it to keep people from coming down here for no reason."

As they got closer to the door; they could hear Dante's Symphony playing. As they opened the door, they could see Adam Anderson over a body in the morgue, acting as if he was coordinating the musical arrangement. They both stood there for a second looking at him and then looking at each other.

"It's about time you two joined me. I was feeling like you didn't want to come and see me," Adam said before the two Detectives could say anything.

As he turned around to look at them, Sgt. Allen could see the body on the table for the first time; it was Marcus. Seeing his friend on the table froze him in place; he couldn't speak or move. Sensing his partner may be struggling with the sight of his friend on the table in front of them, Detective Howard whispered, "Are you alright?" Sgt. Allen simply responded with a nod.

"What is it that you have for us?" asked Sgt. Allen.

"I did as you asked; I tested Mrs. Landry for poison, and it came back positive for Batrachotoxin. I also tested Marcus and he came back positive for it as well. So, the cause of death for both is homicide by poison."

Hearing that almost sent Sgt. Allen over the edge. His body began shaking uncontrollably, he got light-headed, and almost fell, but luckily, he was able to brace himself on table nearby. Placing his hand on Sgt. Allen's shoulder, Howard asked him if he was ok. "Get him some water!" shouted Detective Howard.

"I am fine, I will be okay. Keep going, is that all you found?

Detective Howard interjected, "What the hell is Batrachotoxin and where do you get it?"

"Batrachotoxin is only found in poison dart frogs in Central and South America and the feathers and skin of the passerine bird found in New Guinea. But neither produces the poison naturally. It is based off their diet, the melyrid beetle," answered Sgt. Allen.

"So, we have to find out who not only has poison dart frogs or a passerine, but also has access to the melyrid beetle? That doesn't sound hard at all, in fact given the fact neither are found here, we should check around to see who has bought them. It is just strange that Samuel Johnson would have any of these and if he did, where did he get them from?"

"We never found out and he never offered the information. But we found enough of it to kill the entire city in his house, so he got it from somewhere. Can you continue, Adam?" an agitated Sgt. Allen said.

"I almost missed it initially, but after hearing how this may be related to the Penny case, I remembered some of the victims were injected with the poison behind their ears." He motioned for both of them to come closer as he turned Marcus's head, lifted up his ear and shined the light and there it was a small little red mark behind his ear.

"What are we supposed to be seeing," asked Detective Howard.

"It is a small needle mark. It is where the poison was administered," said Sgt. Allen.

"Yes, it is! There isn't one on Mrs. Landry, so it is likely she ingested the poison by drinking it or some other means. The thing about Batrachotoxin is that it is very rare, so the pool of potential suspects should be small, because this is something that not everyone can get access to. The hard part is identifying who has it. It affects not only the nervous system, but the heart as well. Whoever did this is one sick bastard."

"Is this similar to the original Penny Case?" asked Detective Howard, as he was still trying to process everything that was going on.

"Yes, it is," responded Sgt. Allen. "It is the same poison and the same method of delivery."

With that, Sgt. Allen ended the conversation. Adam didn't have much else to tell them outside of what he had just told them, but he promised them he would continue to do his part and if he came across any other details, he would let them know. So, they both said their goodbyes to the coroner.

"Excuse me, I have to go to the bathroom," Sgt. Allen told his partner as he stepped inside for a second. Once he got inside, he went to the sink and splashed water on his face. He was still trying to process what he had just learned and how everything fit together." The sound of someone banging on the door, snapped him out of his trance. "I will be out in a second, I'm not finished," he shouted back. What he heard next made him feel like he was in nightmare that was only going to get worse.

"We got another body!" shouted Detective Howard back.

Hearing those words snapped Sgt. Allen back to reality. "What do you mean we have another body?"

"That was the Captain. He said he tried calling you. He said we have another body and for us to get 1425 Edgewood Drive."

Hearing that address sent chills down his spine. He knew that address and the person who lived there. Detective Howard could tell from the look on his partner's face he recognized the address and it scared him for a second. "Whose address is this?"

Sgt. Allen looked at him in shock and said barely above a whisper "Judge White's!"

Detective Howard looked at him and asked, "What the hell is going on? It is becoming clear to me that these murders are somehow connected to the original murders. We just have to figure out how."

Sgt. Allen looked at him with a look of hesitation. "I'm not ready to go that far. Who would have had a problem with anything from the trial? Samuel Johnson had no friends or family, and who would want to wait almost thirty years for revenge that wasn't directly associated with him? Besides, Judge White could have just easily died of natural causes, as opposed to being murdered. What were the Captain's exact words?"

"He said Judge White's daughter had found his body at the home and he wanted us to go to the scene, just in case."

"See there, you are jumping to conclusions; how about we go out there and see what happened before we start making assumptions," Sgt. Allen said as he walked away.

Detective Howard just there in the hallway for a moment as his partner walked away. This dance was starting to get old to him and he didn't know how much more of it he could actually take.

As he began walking Adam ran up to him; "Hey Detective one other thing, that I found that was strange there was a feather from a pillow and light bruising on Detective Jones's face as if…."

"Someone had smothered him with a pillow," Detective Howard added, finishing Adam's sentence. That is strange, why would the killer smother him, only to turn around and poison him. Thank you and I know this is going to sound weird, but can you keep this between us for now; something weird is going on."

"I will give you a week. That is the best I can do, and I am only doing this because I am curious as well and I want to run a couple more tests."

With that the two parted in the hallway and Detective Howard proceeded to go find his partner and Adam went back to go run his tests.

CHAPTER 10

THE CAR RIDE TO the crime scene was a quiet one; neither officer saying anything to each other. As they pulled up to the gate to enter Judge White's property, reporters were already out front; someone had leaked word about the Judge's death. As they approached the gate, reporters took it as a cue to run up to the car to attempt to ask them questions about what was going on. As Sgt. Allen let down his window to be asked to buzzed in, one reporter ran up to the window and show a microphone in his face. Not realizing what it was initially, Sgt. Allen punched the reporter in his face. As he looked out the window, he could see the reporter's nose was bleeding and heard him shouting to his camera man "Did you get that? That son of bitch just punched me!"

"I apologize, you scared me. If you don't go shoving things in people's faces, you wouldn't get punched in the face," shouted Sgt. Allen back as he tried to contain his laughter.

"Do you think you should have done that? That will only cause more problems and bring more scrutiny to the case, once everything gets out. In light of everything that is going on, we do not need to make an enemy out of the media," stated Detective Howard, almost lecturing Sgt. Allen.

Part of Sgt. Allen knew the Detective was right, but he didn't care and the fact this officer who was still wet behind the ears was questioning him pissed him off, more than that reporter did. Just as he was about to correct the young officer and voice came over the intercom. "Who is this?" the voice on the other end asked.

Not wanting the reporters to hear what they were actually there for, he simply gave them their names and told them they were there to meet with the homeowner in response to a possible disturbance. The voice on the other end went silent, and just as Sgt. Allen was about to press the intercom button the gate opened. The reporters took this as their opportunity to attempt to enter the property. However, on the other side of the gate were some officers waiting, and once Sgt. Allen and Detective Howard passed, they blocked the road preventing them from passing and starting pushing them back on the other side of the gate.

As they pulled up to the house, they saw the coroner's vehicle and they both wondered how he got there before they did. Once they found a place to park, they got out of their vehicles and started walking towards the house. They thought they heard someone calling out to them.

They kept walking to the door, assuming the yelling wasn't directed at them, but as the person got closer, they could make out what the person was yelling. It was one of the younger officers trying to get their attention.

"Sgt. Allen, the body is not in the house. It is in the back yard!"

Both Detective Howard and Sgt. Allen looked at each other, both could tell the other was thinking what was going on and more importantly what were they about to walk into. They both turned around and walked back down the steps and began to walk to the side of the house. As they both walked around the corner to go to the back of the home, they were taken aback by the back yard.

"This is what 50 years on the bench gets you! This is bigger than the apartment complex I live in! Almost makes you think how much of this was earned looking the other way!" exclaimed Detective Howard.

Sgt. Allen didn't make a comment; he simply looked the Detective and kept walking. He had heard the rumors, but wasn't going to give Detective Howard the satisfaction of knowing he could have possibly been correct. Not out of some sense of loyalty for the judge, but he knew if he acknowledged it, it would lead to the Detective questioning everything the Judge ever did, including presiding over the original Penny Murder trial.

The backyard was massive. It had its own private lake as well as a pool. Off to the side of home was what appeared to be a golf course.

"Hey, it looks like someone is motioning for us down by the lake."

Hercules was standing down by the boathouse trying to get the attention of the Detective Howard and Sgt. Allen.

Are they blind and deaf? Can't they hear and see me? He thought to himself.

"You are right it is. I guess we know where the body is," said Sgt. Allen.

"Nice of you two to finally make it down! I guess in your old age your vision and hearing are starting to fail you," joked Hercules. "Adam is already inside looking at the body. His wife found the body this morning around 11 and immediately called 911."

Sgt. Allen stood and listened to Hercules talk, patiently waiting for him to get to the part about why they were called and what, if anything, was found on the body. However, that moment never came. Before he could say anything though, Detective Howard chimed in; "Sorry to interrupt, but why were we called out here? You haven't mentioned any signatures of the Penny Murder so far. Is the only reason we were called out here because it was an eighty-year old judge who could have died from natural causes and more importantly you haven't mentioned a note."

Hercules looked taken-aback for second. He looked over Sgt. Allen as if to ask who does this Detective think he is and who does he think he is talking to. Sgt. Allen simply shrugged his shoulders. While he didn't like the tone the young officer used, he agreed with what he said. Realizing he was not going to get any help from Sgt. Allen, he stated in an somewhat aggressive tone, "you were not called simply because an eighty-year old judge died, you were called because the eighty-year old judge who presided over the original trial died suddenly, according to his family. He had no known health issues, so his death is somewhat of a mystery right now. To get any other information, you will have to speak with Adam inside. Now if you will excuse me, I have something I need to take care of." With that he walked away towards the house.

After Hercules walked away, Sgt. Allen looked at the young detective and said, "Look I understand your frustration, but you have to watch how you talk to people. These are people that you will have to work with, so establishing good working relationships is key. Good relationships equal trust."

Detective Howard only repeated the word "trust," in a disgusted manner and walked inside, not giving Sgt. Allen a chance to follow up. As they walked inside, they saw Judge White sitting in a recliner and Adam standing over his body, examining it closely. It appeared he was looking for injection sites. As they got closer, Adam turned around startled by the sight of them.

"Hasn't anyone every told you two not to sneak up on someone!" he said

"Our apologies! What do you have so far," asked Sgt. Allen.

"So far I do not have much? No obvious signs of trauma, no puncture wounds found. If he was poisoned it would have been in his drink." As Adam said that he pointed to a bottle of Mitcher's twenty-year-old single barrel and next to it was a glass, that still had a small amount of alcohol in it. "It appears he has been dead about 12 hours, so that would place the time of death around 11 last night. I will know for sure once I get him back to my office and get the toxicology report."

"Looks like we will have an interesting conversation with Mrs. White to find out why she didn't call 911 until this morning. Do you mind if we look around to see if we can find anything that may connect it to the previous murders?" asked Sgt. Allen.

"No go ahead. I am almost finished here."

As the two officers began to look around, they noticed Judge White's extensive adult magazine collection. "When I was a kid, I wanted to collect baseball cards," remarked Detective Howard.

"We are not supposed to be looking his collection of magazines; we are supposed to be looking for clues," responded an aggravated Sgt. Allen.

Detective Howard simply looked at the Sergeant and shook his head, continuing to attempt to find any clues or the calling cards of the Penny Murderer. After what seemed like forever, they both finished searching the boathouse and found nothing. They both had walked back over to the body to see if there was anything on him that was missed, now that Adam had finished his examination of the body.

After a few minutes, Sgt. Allen looked at Detective Howard and said "I guess this was simply a case of an old man dying of old age. There are no signs of the copycat. I will call the Captain and let him know, Judge White was not a victim of this new killer."

"Wait," shouted Detective Howard. On the bottom shelf of the table was a magazine, something about it seemed strange, it was the only one on the table. As he bent down on one knee to pick up the magazine.

Sgt. Allen getting annoyed, simply asked; "What are you doing?"

"Something about this doesn't seem right." Detective Howard picked up the magazine and placed it on the table. It was the 1971 *Playboy* with Darine Stern on the cover. As Detective Howard carefully turned the pages, he began to get disheartened, thinking he may have been wrong. But there it was on the centerfold page a note that read:

A Penny For Your Thoughts; What Happens When You Knowingly Send An Innocent Man To Prison? After finding the note, he began to look on the floor for the Penny. He found it there it was, right next to the Judge's left foot. "I guess someone else thinks Samuel Johnson was innocent. We have to find out who moved this."

"That doesn't mean that. The Judge has sentenced numerous individuals to death over his time on the bench. What about Marcus and Mrs. Landry? Neither of them had any ties to the original Penny Murder case. This is likely the work of some sick bastard. We are going to go to the house and talk to his wife. We will not mention any of this; we will ask the basic questions," Sgt. Allen said in a demonstrative manner.

"So, we are going to treat her differently than the Landrys?" Detective Howard asked sharply. He didn't Sgt. Allen a chance to respond. He simply turned his back and walked out, leaving Sgt. Allen to stand there with a look of anger and disgust on his face.

"Detective, stop! Turn around and look at me. Who do you think you are talking to?"

Not wanting to cause a scene and make things worse for the victim's family or make the department look bad, Detective Howard stopped walking and turned around and simply said, "This is not the time or place for this, we have to go talk to the victim's wife. This is a discussion we can have at a later time."

Hating it, but realizing the Detective was right, Sgt. Allen simply acknowledged it with a head nod. He told himself this would be the last time this Detective talked to him like this. They were going to have a long conversation when they were done here. The rest of the walk back to and inside the house was done in silence.

As they approached the front door, there was a young officer at the door, who told them Mrs. White was inside with some of her family and friends. Judge and Mrs. White had been married for almost sixty years. They were high school sweethearts who ended up getting married the day before Judge White left for Vietnam. The only time they were apart were for the three years he was out serving his country; they made a vow they would not sleep apart from the day he got back and it was a vow they had kept.

"Excuse me, Mrs. White, we are so sorry for your loss. We understand this is a difficult time for you and we would like to ask you a few questions," started Sgt. Allen.

"Can this wait? Can't you see my mother has been through enough," one of her daughters said defensively. But before she could finish her mother simply held up her hand and the young lady stopped talking.

"I appreciate your sympathies and yes this will be a good time to talk. I would like to go ahead and get this over with. We can go to my knitting room so we can have some privacy," answered Mrs. White.

As they entered the room, Mrs. White asked them to sit down and apologized for not offering them anything to drink or eat. They both said that it was not a problem and, given the circumstances, it was understood.

"We understand you have been through a lot, so we will keep this as brief as possible. When did you notice something was wrong?" Sgt. Allen asked.

"This morning when I woke up, Abraham wasn't in the bed. I could tell he hadn't slept in the bed at all last night. We had not spent a night apart for the past fifty years. Yesterday evening, he said he was going to his boathouse to read and I went upstairs to lay down, because I wasn't feeling well."

"Can you tell us what time your husband went to the boathouse last night, the time you went to sleep, and what time you woke up this morning?"

"I think he went out there around 6 or 6:30. I am not sure what time I went to sleep, I took one of my pain pills and fell asleep shortly after, so around maybe 7 or 7:30. I woke up this morning around 9. After waking up, I got worried, so I called Abraham's cell and I got no answer. So, I then called my daughter Trisha. She is the one who spoke while we were in the living room. She is the one who found the body."

"We will need to speak with her as well."

"Okay." After that Mrs. White pressed the intercom on her desk and asked Trisha to come to her knitting room.

"She will be here shortly. Do you have any other questions for me?"

"Yes, we do, ma'am," replied Detective Howard. He could sense Sgt. Allen staring intently at him, it felt as if he was burning a hole in the side of his face. This didn't bother him; he was beyond his partner's attitude. "They will be quick, and we will let you continue to grieve. Has anyone made any threats against the Judge recently? Has he received any strange phone calls?"

"No, not that I am aware of, Abraham has been his same self, there have not been anything of concern. Are you saying my husband was killed? This brought tears to her eyes as she began to think about someone killing her husband."

Sgt. Allen, sensing the interview was about to take a turn for the negative, quickly responded, "No, ma'am, that isn't what we are saying. We do not know what happened to your husband at this time." This seemed to calm her down a little.

"I am sorry, Mrs. White. One last question." How long has your husband been a pervert, he wanted to ask, but instead he said, "How long did your daughter see Samuel Johnson?"

"My, you are an uppity one," replied a shocked Mrs. White.

Her response was one Detective Howard expected. Why else would their daughter have kept it a secret?

Hearing Detective Howard ask that question made Sgt. Allen's blood boil.

"Mrs. White, we have no further questions for you, thank you for your time and once again, we are sorry for your loss."

"Thank you, Sergeant Allen," replied Mrs. White as she got up to leave. She didn't acknowledge Detective Howard, she simply looked at him with disgust as she got up to leave the room.

As Mrs. White was about to open the door, Trisha opened the door and came in. She saw the look on her mother's face, so she asked, "Mom are you okay? What did you say to her?" She asked as she looked at both of the officers.

"They didn't do anything. I am fine, honey, just sit down and answer Sgt. Allen's questions."

"Please have a seat, Mrs. White," Sgt. Allen said.

"You can call me Trisha," she responded as she looked over Detective Howard as if he had done something wrong.

"Thank you! We will not take up too much of your time. We only have a couple of questions for you. Can you tell us what happened this morning and also if your father has any known enemies?"

"In particular anyone who wasn't happy with his presiding over the Penny Murder trial," interjected Detective Howard.

JAMES SMITH

Trisha quickly asked; "What does the Penny Murder trial have to do with this and are you saying my father was killed?"

Sgt. Allen quickly responded, "No that is not what we are saying. We are just trying to get an idea of what happened. We will not know happened until we get the coroner's report. Can you walk us through what happened this morning?"

Trisha, appearing to take a sigh of relief, began telling the officers what happened this morning. "My mom called me this morning around 9:30, crying, saying dad didn't sleep in the bed with her last night, he wasn't in the house, and he wasn't answering his phone. She was afraid he was still in the boathouse and something bad had happened to him. So, she wanted me to come over and check for her to see if I would go check to make sure everything was okay. I got here around 10:30."

"Sorry to interrupt you Trisha, but why didn't you call 911 after your mother called you?"

"I figured dad was in the boathouse, drinking his bourbon and looking at his *Playboys*. But..." she couldn't finish her last statement as she broke down crying.

Handing her his handkerchief, Sgt. Allen told her, "It is okay, take all the time you need, we know this is hard."

"Thank you. I keep thinking what if I would have called 911, would they have been able to get there in time to save him."

"Don't think that, he died last night. There was nothing that you could have done."

Hearing this made her feel somewhat better as she began to continue her account of what happened. "After I got here, I walked to the boathouse and when I went in, I saw him there in his chair, with his Bourbon and thought he had fallen asleep. I called his name and he didn't answer. So, I walked over to him was about to shake him, but when I touched him, his skin was cold, and I knew he was dead. That is when I called 911."

Sgt. Allen, wanting to let her get back to her mother and help her grieve was about to close the interview, when Detective Howard interjected with another question: "Did you touch or move anything after you found your father?" He could sense she was hesitant to answer the question, "It is okay if you did, we just need to know?"

After hearing his reassurances, she said, "Yes, I did, I moved the *Playboy* off his lap, closed it and put it on the bottom shelf on the table. I am sorry, I just didn't want anyone to see him like that, looking like some sort of sick man."

Trying to comfort her, Sgt. Allen said, "It's okay we understand, thank you for being honest with us. Thank you for your time, we will be leaving know. If you or your mother can think of anything else, please call me and let me know," he said as he handed her his card.

The walk back to the car and the first ten minutes of the car ride were done in silence. Each one not wanting to hear what the other had to say. Until finally, Detective Howard asked; "Do you have a problem with me?"

"Yes, I do. I have a problem with you thinking you know everything. I have a problem with you acting as if the person responsible for the murders almost thirty-years ago wasn't put to death. You do not know everything or how to talk to people around here."

"So basically, you have a problem with me doing my job."

"No, I have a problem with how you go about doing your job."

"You do realize I am only asking questions that any reasonable person would ask. What do you think will happen once all this comes out? Do you think everyone will share your belief? No, they won't. What do you think the best way to eliminate the perception of bias and to show you have an open mind? Whether you like it or not, and sorry if it hurts your feelings, but guess what, the original case will be put under a microscope. So instead of you fighting me about how I am acting, why don't you ask yourself, why do you not understand this."

Hearing what Detective Howard said, he realized it made sense. In fact, it is the same speech he had given multiple times over his career to detectives who were too invested in a particular outcome of a case. He realized that in order to get Detective Howard and anyone else with doubts about the guilt of Samuel Johnson, he needed to take his advice.

"We will try it your way, but we have to establish a line of questioning for the future. We can't keep going in acting as if we are on different pages. Also, until we get the coroner's report when there is no obvious sign of a homicide, we do not tell the family the victim was murdered. We both can be 100% sure, but until the coroner confirms it, we will only speak of it between the two of us."

"I'm fine with that. I think that is a good idea."

They spent the rest of the car ride discussing strategies and trying to identify people they need to speak with. The first person they needed to speak with the Samuel Johnson's lawyer, Garret James.

CHAPTER 11

It had been a couple of weeks since she found the bank statements in Marcus's office. She had recognized not only the name on the account, but also the bank and the person responsible for handling the account. She sat on the plane and couldn't help but think about how much her life had changed over the past month. One minute she was ecstatic, and her life was moving in the direction she had always dreamed, both personally and professionally, and the next she was burying her husband. She had told Patrice and Alan she was taking the trip as a getaway from everything that had happened. And while that was partly true, the main reason was to find out more about the bank account.

As Nicole sat, waiting to reach her destination, she thought back about the funeral. She almost didn't show up. She and Marcus had talked before and neither one of them wanted a big funeral, they both just wanted something simple. They both joked they would be happy to just be placed in their grave, in a pine box, in the middle of the night, with no one else there. However, she relented because she saw the look on his mother's face, when she first told her she wasn't going to have a big funeral. She couldn't stand to see her in any more pain than she already was. She thought Marcus would have been okay with it, because next to her, he loved his mother more than anything.

While initially she was against the whole idea of a big funeral, she was glad that she did it. Of course, seeing his casket in the front was hard for her. But something strange happened; listening to everyone tell their stories about their memories with Marcus and seeing other people grieve made her feel better. She realized she was not alone. The most moving part was Mrs. Amanda Turner. She was a like a mother to the both of them. She was eighty-three years old and had met the two of them at church. From that day on, she adopted both of them. They would always speak when they went to church and on those days where they didn't show up, she would call them to ask were they okay and when they said okay, she would recap the service for them.

Mrs. Turner gave an amazing eulogy; there was not a dry eye in the church. Then she sang "Amazing Grace." Nicole hadn't realized Mrs. Turner could sing that well. She could hear her singing it right now, but her moment of reminiscing was cut short, as the pilot came over the intercom; "We are getting ready to make our descent to Lynden

Pinding International Airport. Thank you for flying Delta and enjoy your stay in the beautiful Bahamas.

Walking through the airport brought back memories. She and Marcus used to come to the island multiple times a year. They had fallen in love the first time they came and made a point to come back. It was a second home for them. Over the years, they had made some wonderful friends and she was on her way to see one of them right now. She had finally made her way through the airport and got her luggage. As she walked outside the smell of the ocean hit her. She told the driver to take her to Cable Beach.

As she sat in the back of the cab, she looked inside to make sure the contents were still there. After seeing they were, she held her back close to her, a tear running down her cheek. Although Marcus had died almost a month ago, it was still as if she was in a bad dream, waiting for someone to wake her up. But as she held her bag close to her, she realized this was not the case. In her bag were the ashes of her husband. He had told her, when it was time, he wanted his ashes spread in the place where he found true happiness.

Cable Beach was the spot he had proposed to her. The proposal was a shock to her, they had only been dating a couple of months, but he told her he knew from the moment they met she was the one. She could picture the moment he proposed; him down on his knees, the sunset in the background, the smell of the ocean, and her feelings of nervousness and excitement as she realized what was happening. In that moment, she realized how much she loved him and what she was truly missing her life. When she met him, she didn't expect to find love. In fact, while he fell in love with her at first sight, it took some time for her to come to that realization. She didn't realize how much she loved him and wanted to spend the rest of her life with him until she saw him about to propose.

She didn't realize it, but a steady stream of tears had started flowing down her face. Not only was she thinking about Marcus, but also her father. The two men in her life who she loved more than anything were taken from her too soon. She thought about how much they both were alike, but different. She thought about how her father would have been overprotective in the beginning and how much he and Marcus would have not liked any other. But as they got to know each other more, how much they would have started to get along.

"Ma'am, we are here," the cabbie said, snapping her out of her thoughts.

"Can you wait here, until I get back?" She asked as she got out of the cab, with her bag in hand. As she walked out to the beach, it was still as beautiful as that magical night. There were a few people there, but not too many. So, she was able to find a secluded section to do what she had come to do. She lifted the urn out of the bag, placing the bag on the ground, taking her shoes off as she started walking towards the ocean. As she got closer to the ocean, the warmness of the water covering her feet, and up her legs as she started walking deeper into the ocean. She paused for a second, this was it. This was goodbye! She didn't know if she could do it; she wasn't ready to let him go.

"I am not ready to let you go! You lied to me, you said you would never leave. I hate you," she screamed out, as she began crying. This moment was so much harder than she realized it was going to be, all those pent-up emotions came flowing out. She almost turned around, and got out of the water, with her husband in her hands. But she looked up and saw dove flying by, and it brought a smile to her face. You always knew what to do, she thought. She unscrewed the top, saying a prayer in the process and telling her husband how much she loved and missed him. And with that she began to shake the remains of her husband out. His ashes caught in the wind as he was blown out to the ocean. "I love you," she whispered, and she stood there for a few moments just watching, as if he would somehow magically appear.

After a few moments she turned around and headed back to the beach, grabbing her belongings and heading back to the cab. "Take me to First Caribbean International Bank," she said.

Sitting in the cab her focused shifted from burying her husband in the ocean to what was on the bank statement. What did you get yourself into, Marcus? she thought.

Could this be what got him killed and if so why? What does all of this mean? She didn't know the answer to any of those questions, but she told herself she was going to find out.

Just then the cab pulled up to the bank and she got out and proceeded to walk towards the back entrance. She felt a combination of guilt and nervousness. While she had told her friends she would be visiting the island, she didn't tell them the entire truth and that she would be showing up to one of their jobs. While it would be nice to catch up with old friends, that wasn't the only reason she was coming to see them. She had to find out what the bank statements meant.

As she opened the door, she looked around trying to identify her friend. After a quick scan, she saw him. James (Billy) Wallace was the brother of Harry Wallace, but they had had a falling out ten years ago. The only people who knew the reason were Nicole and Marcus. Billy told everyone he was moving to the Bahamas because the job opportunity he was being offered was too good to pass up. While the job was good, the real reason was he wanted to get as far away from his family as possible. He was offered the position of Branch Manager, and after diligently working there for five years, he was made the Manager overseeing all of the bank's branches in the Caribbean.

Their eyes locked on each other at the same time. She could see he was in with an employee, as he gave her the wait a minute finger. She didn't mind; she knew he was

busy and her showing up to his place of employment without telling him, didn't help things. So, she decided to call
her friends and let them know she had made it safely. One
of the conditions for her being able to travel alone was she
had to call and check in with Patricia and let her know
where she was and that she was ok.

As she was getting off the phone with Patricia, she felt
someone touch her on the shoulder, so she turned around
to see who it was.

"Hello stranger, how are you doing?" Billy said as they
gave each other a hug. "Come on, let's go to my office and
talk."

As he closed the door behind them, he asked her, "How
was your flight? I wasn't expecting you to see you today."

"My flight was okay. I decided to surprise you, if that
is okay."

It was something about the way she said that caused
him concern. "What is really going on? Is it something else
about Marcus's death? You know you can talk to me about
anything?"

In some way Nicole felt relieved that he could see
something was going on. She didn't have to beat around the
bush and try to small task. She wanted to get right to the
ask. "I had another reason for coming to see you, outside
of a friendly visit. I need your help." Billy looked puzzled as
she continued not understanding how he could help her. I
found this in Marcus's office hidden and I think it may have

played a part in his death," she said as she handed him the documents.

Billy started looking at the paperwork and his initial response was, "What the hell!" Billy exclaimed as he looked at the name. "What the hell is Marcus doing with my brother's bank statement and more importantly how does he have an account worth over twenty million dollars?"

"So, you didn't know he had an account with your bank."

"No, I didn't. You know both me and my brother haven't been close since he disrespected my wife."

"I was hoping you could tell me when the account was opened and who the account belongs to that has been depositing two hundred and fifty thousand dollars into twice a year, for the last four years."

"You know I am not supposed to be doing that, I could get into a lot of trouble. Also, the banks in the Cayman Islands are used because of their notorious customer privacy."

Hearing that, Nicole's heart sank. "I'm sorry, it was a long shot; I just need to get answers. It wasn't a wasted trip. At least I will get to see my friends," she said trying to cheer herself up.

"Hold up, I didn't say I couldn't or wouldn't do it. I just said I am not supposed to do it, and besides I am not going to fire myself."

A look of relief came on Nicole's face. "Thank you so much! I don't know how I can ever repay you."

"You can join us for dinner tonight; Kiesha is excited you are here and will joining us for dinner tomorrow. I figured you would be tired tonight and wanted to just relax. I must confess also, I already told Kiesha you were coming, so you have to come."

Nicole looked at him with a laugh and said, "I love you and what time do I need to be there?"

"I love you as well and will do whatever I can to help. Dinner will be 6:30, so Kiesha would like you there by six o'clock. Now get out of here and go relax and I will see you at dinner tonight."

"I will see you tomorrow," she said as they hugged and said their goodbyes to each other. As she got into the cab and looked back at her waving friend, she thought of how lucky she was.

Billy went back inside and sat down at his desk. He couldn't believe what was in front of him. "What has my brother gotten himself into?" he thought. As much as he couldn't stand his brother, he still loved him and, in that moment, he was faced with troubling option; he could go against his family or he could go against someone who had become family.

He knew what he had to do; he picked up the phone, calling his secretary and asking her to get him the phone number to the Cayman Island National Bank.

CHAPTER 12

As both Mr. and Mrs. Miller sat in front of each other, they never imagined they would end up in this position and they both wondered who this masked man in their living room was and how did he got into their home. The Millers had been married for almost twenty-five years, and surprisingly they both loved each other more today than they had when they first met. Patrick and April Miller were both teachers at Monroe High. In fact, they first met each other in the hallway, walking to their respective classes. Patrick thought she was the most beautiful woman he had ever seen and April's first thought about him, was "a male teacher, he won't last long." In fact, she had placed money in the school's pool on how long he would be there.

They would pass each other in the halls and see each other in the teachers' lounge. While their interactions were always cordial, they never went much further than the usual talk about school or students. This was not for a lack of trying on her part. She had found herself drawn to him, not because of his good looks, but because of how intelligence he was. However, there was a problem that prevented him from reciprocating her feelings: he was in a relationship. So, she left it alone, because she didn't want to be accused of ruining his relationship, especially since he was seeing another teacher.

However, the roles were reversed a few months later, when he was no longer in a relationship, but she was. He had always found her attractive, both mentally and physically, from the moment they first met. But when his relationship finally ended, he thought he had missed his chance with her, because she had started seeing someone.

That was their dance for the first couple of years, when one was not in a relationship, the other one was. They would have probably never been together if not for cruel fate. She had finally met someone who she thought she could spend the rest of her life with. In fact, they were engaged to be married, but he died tragically in car accident. It took her forever to get over it, but there he was as a friend, helping her to get through it. She could feel he was doing it out of the kindness of his heart and not for any other reason.

A few months after her fiancé's death, they both were working late one night during a severe storm. During the storm, the power was knocked out and neither one knew the other was in the building. It was not until they wondered out into the hallways, did they know the other was there. They couldn't leave, because the storm was so severe, so they both sat in the teachers' lounge and talked for hours. They talked well past the storm ended and afterwards they realized how much they had in common and how much they liked each other.

That night was the first time they made love. It was beautiful, the sound of the storm, being in each other's arms, was the best night of her life. She fell in love with him that night. It was a combination of not only that night, but everything that he had done for her since the death of her fiancé.

On the night of their wedding, he gave her a present. It was a card and inside the card was envelope. The card was homemade and confusing, she expected it to be one professing his undying love for her. However, when she looked at and read the card, she got angry. She didn't understand it; the front of the card read "On the morning after our wedding there is just one thing I want to do." As she opened it, the next page said "No, it isn't breakfast in bed, it isn't even to hold you." The last page simply said, "Run to the bank," and there was a picture of a guy running to the bank with a check in his hand. After reading she looked up at him and saw him smiling and that only made her even madder. He motioned for her to open the envelope inside the card and when she did, she found a check, which was even more confusing.

He simply looked at her and told her to read the check. When she started reading it, she couldn't believe it, and in that moment, she started laughing and was soon joined by him. It was the check from the bet about how long he would last at the school. He explained to her how he found out about the bet and bet on himself, he had placed a bet of over five years. She had wondered for a short time about what had happened with the bet but had forgotten about it. That night they made love all night and, in the morning, they had breakfast in bed and laughed together. They still had the card and check to this day; it was sitting on the mantle, wrapped in plastic.

Now those were the only things she could focus on, as she sat bound and gagged in her chair, trying to figure out what was going on. She was terrified, not only for herself, but for her husband. She couldn't see him and feared the worst. Suddenly a masked intruder walked in front of her. In her mind she was asking what they were doing and what did they do to her husband, but it only came out as garble, with the gag in her mouth. The intruder got closer to her and she got even more scared. As the intruder reached their hands out, she flinched, fearing the worst. However, the intruder was only turning her chair. As she opened her eyes, after closing them in fear, she saw her husband. He was sitting in front of her in his chair tied up, same as her, the only difference he was hunched over as if he was dead.

Tears began to stream down her face as she feared the worse. Then after what seemed like an eternity, she saw him began to move, as if he was waking from a long sleep. She started screaming his name through the gag, but was only able to get out unintelligible sounds. The intruder walked over to her, placing their hands on their lips in shushing motion, as they nodded their head up and down to make sure she understood. When she nodded her head in agreement, they began to remove the tape and gag from her mouth.

"Why are you doing this to us? We have never hurt anyone, and we do not have any money. You can have anything you want, but please don't hurt us," she said.

The intruder simply looked at her from behind the mask and walked over to her husband. Once he was in front of him, he repeated the same process he did in front of her. Once Mr. Miller nodded in agreement, he removed the tape and gag from his mouth.

Once the tape was removed, Mrs. Miller blurted out, "Are you okay honey, can you hear me?"

The intruder walked over to her forcefully, grabbing the tape as if he was about to put it back on her mouth. Only pausing when he heard Mr. Miller say, "Please don't do that. I am okay honey, just do whatever they ask."

This seemed to calm the intruder as they put the tape back down and sat down on the table in the living room.

"I have a question for you Mrs. Miller. If you answer truthfully, I let your husband live. You lie to me, he dies. Do you understand?" they asked as they looked at Mrs. Miller.

Mrs. Miler nodded her head yes, as tears began to flow down her eyes. All Mr. Miller could do was to sit and watch, wishing he could do something to protect his wife.

"It is a simple question; why did you do it?" the intruder asked.

"Why did I do what?" responded Mrs. Miller.

"You know what I am talking about." Mrs. Miller got a confused look on her face as she honestly had no idea what they were talking about. Mr. Miller simply looked at her with a look of surprise as he tried to figure out what they were talking about.

"It is obvious she doesn't know what you are talking about. You have the wrong person, if you let us go, we won't say anything to anyone. We understand you made a mistake, someone did something bad to you. But you can't punish us for something someone else did."

The intruder looked at the both of them and said, "You are right. I made a mistake; I am so sorry. I will let the both of you go." The intruder paused for a second and acted as if he was about to untie Mrs. Miller, begore he said, "Do you both think I am stupid? I didn't get the wrong person. You both have no idea how long I have been waiting and dreaming of this moment. You both will pay for what you did."

Both Mr. and Mrs. Miller could feel the anger in the intruder's voice and both of them were scared for the other.

"We can talk about this. Tell us what you are talking about, we didn't do anything to harm you intentionally," Mr. Miller said, his voice noticeably shaking.

"You are right, you didn't harm me. You hurt people who I loved more than you could possibly imagine. So, I will ask you again, why did you do it? Do not give the you do not know what I am talking about excuse. Twenty-four years ago, to the day, you lied, and it got someone killed!"

All of sudden a look of sadness came over Mrs. Miller's face as she realized what today was. Tears began streaming down her face, she couldn't hold her head up. She could only say I am sorry over and over again, barely above a whisper.

"Now you remember, don't you?"

Mr. Miller, not knowing what was going on looked over at his wife confused. "What is he talking about honey, what is going on?"

"Cut the act, Mr. Miller. You are as bad as she is. What she did was bad, but what you did was even worse."

Hearing that caused Mrs. Miller to look up in shock. "What is he talking about, Patrick?"

"Nothing honey, don't pay any attention to him. He is crazy, he is just saying a bunch of nonsense."

"Why don't you ask him where he was the night your fiancé died?"

A look of shock and concern came over Mrs. Miller's face as she tried to process everything that was going on. She had forgotten she was tied up and being held hostage. She was only focused what she had just heard and trying to figure out what it meant. "Patrick, what the hell is he talking about?" She then looked at the intruder and asked, "What are you talking about, why are you doing this?"

"Honey, look at me. Do not pay any attention to him, he is just saying this to get you upset with me."

"Look at you two. You built this facade like you two were this perfect couple and these perfect people. Yet, you both were keeping these secrets from each other and you both are killers! But maybe that makes you perfect for each other."

"Who are you to lecture us? You broke into our home and our holding us hostage," Mr. Miller responded angrily.

"I know what I did, but when are you the two of you going to take responsibility for what you did. In particular you, Patrick, either you tell your wife what you did, or I will!"

Mr. Miller could tell the intruder was serious. He paused for a second and tried to gather himself. "I am sorry honey, I had to do it. I loved you and it was the only way I could have you," he said as his voice began to trail off.

Realizing what he was about to say, Mrs. Miller began crying uncontrollably. "No, tell me you didn't do it. Tell me you didn't," she kept repeating over and over again.

"He didn't love you. He was cheating on you and he wasn't going to stop. I tried to talk to him. I tried to get him to stop and I wasn't going to let him hurt you. He wasn't supposed to die, he was only supposed to get in accident."

Hearing that Mrs. Miller got quiet and couldn't say anything. She couldn't even look at her husband. She simply sat in the chair with her head down.

"April, please say something. Please! It was accident."

"I don't think she wants to talk to you anymore," the intruder said.

"Fuck you, you bastard. You did this, we were happy until you came here and did this."

"My loved ones were happy, until you two ruined their lives. So, guess what? I do not feel an ounce of pity for either one of you. You did this to yourselves." With that the intruder got up and walked over towards Mr. Miller. Standing in front of him, the intruder bends down and placed their hand behind his ear.

"Ouch, what did you do to me?" Mr. Miller said as he felt a sharp pinch behind his ear.

"I put you out of your misery," the intruder said as he walked away.

All of sudden, Mr. Miller's chest got tight and it felt as if his throat was closing. He could no longer talk and was only gasping for air. Hearing this snapped Mrs. Miller out of the trance she was in.

"Patrick, Patrick! What did you do to him you bastard? Patrick please don't leave me."

It was too late; she saw his head fall down and this time she knew he was dead. She began to cry uncontrollably.

"Now you see how it is to lose someone you love at the hands of someone else."

"What do you want from me? You ruined my life and for what a mistake I made twenty-four years ago?"

"Yes," the killer simply said as they got up and walked towards her.

As the killer got close and reached their hands behind her back, Mrs. Miller flinched as she expected to fill sharp prick at any moment. But it never came as the killer simply untied her. The killer didn't say anything, they simply walked towards the front door. Before leaving out they removed their mask and turned around, revealing their face to Mrs. Miller.

Mrs. Miller sat there in shock as she said, "You look just like them!"

And with that the killer was gone as quick as they had come in. As the door closed, Mrs. Miller got out of her chair and ran over to her husband and tried to wake him up. Then all of sudden she could feel her breathing slowing down, her chest tightened, and she fell to the ground; the last thing she saw was her husband in his chair dead.

CHAPTER 13

IT HAD BEEN A couple of weeks and word about the new Penny Murders had not reached the public. Both Sgt. Allen and Detective Howard were surprised but thankful. Neither one wanted to deal with the media or public attention that would follow. Detective Howard and Sgt. Allen had placed a renewed focus on their partnership. They had started working and functioning as a team. While there were still some issues to work through, they had started to do a better job of communicating with each other. Over the past couple of weeks, both detectives had been working hard to find any possible leads, combing through pictures, revisiting crime scenes, recanvasing the areas, trying to find any new information or find something that may have been missed. However, they had no luck.

At the behest of Detective Howard, they had started looking over the old case files and identifying witnesses or anyone who may have been involved in the original trial who they could speak with. First on the list was Garret James; he was Samuel Johnson's lawyer. Samuel Johnson was a court-appointed lawyer who had voiced his displeasure with being forced to defend him. Detective Howard wanted to speak with him not only about his defense of Samuel Johnson, but to also see if they could identify anyone who may have had an issue with the results of the trial.

Shortly after the trial ended, he had moved to Jacksonville, Florida and opened up his own firm. Over the past twenty years, his firm had grown to one of the largest in the state of Florida. Detective Howard had voiced how unusual this was and how something about the move didn't seem right to him. He had even gotten Sgt. Allen to agree with him. The Captain had agreed to the trip, but he told them they better come back with something, or else they would be on traffic duty.

They had been in the car for about three hours and were getting closer to their destination. They had spent the first part of the drive not talking about the case, but trying to get to know more about each other. Sgt. Allen learned that Detective Howard didn't know his father growing up and that he didn't find out until he was adult the reason why. He had heard the painful story and he could see and feel the sadness in Detective Howard as he talked about it. Detective Howard had told him how he was told his mother died during childbirth and his father didn't want him, so he grew up in foster care. But he later learned that his father didn't know he had a son. After realizing that he went on a long search to find his father. He told him about the feeling of joy that came over him when he found out who his father was, but that feeling turned to sadness when he learned that his father was dead; he had been murdered.

Sgt. Allen learned this was the reason Detective Howard became a police officer. He had grown up wanting to be an engineer, but all of that changed after he learned of his father's murder. He couldn't prevent or solve that crime, but he could do those things for others. Sgt. Allen told him about what happened to his family and how he almost didn't recover. After talking about each other's personal tragedy, they both came away with a better understanding of each other.

After their talk they both went silent for a while, needing a moment to process everything the other had told them, as well as a moment to recover from talking about their own losses. Breaking the silence of the drive, Sgt. Allen spoke. "So, when we get there, we have to make sure we do not turn him off to us immediately. I only interacted with him briefly at the original trial, but from what I remember from the stories told to me by other people he was a bit of a hot head, didn't take to well with being questioned, and was ambitious."

"How do you want to play this?" Detective Howard asked.

"I think we should be honest. We have been lucky that word hasn't gotten out yet, but let's face it, we are on borrowed time. I think by being honest it may jog his memory about something that didn't seem quite right at the time and provide us with a lead that can help us in this case."

As Sgt. Allen finished his statement, the GPS came on and indicated they were approaching their final destination. As they turned into the parking lot and found a parking spot, they both went over the plan one last time, before exiting their vehicle. Unfortunately, for them there were no parking spaces near the building, and it was one of the hottest days ever in Jacksonville. The temperature was 114 and the humidity was 98%. They both were sweating uncontrollably as they walked to the building, both wearing a suit, with jacket.

Detective Howard said, "Damn its hot. Did we go to hell and no one tell us?"

"Yea, we probably could have worn something less hot today."

As they both entered the building the fresh breeze of the air conditioner was a welcomed feeling. They instantly felt a sense of relief, however, their clothes were soaked.

"Good afternoon, gentlemen. It appears you two may not be used to this wonderful Jacksonville weather," said the gentleman behind the welcome desk.

"No sir, we are not," they both replied as they walked towards the desk.

"How can I help you good folks today?"

"We are here to see Mr. Garret James. He is expecting us." replied Sgt. Allen.

"Let me just make a phone call to verify and I will send you on your way. What are your names?" asked the guard behind the desk.

Both officers gave him their names and he called someone, and they could tell by the conversation, the person on the other end verified they did have an appointment.

"Both you gentlemen are good to go. The elevators are down the hall, to the left. You will be going to the twenty-first floor, the penthouse. Once you get off the elevator, someone will be there to guide you the rest of the way."

They both said their thank you and found their way to the elevator. On the way up, they both thought to themselves of how Garret had come a long way from being a public defender in Monroe to the managing partner of one of the largest firms in Jacksonville. As they looked out the elevator, they could see not only the parking lot, but also the St. Johns River. They both stood on the elevator and thought how lucky they were there were no other people and the elevator went straight to their floor without any stops.

The sounds of bells indicated they had reached the twenty-first floor. As they walked out of the elevators, a set of glass doors were in front of them, with the name of James's Legal Group in gold on the door. They could see another welcome desk in front of them, and a multitude of people of walking around talking.

"Welcome to the big leagues," whispered Sgt. Allen.

As they walked through the door, they were greeted by the secretary. The secretary was in her early twenties and could have passed for a model. She was sitting down, but they both could tell she was a tall woman and had mocha skin. Detective Howard tried hard not to stare at her, but he could have sworn she caught him looking and smiled at him.

"My name is Elizabeth Johnson, and welcome to James's Legal Group, how may I help you today?" she said.

Detective Howard still staring at the beautiful woman in front of him, was unable to speak, so Sgt. Allen spoke up. "This is Detective Howard and I am Sergeant Allen; we have an appointment to see Mr. James."

"Give me one second, let me check to make sure he is available." With that the secretary picked up her phone to call who they assumed was Mr. James. After a few moments she placed the phone down and said, "If you will follow me, I will take you to his office."

With that they followed the secretary. They followed the secretary through the rows of the desks, they were amazed at how many people actually worked in the office. Everyone worked out in the open; there were no closed offices.

As she was taking them to Mr. James's office, she realized they were looking around confused as to the layout of the office. "Mr. James's doesn't believe in closed offices; he thinks everyone working in the open makes communication easier and people don't get trapped in their own little words. He is the only one that has his own office, one of the perks of being the boss," she said.

The doors to Mr. James's office were massive and beautiful. They were made out of Pakistani wood from what appeared to be the 17th century and appeared to be hand carved. Once they got to the door, Mrs. Johnson knocked and said, "Detective Howard and Sgt. Johnson are here to see you sir."

They could a hear a voice from the other side saying come in. As they walked inside his office, they noticed it was massive. His floors were glass tile, a mixture of white encompassing a black square with the letters GJ engraved in the floor. He had an Enloe 4 Piece Living room set as office furniture. His office was nicer than most people's living room. Mr. James was sitting behind a German Biedermeier Mahogany Kneehole desk. Garret James was in his early sixties, but it was obvious that he had had extensive facial surgery over the years. His skin was pulled so tight that it appeared it hurt as he talked. He had an over done artificial tan.

"Welcome gentlemen, please have a seat. May I get you both something to drink? We have some Fillico." Seeing the look of confusion on both the officer's faces, he said, "It's bottled water, a very expensive bottle. But it is worth every penny."

They both politely declined.

"Mrs. Johnson that will be all for now," Mr. James said.

Once she closed the door, Sgt. Allen began speaking. "Thank you for taking the time meet with us. We understand that you are a very busy man, so we will try not to take up too much of your time."

"It is my pleasure. I must say I was shocked when I received your phone call about a case that happened over twenty years ago. I am surprised to see you still on the force, Sergeant Allen, I thought you would have moved on to bigger and better things by now."

"No, I am still here doing what I love."

"I can respect that; now how may I help you two?"

"Full disclosure; the reason we are asking about the original case, is it appears we have a copycat. Someone is copying the signature of Samuel Johnson and we wanted to talk to you to see if there was anything that stood out during or after the trial or was there anyone that took an unusual amount of interest in the case or someone who expressed their strong opposition to the verdict."

The attorney sat there for a second trying to process what he had just been told and then after a few moments he finally spoke. "Are you sure it is a copycat?" was his first question.

This was usually the moment when Detective Howard would interject and share his doubts about the original trial, but this time he just sat there and let Sgt. Allen answer the question.

"While the signature is the same, we have not found anything that would lead us to believe this was anything but a copycat."

The attorney was still in shock, but he managed to speak. "I am sorry, I am a bit surprised; I understand your saying you believe it is a copycat. However, he always said he was innocent. Hearing this makes me wonder; did I get an innocent man killed? This is a bit perplexing and I am having a hard time processing it right now."

"We understand take all the time you need."

"To answer your question, there were some weird things that happened during the trial and there were a couple of people who expressed their objection to the verdict and displeasure towards me quite forcibly. I believe I still have some of the letters that I received over the years, I will gladly give those to you, if you think it will help."

"We would greatly appreciate that."

With that he picked up his phone and called his secretary and told her to get him the Samuel Johnson file. Once he put the phone down, he looked up at the two officers and said, "there were a few things that stood out. He claimed that he was having an affair with two of the victims and there was even talk about Mrs. Trudeau being pregnant with his child. However, the judge refused to let me present the evidence at trial, because as he put it, he was not going to let his daughter's name be sullied by the lies of some, forgive me for this, but this are his words. He finished that sentence off with the N-word."

"What are you talking about, there was never any mention of Mrs. Trudeau being pregnant," a shocked Sgt. Allen responded.

"Exactly, and Judge White wanted it that way. The family said they had proof she couldn't have been pregnant, since she never missed any time from school and there were no records of her having a baby. That was more than enough for the judge to rule it inadmissible. The whole trial just didn't sit right with me and immediately after it was over, I had to get out of town. There was no way I would have been able to practice law in town again. I would be forever known as the lawyer who defended the black man who killed white women."

"Why do you think he said that he had an affair with both of those women?" asked Detective Howard, finally speaking.

"I am not sure. He didn't have any proof and neither woman admitted to it, so you could tell the jury didn't believe him. It only made the jury hate him that much more. I tried to tell him, that he should not mention it when he took the stand. But he wanted to, even after I told him he would only hurt him."

Before either officer could say anything, Sgt. Allen's phone rang. It was the Captain and his words sent Sgt. Allen into a state of shock; "Get back here! We have two more bodies, a Mr. and Mrs. Miller. They were both teachers at the high school and someone leaked it to the press. They know everything and are about to publish a story."

After getting off the phone, he thanked Mr. James for his time and looked over to his partner and told him they needed to get back, because shit had hit the fan. As they were getting ready to leave out, Mr. James told them to stop by his secretary's desk on the way out and she would give them a copy of Samuel Johnson's file. With that, they both left his office. Once they got to the secretary's desk, Detective Howard remembered he left his pen in his office. It was a gift from his mother before she died. So, he told Sgt. Allen he would be back he had to go get his pen.

As he walked back to his office and he got closer to the door, he could hear Mr. James talking from behind the door. He got closer and could tell Mr. James was close to the door as he heard him say, "They just left, I told them everything you told me and they bought it." That was all he could hear as it appeared that was the end of the conversation. Not wanting to be seen by Mr. James as he opened the door, he ran and ducked behind an empty desk, just as the door opened. Once he saw he had left he made his way back to the front desk. In the rush to not be seen and trying to process what he had heard; he had forgotten all about the pen. As he walked back to the front he was still shaken, and he looked out of it.

"Are you okay?" Sgt. Allen asked with a look of concern, as he saw the look on his partner's face.

Hearing those words made him snap out of his trance. "No, I am good. On the way back, everything hit me that is going on and I got lost in my thoughts for a moment."

With that, they both headed out of the building and into the madness ahead.

CHAPTER 14

As NICOLE SAT IN the car in the on the way to the Wallaces' house, she couldn't help but think about all the good times, she and Marcus had had on the island. She had spent the day trying to keep her mind off the information Billy found. She tried to go out and see the island in an attempt to take her mind off of it, but she found herself going to the places she and Marcus use to go together on the island. She didn't know what was worse, the feeling of sadness brought on by thoughts of her and Marcus, or the feeling of anticipation that she may find out what may have gotten her husband killed.

As she walked to the door, she could smell dinner. As usual Keisha had outdone herself. She didn't realize how hungry she was until she smelled the food. She had not eaten anything all day. As she approached the door, she could see Billy dancing with their two daughters, Zoey and Tyra. She paused for a second and thought about her and Marcus and about how they wanted to have children, but hadn't been able to. A tear streamed down her face as she realized it would never happen.

"Auntie Nicole," she could hear a voice calling her name and the sound of feet running to the door. The door opened and there were two of the most beautiful kids she had seen.

"Hello, my two princesses. My god, you two have gotten so big since the last time I saw you."

"I am the tallest."

"No, I am the tallest."

"I am the tallest," Billy said as he walked up behind them. "Now go wash your hands before dinner. Would you like kids? We are having a two for one special."

"Stop trying to pawn our kids off on Nicole," a voice from around the corner said. It was Kiesha. As she came from around the corner, they both embraced. "Thank you for coming and I am so sorry about what happened to Marcus. I am sorry I couldn't come to the funeral."

"Its okay, Billy explained the reason to me and I understood. Thank you for having me. Do I smell what I think I do?"

"Of course, I made your favorites: Conch Fritters, Jerk Chicken, Pigeon Peas and Rice, Baked Macaroni and Cheese, and for desert: Bahamian Guava Duff."

"I love you!"

"What about me?" asked Billy.

"Aww is my poor baby jealous," Kiesha replied jokingly. "Come on let's go to the table, so we can eat and catch up. I know you two have something you need to talk about. But it will have to wait until after dinner."

"Fine by me, dinner smells too good to wait," Nicole responded.

As they all sat down at the dinner table to eat. The food was amazing, but it felt good to be around friends, and not have to think about what all she had been through. It was nice to sit there and listen to their family stories; she listened about trips they had been on, she was entertained by stories told by Zoey and Tyra, they both wanted to tell her the same stories. She would listen to both of them tell them, because the whoever told the story first didn't tell it right, so the other twin would have told it the correct way.

After dinner they moved to the living room, where an intense dance battle was held. She sat back and watched them and thought about how much Marcus would enjoy this moment with her. She could feel a tear streaming down her face, she wiped it away quickly, not wanting to ruin everyone's good time.

"Billy, how is it that you married a black woman, moved to the Bahamas, and you still have no rhythm?" a joking Nicole asked.

"I ask him the same thing every day," a laughing Kiesha responded.

"I have rhythm, you both just can't appreciate it with your untrained eyes. Daddy has rhythm, doesn't he girls."

"Mommy says it's not nice to lie," responded Zoey.

That made everyone in the room laugh. "That's right baby, don't lie," a still-laughing Kiesha responded.

"Not my girls too, ouch that hurts."

"We still love you daddy, but you can't dance," the girls responded as they gave him a hug.

"Alright girls it's time to go to bed."

"Please mom, not yet, can we stay up a little longer?"

"No, you can't. Say good night to daddy and auntie Nicole."

They both said their good nights and went to their rooms to put on their pajamas to get ready for bed.

Kiesha said, "I will put them to sleep so you two can talk. I will be back once I put them to bed."

As Kiesha walked down the hall to the girl's room, Billy motioned for Nicole to follow him to his office. Once Nicole entered, he closed the door.

"Would you like a drink? I have your favorite, home-made Goombay Punch."

"You know I would," Nicole responded.

As he poured them both a drink, he began talking. "You know I was surprised when you showed me the banking information. I had no idea he was using one of the branches in Caribbean and I am pretty sure if he had known I was the branch manager, he would not have put his money in the account, or should I say he would have withdrawn it."

Nicole looked puzzled with that last statement.

"Yes, that account has been open since 1993. This is where it gets even crazier, the name on the account of the person making those deposits is Governor Landry. The first payment was for one-hundred thousand dollars, and there were deposits of one-hundred thousand dollars every year, up until the last six years, when the deposits increased to two-hundred and fifty-thousand dollars twice a year."

"Why was Governor Landry making these payments to your brother for almost thirty years?" Nicole asked, as she stood shocked, trying to absorb what she had just heard, trying to figure out what Marcus got involved in and found out.

"That isn't even the weirdest part."

"What is?" she asked as she sat there waiting for him to tell her.

"I called the Cayman Island National Bank, by the way you owe me a bottle of Macallan's. I had to promise my friend in the back a bottle in order to get him to give me this information," he said with a smile on his face.

"I will send you a bottle as soon as I get back."

"Don't worry about it, I still have the last bottle you sent me. So, my friend was able to tell me the name on the second account was Abraham White."

"Wait, you mean Judge Abraham White?"

"Yes, the one and only, and get this, he started receiving payments from him the same year as he did from Governor Landry."

Nicole sat there for a moment trying to process everything she had just been told. "What happened in 1993?" she whispered.

"I do not know, but I know if it involves my brother it is probably not something good."

"Were you able to find out anything about the third account?"

"Unfortunately, that one is still a mystery. The only thing I can tell you is my brother started making deposits into the account in 1993. He has transferred a total of four million dollars to the account since then."

Nicole sat up with a renewed sense of understanding, not because of the four million that had been transferred to the account, but because of the year 1993. "Did you say 1993?" she asked already knowing the answer.

"Yes, I did. What was so significant about the year 1993?"

"That was the year of the Penny Murder trial," she said with a look of shock. Nicole sat there in shock as she tried to process what it all meant and why did Marcus had this information. She was sure the reason he was killed because he found out something from the old trial, but she still had no idea what it was. She was trying to play it out in her head, how Marcus found out and what exactly did he find out that got him killed.

"This all seems a little too connected to be a coincidence. Marcus never said anything to you about any of this?"

"No, he didn't, and you are right, this can't be all a coincidence. All I know is this is what got him killed. I do not know how all of this fits, but I know it has something to do with the Penny Murders." In that moment she realized Billy didn't know everything that was going on back on home. So, she decided to tell him right now. She told him about how Marcus, Melissa Landry, and Judge White were all killed by the same person, someone copying the Penny Murders.

"Wait, so you are telling me the same person killed Marcus, Melissa Landry, and Judge White? And to top it off, they are copying the Penny Murder. What the hell is going on? What have you gotten me involved in?"

"I know, I am sorry. I didn't realize you would find all of this out. I have no idea what is going on. I am still trying to process all of this. I am sad and pissed that Marcus was doing all of this and he didn't tell me. We used to tell each other everything and we promised we would never keep secrets from each other," she said as tears began flowing down her face.

It hurt him to see his friend crying like that. He got up from behind his desk and gave her a hug and told her everything would be okay and that he and Kiesha were there for her and would do whatever they could to help.

Hearing those words made her feel better. Just then Kiesha came into the room. "Hey, you guys you need to see this," she said as she held up her phone in front of them. It was a breaking news video on Facebook, a friend of hers had shared. The news anchor stated that Mr. and Mrs. Miller, both teachers at Monroe High, had been found dead in their homes. The news anchor continued by saying the suspect behind their deaths is the same person behind the murders of Detective Marcus Jones, Mellissa Landry, the daughter-in-law of the former Governor Landry, and Judge Abraham White. The last words out of his mouth before the video ended were the most significant. His last words were the murders were suspected to be committed by someone copying the Penny Murders from the 90s.

They all sat there in silence for a few minutes, then finally Billy spoke. "Nicole, I know how much you don't want to, but you need to leave this alone. You need to give this information to the police and let them handle it. We do not want anything to happen to you, we can't stand to lose both you and Marcus. This has obviously grown, and you have no idea who is involved and what any of this means."

Nicole appreciated his concern, but she couldn't leave this alone; she had to see it through and besides, she didn't know who she could trust. If Marcus didn't tell anyone then apparently, he didn't know who he could trust either, and that included Sgt. Allen. "I appreciate your concern, but I can't leave this alone. I have to find out what happened to Marcus. I will be careful, but I can't stop."

Kiesha barely let her finish before she went over to her and gave her hug. As she held her in her arms, she said to her "promise us you will be safe. I know you won't stop; I wouldn't stop either. But you have to be careful, do not put yourself in any unnecessary danger. If you need us, you know we are here for you."

"Thank you and I promise." Nicole said as they let go of the embrace. She understood their concern and she appreciated their concern. "Did either of you know the Millers?" she asked.

"Yes, we both were in their classes. It is crazy that they both are dead. Who would want to hurt them? They were two of the nicest people in the world and would never hurt anyone. They loved each other more than anything," Billy replied.

"Somehow, they are connected to all this as well, I just have to figure out how. I am sure nothing the killer has done so far has been random, there has to be a reason for each victim."

"And we are here to help you try to figure it out," Kiesha said as she looked at both her and Billy. With that they all spent the rest of the night and most of the morning trying to make sense of everything together.

CHAPTER 15

IT HAD BEEN A day since the information about the case had been linked. The city was turned on its head, people were in a panic, the department was inundated with calls from scarred and irate citizens. The reemergence of the Penny Murderer had awoken those voices in the community that claimed Samuel Johnson was innocent. Sgt. Allen could barely make it to work, trying to navigate the protests. It was almost impossible to turn into the parking lot at the precinct; protesters were standing out front demanding justice, calling out those who they claim put an innocent man to death.

As he got out of his vehicle all other sounds were drawn out by the protesters. So much so that he didn't hear Detective Howard calling his name. In an attempt to get his attention, Detective Howard touched his shoulder. However, this gesture didn't have the intended effect. It scared Sgt. Allen half to death and he turned around ready to fight. He was pissed, but relieved it was Detective Howard. They didn't even bother try talking outside, they both looked at each other and acknowledged they should probably get inside.

They didn't have time to talk once they entered the building. As soon as the door closed behind them, they saw Captain Brown in the hallway and he motioned for both of them to follow him. As they walked through the door, they were caught off guard by all of the people inside the squad room. There was the Chief of Police, the three Assistant Chiefs, the Mayor, the District Attorney, and former Governor Landry. Detective Howard could understand the reason for everyone else inside the room, except for a retired Governor. He was even further shocked when he spoke first.

"Where do we stand with the investigation? What have found out about the murder of my daughter?" Governor Landry demanded.

Seeing his partner was a bit shocked by what was going on, Sgt. Allen answered, "We are still trying to find out why each person was targeted. We have not found a connection between any of the victims yet. The two newest victims were both schoolteachers and were loved by everyone in the community. Two of the victims had some sort of connection to the original case; your daughter, Mrs. Landry, by her association to you and Judge White, who was the sitting judge on the case. We do not know how Detective

Jones fits into the picture as well. The notes indicate the victims all did something the killer believed to be wrong on some level. We do not know about the last two yet. The first three victims were all killed by Batrachotoxin, the same poison used in the original murders. Additionally, Mr. Garret James gave us his file from the original trial, and we have not had a chance to go through it entirely to identify any potential leads."

Harry Wallace growing angrier by the second and already growing frustrated with how this was being portrayed by the media against him. He used the original case as a springboard to starting his career in law; in fact it the case is the reason why no one ever runs against him for DA. "So, basically, you have nothing. What happened to Nicole Jones?"

Detective Howard growing impatient with this inquisition stated, "As you know investigations take time sir, especially when there is nothing obvious link in the cases. I am sure you understand this, having worked on the original case. Especially considering it took, what, seven years to catch the original killer." The detective knew the last part was unnecessary and would hear about it later, but he didn't care. He didn't appreciate being ambushed like this and being questioned by people who were not a part of the investigation.

Captain Brown cussed to himself after hearing the young detective speak and knew it would cause issues. So, before the DA could respond, he said, "We talked about Nicole before, she is not a suspect at this time. If anything changes then we will reevaluate, but I do not see the need in bringing her in and wasting time, that could be spent doing other things."

"What about the baby? The lawyer for Samuel Johnson said there was a talk of potential baby in the original trial. If there was a baby, then maybe that person grew up wanting revenge," said Detective Howard.

"How dare you disrespect her and her family by even mentioning that lie. There was no baby. She would not have laid with that filthy animal. This is the last time you will mention that," Governor Landry said angrily.

Detective Howard was taken aback by the Governor's response, but he was still undeterred as he asked his next question, "What if Samuel Johnson was innocent?"

Harry Wallace looked at the detective and said with disgust, "What if Samuel Johnson was innocent? You were not there, so I will not let you sit here and question the work of all of those involved in the original trial. Samuel Johnson was guilty, I knew it, the city knew it, Samuel Johnson knew it, and your partner knew it," he said, looking at his former partner.

Realizing the situation was about to get out of hand and to protect the young detective, Sgt. Allen said, "If that is all you have for us, we need to go see Adam, so we can get the details about our two newest victims so we can continue our investigation."

Captain Brown said, "Yes it is, and keep us updated."

With that the two officers walked out of the office. "What the hell was that?" snapped Detective Howard.

"Welcome to how things are done in this department. As you can see, the Governor and the DA run this city," replied Sgt. Allen. "Now let's go find Adam, so we can find out what happened to the two newest victims."

As they walked into the coroner's office, they found him sitting behind a pile of paperwork with a sandwich in one hand and a pen in another.

"Good morning gentlemen. How is your morning going," Adam said with a sheepish grin.

Sgt. Allen responded with a laugh, "Fuck you. What do you have for us?"

"I can feel the love in the room. Not much, the victims died around 10 am yesterday. It appears that both victims were poisoned, but I am still waiting on the lab results. Follow me and I will show you the bodies."

They both looked at each other and followed behind the coroner, as he led the way with his sandwich in his hand. He ended up taking them into the room with the bodies and pulled back the sheets, revealing the naked bodies of Mr. and Mrs. Miller.

He first showed them Mr. Miller body. "As you can see, he has the same mark behind his ear as previous victims, indicating the poison was potentially injected behind his ear. Outside of that, there is nothing unusual about his body." Next, he showed them Mrs. Miller. "Mrs. Miller, unlike her husband, doesn't have any distinguishing marks on her body. So, it is likely she was poisoned in some other manner, possibly a drink. But I can't be for certain at this time."

"So, you can't tell us nothing else?" Sgt. Allen asked hoping there was something else.

"Unfortunately, that is all I can tell you at this time. If I get anything else, I will let you know."

With that the detectives said their goodbyes and left the morgue. As they walked out of the office Detective Howard asked, "What does the DA have against Nicole Jones?"

"It's simple, she use to embarrass him in the courtroom. He has been looking for any excuse to embarrass her and this is his opportunity. But don't worry about Nicole, if there is one thing, I have learned about her, she can take care of herself and prefers it that way. Let's go by forensics to see if they have anything."

As the two officers walked up the steps to the third floor, Sgt. Allen's phone rang. It was a number he didn't recognize, he almost didn't answer it, but something told him to. It was Nicole.

"Where are you," he asked.

"I am out of town; I went to go visit some friends. I have to speak with you when I get back, its important. It's about something I found out here."

"What are you talking about?"

"I can't talk to you about over the phone. I will call you when I get back."

With that Nicole was gone. Sgt. Allen thought to himself, what could she have found out and why couldn't she tell him now?

"Is everything okay? Who was that?" asked Detective Howard.

"That was Nicole, she said she had found something and needs to speak with me when she gets back."

"Did she say what she had found?"

"No, she did not, and she didn't say where she was either."

As they walked into the Forensics office, they saw a couple of officers and civilians at their desk working, none of whom even bothered to look up at them. When they got to Sgt. Raymond Franks's office, he had his back to the office, typing intently on his computer, listening to some Thelonious Monk. Sgt. Franks had been on the force for ten years and he had spent most of his time in the unit. He loved it, even though it wasn't like CSI. He fell victim to the line of thought he would be doing the same things as the people in the show. He turned around when he heard a knock on the door.

"Sgt. Allen, I was expecting to see you. I see you brought a guest; this must be your new partner, Detective Howard. I have heard good things about you," Sgt. Franks said as he extended his hand out to shake the young officer's hand.

Detective Howard responded, "Nice to meet you."

"You say that now, wait until you get to know him," Sgt. Allen said as both he and Sgt. Franks began laughing.

"Have a seat," Sgt. Franks said to them as he reached behind him to pull a box off the desk behind him. "We just finishing checking the note and penny, as well as some other things found at the scene. Just like the previous scenes, the killer did a good job of wiping or not leaving any prints or any evidence. However, we found a found an eye drop bottle in the kitchen, and it had a partial print."

Both Sgt. Allen and Detective Howard looked at each other and then looked at Sgt. Franks. Could this be the break they needed to help break this case open?

"We checked it against both of the victims, and it didn't match either."

Allen and Howard got excited hearing that, they had finally gotten some good news and a potential break in the case.

"We entered the print in the system to see if we get any hits and we also are testing the contents of the bottle to see if it is in fact the poison, or simply eye drops. We should have something on both by the end of the day." Sgt. Franks also reached inside the box and pulled out two plastic bags. "Here are the two notes that were left at the scene, as well."

Sgt. Allen took the notes from Sgt. Franks and as he looked at them. The first note read; "Penny for your thoughts; what happens when your wife commits a sin and you cover it up?" The same as the previous notes, Sgt. Allen had no idea what the notes meant. The second note read: "Penny for your thoughts; what happens when you can save a life, but you remain silent to protect yourself."

"Just like the previous victims, Mr. and Mrs. Miller apparently did something the killer viewed as a crime worthy of murder. What are we missing? Something about these murders has to link together, we are missing it. We have to figure it out," stated Detective Howard.

"You're right, but what do a cop, the daughter-in law of a retired Governor, a Judge, and two teachers have common? We are going to have to go through the histories of all the victims again, and see if there is something we missed," responded Sgt. Allen.

Detective Howard said in a questioning manner, "Is it obvious the sin he knew his wife committed is tied to her not saying something about a previous murder?"

In that moment, Allen's phone rang. As he picked up the phone, he recognized the voice: Tina Montgomery, one of the Department's Crime Analysts. "Excuse, I will be back, I have to answer this," he said as he excused himself from the room.

"So how are you enjoying working with your partner?" Sgt. Franks asked.

"So far, so good. We have our challenges, but that is to be expected with any new partnership. We both have to figure each other out and it doesn't help that I have doubts about the trial and conviction of Samuel Johnson."

"How so?"

"There were just somethings that I think were a bit sketchy in the investigation and the trial, seems like it was sham. Everyone involved had already made up their mind he was guilty and everything was set up to make sure that outcome was reached."

"Those are valid points, but from my understanding they had eyewitness testimony, as well as evidence indicating he was guilty."

"True, it could be that I am way off-base, but I like to verify things, instead of just taking everyone words. You know the saying, trust but verify."

"I understand but you will have issues in this department if you try to verify everything. You will not make many friends."

"I guess that isn't a problem for me, because I am not here to make friends."

"While you may not be here to make friends, you do have to work with these people. In the world of law enforcement, you don't want to make non-friends. If you do, you will make this job harder than it already is. You can't do this job alone; you need to be able to rely on others and others need to be able to rely on you. Just something to think about."

"You are right, but I can't let people's hurt feelings get in the way of me doing my job. If people get their feelings hurt, then so be it. I am here to solve cases and make the city safer, not to appease people's fragile egos."

Sgt. Franks realized he was not going to change the opinion of the young detective, so he decided to change the subject. They took this opportunity to get to know each other, as they both would be with the department for the foreseeable future. In the course of the conversation Detective Howard learned that DA Harry Wallace and Sgt. Allen had a falling out, shortly after the original trial. No one knew the reason why and neither of them ever said what the cause was. Everyone thought it was strange, because the two of them use to hang out all the time, even when they were not working. There were those who thought it was because DA Wallace took most of the credit for the case and used it to advance his legal career.

After about fifteen minutes, Sgt. Allen returned back to the office. "We have to go; we have a potential lead about the source of the poison. I was just on the phone with one of the analysts and they passed along information about a Thomas Rice. He is involved in the black-market sale of exotic animals. They were able to find an old ad he posted two months ago, trying to sell a poison dart frog, with beetles.

He has no priors and is originally from Florida. He lives just outside the city, so if we leave now, we can get there within the hour."

An excited Detective Howard, stood up and said, "What are we waiting for? Let's get out of here and go talk to him."

"Sergeant Franks, when you get the results on the print and whether it was poison or not, give me a call," Allen said as he walked out the door.

As they were leaving, Detective Howard's phone rang. It was a quick phone call and once he got off the phone, he said to Allen, "Something has come up. You can handle this by yourself, right?"

Sgt. Allen felt a sense of happiness and confusion. Part of him was glad to be able to conduct the interview alone, without having to worry about his partner messing up. However, he was confused because he wondered what could possibly make him want to miss this. However, he didn't have time to figure out what that reason was. "No, I got it. Go take care of what you need to. I will let you know what, if anything I find out."

"Thank you! I promise this won't happen again, but it is a family emergency."

With that the two officers said their goodbyes, one to go interview a potential witness and the other to go take care of a family emergency.

CHAPTER 16

IT HAS TAKEN ME longer to find his house than it did to actually get here, Allen thought to himself. It had taken him about thirty-five minutes to get to the area of the house, but he had spent almost as long trying to find it. Thomas Rice was a thirty-nine-year-old white male, never married, no kids, and a bit of a recluse. His home was deep in the woods and his address didn't show up on GPS. "I have to find this place before it gets too late, I will never find my out of here in the dark," he whispered to himself.

There in the distance, he thought he saw a sign. As he got closer, he realized he did. The sign said no trespassing, all violators will be shot without question. When he saw the sign, he started thinking maybe it wasn't a good idea to come out here by himself. As he kept driving, he saw a house in the distance. The house itself didn't look like he thought it would. He was expecting to see a half-decaying log house, with a bunch of clutter in the yard. Instead he saw a modern-style home, fairly new. It looked like it was almost five thousand square feet at least. Behind the home was a large building. Sgt. Allen assumed this was where he kept the animals.

As he parked his car, he saw someone come outside the house with what appeared to be a shotgun. Not wanting to get shot today, he turned on his loudspeaker; the first time he was glad that he had had it installed in his car. "This is Sergeant Allen, with the Monroe Police Department. I am here to see Thomas Rice."

He could see the person on the porch saying something, but he couldn't hear what they were saying, so he opened his door so he could hear them.

"I am going to need to see some identification," the unknown gentleman said.

"Is it okay if I walk towards your porch and show you?"

"Yes, come on, but no sudden movements."

As Sgt. Allen walked to the porch, he had his ID in his hand out in front of him, so the unknown person could see his badge. "As he got close enough for the person to see his badge he said, "I am Sergeant Allen and I am looking for Thomas Rice. Is that you?"

"Seems legit. What do you want with Mr. Rice?" the unknown gentleman asked.

"I just need to ask him a few questions."

"Questions about what?"

Not really wanting to play twenty-one questions with the gentleman, Allen said, "I am here to ask him about the sale of poison dart frog. Before you ask, I do not have a warrant, but if you would like I could get one. I know all about your business and honestly, I do not care. But what I do care about, is that he may be able to answer some of my questions and provide me with some answers about a potential killer."

Hearing that last part troubled the gentleman. The look on his face changed and his voice became more rushed. "I am Thomas Rice, but I do not know anything about a murder. I only sell animals; I do not kill anyone."

"I know you didn't kill anyone, but I was hoping you could give me the names of the individuals who you have sold poison dart frogs to." Sgt. Allen got the sense Thomas was about to get amnesia. "The part about me not caring about your business can change if you do not want to answer any questions. I found your ad online about selling one, I have a screenshot of the add, along with the IP tracing it back to you. I can make a phone call and get a search warrant and have this place swarming with cops, and since the trafficking of illegal animals is a federal offense, you will have to deal with the federal government and I am sure you do not want that." He had made the part about the IP address up and he didn't even believe himself about being able to get a search warrant based off the information he had, but he had to give it a try, because he didn't want to come back out here.

Thomas paused for a second, as he considered what the officer said to him. He was also impressed that he was able to find his ad, because he had placed it on the dark web. "I don't have the person's name. I don't get their names and I do not give them mine. All sales are done with cash. In this business you don't want to leave a paper trail, don't want to leave anything that will connect me or the buyer."

Hearing that, Sgt. Allen's hope disappeared. Another dead end, he thought.

"I can't give you the person's name, but she…."

"Did you say she?"

"Yes, she mentioned that it was for scientific purposes and she would double the payment amount if I could get her some melyrid beetles as well. It took forever to find those things; I had never heard of them before. I should have charged her more, because after finding them and having them shipped here, I barely made a profit."

"The beetles are where the poison comes from, without eating them; they are just regular frogs." The fact he didn't know this last part made Sgt. Allen question how much of an expert this guy really was. "Can you describe the woman for me?"

"I didn't know that. She seemed like an average woman, I can't remember every detail, only that she was white,

probably late thirties, and about my height or a little short-
er. I am 6', so she is about the same."

"That's all you can tell me about her? Where and when
did you meet? How did she contact you?"

"Yes, that is all I can remember. I didn't really pay much
attention, this wasn't a date, I just wanted to get my money and get out of there. We met at Wal Mart, about two
months ago. The majority of our communications were
done through a secured website that deletes messages after
forty-eight hours."

Hearing that, Sgt. Allen thought to himself, he just
couldn't catch a break.

"Wait, she did give me a phone number to contact her
once I got the beetles. I think I may still have it, give me a
second."

With that Thomas went inside the house. After what
seemed like forever, he came back out with a piece of paper
with a number on it.

"Here you go, this is the number she gave for me to
call her."

Sgt. Allen looked at the number and figured it was a
burner, but at least it was a start. "Thank you and if you can
think of anything else, please call me and let me know," he
said as he gave him one of his cards.

As he got inside his car to drive off, he couldn't help but
think about what Mr. Rice had told him. "It was a woman."
He didn't know why that part stuck out to him, even if it

was the killer, but he knew he had to figure it out. In that moment, he also wondered where his partner was. But he couldn't focus to much on that, he finally had something to work with. So, he picked up the phone and called Diana. "It's Mike, I have a phone number I need you run for me, and I need for you to tell me what you can find about it. The number is 912-555-7234. I have to go, but call me as soon as you find out something."

"Okay Mike, I will let you know what I find immediately."

After getting off the phone with her, he decided to call the Captain and tell him what he had found out. "Hey Captain, I am just leaving Thomas Rice's house. He sells exotic animals. Diana found an online add he placed a couple of months ago trying to sell poison dart frogs."

"What did you find out?" asked the Captain.

"He couldn't give me a name, but get this; the person that he sold the frogs to specifically asked him to get some melyrid beetles."

The Captain already knew the significance of the beetles, so this further piqued his interests. "Was he able to give you anything about the person who bought them?"

"He was able to give me a phone number. I just gave it to Diana. I fear it may be a burner, but at least it will be a start. If it is, I will be able to track where the phone was sold and hopefully, can get an ID using that information.

And Captain, get this, he said the person he sold it to was a woman."

"A woman? So are you telling me the killer is a woman?"

"I am not sure, but the person who bought the only source of the poison in the region is a woman, so we will see where the cards may lie."

"Do you want me to get a warrant for Thomas Rice?"

"No not yet, I fear if we do and he is arrested, we will not get anything else from him. At least this way I have the ability to go back and ask him questions and can use the potential arrest as leverage. But what you can do is get me a warrant for his phone records, I want to know who he called when I left."

"No need to say more, I will get that done. Is there anything else?"

"No that is all."

After he got off the phone with the Captain, his phone rang, it was Diana. "Tell me some good news please," he said hoping she would provide him with some good news.

"I was unable to give you the name of the phone's owner. It is a prepaid phone, so there is no owner information. However, I was able to get the location the phone was purchased. I am texting it to you right now, so you can try to get the purchaser's information, the date it was purchased, and hopefully if it is still available, any camera footage. I have also passed the information to Hercules and let him know what it was for and he is working on getting a warrant, just in case there are any issues."

"Thank you so much! You are my hero." Shortly after he got off the phone with Diana the address came through on his phone: 374 Winchester Drive, Johnny's Quick Stop. He knew the address well; it was where he had gotten his coffee from every morning for the past ten years. He had a good relationship not only with the people who worked there, but the owner as well. He had always prided himself on his relationship with everyone in the community. On the way to the gas station he called the owner to let him know what he needed, to speed up the process.

As he walked inside, he saw Tonya Blackshear behind the register. She was a senior in high school and had been working here for the past two years to save up money for college.

"Good evening, Sgt. Allen! Mr. Johnson already called me and let me know what you needed. I looked through our records to see if the person who bought the phone used a credit card. No luck; they paid in cash. I have set up the camera in the back for you. I have pulled up the date the phone was purchased, so all you have to do is press play and everything should be in order."

"Thank you, Tonya, you are a life savior. How is the family doing; are you keeping your head in the books?"

"You're welcome! Everyone is doing okay, mom has started a new job, and my dad actually gets back this weekend from his deployment. You know I am, still got straight A's and in the running for Valedictorian."

"Awesome! Keep up the good work! Tell your parents I said hello; tell your mom I said congratulations and tell your dad I said welcome home." With that he walked to the back and pulled up a chair and got ready to watch the video. On the tv was a sticky note with a time on it; Tonya had written the time of purchase on it. The phone was purchased at 10:23 am, so he fast-forwarded to 9:45 to make sure he caught the person entering the store. For the first ten minutes there was no action, no one entered or left the store. Then at 9:57, more people started walking inside the store. However, there was no one that fit the description given by Thomas Rice or who stood out to him.

Then he finally saw someone come in who could possibly be who he was looking for. However, they were wearing a hat, so he couldn't see their hair or their face and it didn't help that the person didn't look up at the camera. He could tell from the way the person walked, they were a female, which made all of those things even more suspicious. He tried following the person as much as he could while they were on screen, with the hopes he could get a good picture of their face. As they got to the register, he realized this had to be the person, because no one else had come that fit the description. Then he looked at the time, it was 10:22, and they were at the register and he saw them getting a cell phone.

"Come on, turn around; you son of bitch! Come on show me your face!" He whispered to himself. They made their purchase and they still had not shown their face and as they were walking towards the door, he had given up hope, then the individual turned around. Whatever excitement he had went away immediately as he was still unable to see her face. Defeated, he got up and left the store. As he walked out the store, he cursed as he lost what he considered to be a good lead. As he walked to his car, he looked across the street and saw the Monroe Bank. In that moment it him as he picked up his phone.

"Diana, I need you to do something for me."

CHAPTER 17

As DETECTIVE HOWARD SAT there waiting, he couldn't help but feel some ounce of guilt at what he was doing. Trisha White, the daughter of Judge White, had called him and told him she wanted to meet with him and only him. She stressed that she did not want Sgt. Allen there and if she saw him, she would leave. When Howard first heard that, it was a shock to him. He tried to wrap his head around that statement and try to figure out why she didn't want his partner to be there. He didn't know, but he would be sure to ask her. He initially felt guilty about not telling his partner, but that went away, once he realized there could possibly be something, he hadn't told him that was important.

She had told him she wanted to meet at Cedar's Point. He had never heard of the place before that, but when he got there, he realized why she wanted to meet there. It was a secluded location, and provided privacy. He had gotten there early; they were supposed to meet at 3 pm, but he had arrived at 2:15 pm. He wanted to make sure he knew how to get there and also wanted to look through the Samuel Johnson file.

After hearing Garret James's phone conversation, he realized the information in the file was information that both Mr. James and the unknown caller wanted them to see and not necessarily information that would be pertinent to the investigation. As he went through the file, it was obvious the information given was meant to paint a certain picture. He looked at the file and commented to himself that if this is the file that was used during the trial, Samuel Johnson didn't stand a chance.

He realized he wasn't going to get anywhere with that information, but he knew someone who could help. So, he picked up his phone and called Elizabeth Johnson. She had passed him her phone number as they were leaving, so he figured there was no time like the present to see if she was free tonight. He felt a little guilty, because he was going to use her. While part of the date would be business, he did have legitimate interest in her and wanted to go out with her. So, he was happy when she said she was free and she would love to see him tonight. As they were finishing up making plans, he saw Ms. White walking towards him. He said goodbye just as she walked up.

He hadn't realized it when they first met, but she was a beautiful woman. She was six feet tall, had short red hair, and a nice shape. She was wearing a luscious, red, lace romper with black heels. She walked with a sense of confidence that was exciting. He had learned that she was a chemical engineer in California and she was only here visiting her family. He felt bad for her and could relate to her and the pain she was going through right now.

"Hi, Ms. White," he said as she approached. He reached out to shake her hand and to help her find her seat.

"Hi, I know you must be wondering why I am meeting you like this."

"I was, just a little bit, especially given our last interaction."

"I apologize for how I reacted to you."

Detective Howard cut her off, "No, you have no reason to apologize. With what you were going through and everything else you have been through I totally understand. I apologize, I could have handled things a little better."

That seem to put her at ease a little bit as a slight smile came across her face. "The reason I wanted to meet you, is because there are some things I wanted to clear up and some information I need to provide you. My mother wouldn't like that I am here, and I am sure my dad is rolling over in his grave right now." She began to cry after that.

Detective Howard feeling a little bit uncomfortable and not really knowing what to do, gave her his handkerchief and tried to comfort her and let her know everything would be ok. "I understand that you have been through a lot and if you want to, we can do this at a later time. We can just sit here until you are ready to talk, or you are ready to leave. It is up to you, no pressure here."

"You are sweet to say that," she said as she put her hand on his knee. "I think I am ready to do this. But you have to promise me this, no one can know that I told you this."

Seeing the look of concern and fear in her eyes, he agreed to her conditions.

"My family hasn't been as honest with you or the police department as they should, and I fear that is the reason my father was killed." She paused for a second to gather her thoughts and get herself together.

Detective Howard sat there listening intently trying to take everything in and hear what she had to say.

"All those years ago, after my sister's death they left out some details. I was only twelve at the time, my sister was ten years older than me, I remember hearing her and my parents arguing before her death about making the family look bad. This was before her trip to Europe, which was strange because it was during the school year, but the story everyone told it was because she had a once in a lifetime opportunity to intern at one of the largest modeling agencies in Europe.

"What do you mean, she said because she loved him? Wasn't she married to Victor Johnson at the time?"

"Yes, she was. But my sister wasn't happy with him. She only married him, because it was what our families wanted. She and Victor grew up together, and with his family connections and ours, it was foregone conclusion they would marry each other, once they got older."

"Are you saying your sister was having an affair? Do you know who he was?"

"I believe so and no I do not know who she was having an affair with. I only know it was someone my family didn't like. I had seen her on the phone sometimes and heard her mention the name Adrian. I never heard a last name, only the first. Whoever he was, I got the sense that she cared for him deeply. Before my dad's death, I heard mom and dad arguing. I heard mom say they should have told the truth in the beginning and then my dad says; forgive me for this, these are his words not mine. I would never say this otherwise."

"It's okay, I understand. Go ahead and say what you need to say."

"Okay. He said so everyone could find out my daughter was sleeping with a nigger!"

Even though it was part of the story and not directed at him, hearing that word still caused him to frown. Seeing the look on his face and the pain it caused, Mrs. White apologized again. Hearing her apologize again made him felt better, but there was no need for her to apologize, those weren't her words.

"I do not know what any of that means or how it all ties together, but I get the feeling it is connected somehow. I couldn't stay quiet any longer and had to tell someone."

"I am glad you told me and thank you for telling me. Forgive me, but why are you doing this? I got the sense you didn't like me all that much when I interviewed you after your father's death."

"I didn't like you, you brought back all those memories I had repressed, and I hated you for that. But once I got past that, I realized I had to tell you for my sister."

"But why tell me and not my partner or anyone else?"

"I am not sure if you know this or not, but there are those within in the department who are not the most trustworthy and I am not so sure about your partner. I remember hearing my father mention Sgt. Allen's name before and I remember talking to him after my sister died. Something never felt right whenever I talked to him and that feeling returned when I saw him that day my father died. I know this is your first case and you are new to the department."

Detective Howard looked shocked at her last statement.

"I am sorry. I know he is your partner, but I am being honest: he was hiding something."

Detective Howard couldn't tell her that he felt the same way. "It is okay, I am just glad you trust me enough to tell me. I promise no one will know that we talked today or at all."

"Thank you and I believe you. Do you mind if we just sit here for a few minutes, in silence; I like the view from here. He hadn't even noticed, but the view from there was beautiful. However, the view was the last thing he wanted to focus on. But with her sitting next to him, placing her head on his shoulder, all he could do was to look at the view and feel validated. "I knew there was something that was not being told and I am glad I am not the only one who feels this way about Sergeant Allen," he thought.

After they had sat there for another thirty minutes in silence, Trisha said, "I need to go, I didn't realize it was so late. Thank you for taking the time to listen to me and for sitting with me afterwards. I needed that."

"It was my pleasure and if you think of anything else, please let me know. Can I walk you to your car?"

"No that is okay. Thank you for asking, I don't want to take the chance of anyone seeing us together." She realized how that sounded after it came out of her mouth. "I am so sorry; I didn't mean it like that."

"It's okay, I know you didn't. I will just sit here and enjoy this view for a few more minutes."

With that they both said their goodbyes and Trisha gave him a hug, which caught him off guard. As he watched her walk away, he couldn't but feel sorry for her. She had grown up in that house and had to live with that secret for all those years and never had anyone to talk to about. He could sympathize with what she was going through. As he sat back down, he pulled out his notebook and began to strategize how he would deal with the new information he learned today.

After he finished, he walked to his car and began his drive to Jacksonville for his date.

CHAPTER 18

ARTHUR LANDRY WAS ENJOYING the single life. He loved his wife and he missed her; her death had hit him hard. He was still a womanizer, but he blamed himself and his father for his wife's death. He wasn't out of town for business, he was actually at a hotel in the city with a woman whose name he didn't even remember. Prior to his wife's death, he was having multiple affairs, with no care about what it was doing to his wife.

To try to ease the pain of his wife's death he had turned into an alcoholic. His mother-in-law had taken the kids because she saw what he was becoming and didn't want the kids to see it. He didn't want them to see it either, which is why he didn't fight it. He had been drunk every day since his wife's death; the only exception was her funeral. His father tried talking to him as only he could. He called all kinds of names and told him how much of a disappointment he was. In the past those words would have stung and been enough to get him to listen, but now he didn't pay them any attention.

He hated his father now; he blamed him for his not only his wife's death, but also the way he had treated him his entire life. His father was demanding and gave him no options on what he would do in life. His career and the woman he would marry was planned out for him as a kid and there was no deviation from the plan. The fact he was forced into the marriage played a large role in his frequent affairs; it was his way of rebelling against his father.

The death of his wife and the reasons behind it had opened his eyes to everything his father had done to him and for him. He didn't realize how much he hated him until this moment. Now he could not stand the sight of him and he told him so. His father looked at him and reminded him of what he had done for him all those years ago and that if he didn't watch it, he would make sure he would go to prison for what he did.

Now his nights were spent with a bottle of Macallan's and nameless beautiful woman. This night was no exception. He had used a service to find this one, whose name was Cherry. She was lying on the couch wearing only a sheer robe on with a thong underneath. On most nights he would be next to her on the couch, his hands all over her, but tonight he wasn't in the mood. As he stood in the kitchen with his drink, he grew more and more angry. He didn't know why, but all of sudden he felt this rage overcome him.

Arthur slammed the glass down, breaking it in the process. He was so enraged he didn't even realize it. With blood dripping down his hand onto the floor, he walked over to her. "Wake up you bitch!" He began yelling at her, startling her in the process. She had no idea what was going on as she looked at him in shock.

Seeing her not moving only made him madder. He reached down grabbing her by her neck as he started screaming; "Why did you do this to me, Laura? I loved you and you would rather lay up with him?"

Cherry had no idea what was going on. All she could do was close her eyes and scream out for him to stop and try to hold up her arms to block his punches. In that moment she was certain she was going to die, then all of sudden the punches stopped, and she didn't hear him anymore. She slowly opened her eyes and started screaming even louder when she saw a masked intruder standing in front of her and Arthur lying on the floor motionless.

"Calm down, I am not going to hurt you," the masked intruder said as they handed her, her clothes. "You can go, I will take care of this. You are safe now."

Cherry sat there for a moment confused. Was this person her guardian angel? She didn't even care what that meant for Arthur. She jumped up and said thank you, even giving the masked person a hug. Afterwards, she hurriedly put on her clothes and left the house. Once she had left, the intruder put Arthur in a chair, handcuffing his hands behind his back. Afterwards they just sat there waiting for him to wake up. They decided to pour themselves a drink while they waited.

After about fifteen minutes, Arthur began to slowly awaken from his slumber. He was still a little dazed initially, as he tried to figure out what was going on. He tried to rub the back of his head, but he was unable to move his hands. As he realized his hands were handcuffed to the chair, he began to shake violently, trying to get his hands free. Then he heard a voice in the background that sounded familiar.

"Calm down Arthur, you are not going anywhere. You are only going to hurt yourself."

"Who the fuck are you and what are you doing in my home?"

"I am the person who is making things right. You sinned, just like the rest of them. Only unlike the rest, you physically killed someone."

"What the hell are you talking about? I didn't kill anyone, but when I get out of this I will kill you. And I will enjoy it. I am going to make it be slow and painful."

The intruder let out a laugh as they walked over to Arthur. As they bent down to eye level, they calmly said, "Do you honestly think you are going to get out of this?"

The way they said that scared Arthur. He went silent for a moment and couldn't move. He didn't want to die, not like this. In that moment he not only feared death, but he realized he was face to face with his wife's killer. "You killed my wife," Arthur said with a look of defeat and despair."

"Yes, I did. What do you care? You stopped loving her a long time ago, and besides, she was just as guilty as you."

"What are you talking about? You killed her because of my father, the note you left even said so. What kind of monster are you,m punishing Melissa for something she didn't even do? My father is the monster! Why are you not with him instead of being here with me, and why would you kill Melissa for his actions? She never did anything to hurt anyone!"

The killer stood there for moment and let out a small laugh. "I didn't kill her for something your father did. Sounds like you didn't know her as well as you think you did. She was keeping a couple of secrets from you and you thought you were keeping secrets from her."

Arthur sat there for moment, trying to process what he was just told. "Liar, she didn't have any secrets, she told me everything."

"Let's move on, we will get back to that later. Are you ready to admit what you did twenty-six years ago?"

Arthur's eye lit up for a moment as he began to think. "I don't know what you are talking about. I didn't do anything twenty-six years ago that is worth my dying for."

The killer looked and him and simply said the name, Laura Johnson.

Hearing that name brought back memories. Arthur just sat there unable to speak or move. He always knew that eventually someone would find out what he had done. "It was an accident; I didn't mean to do it. I loved her."

The killer didn't say anything, they walked to the kitchen and poured a drink for the two of them. As they walked back into the living room, they went to hand Arthur the glass, but they realized his hands were still tied. "I forgot, it looks like you may need a little help to drink this," they said as they placed the glass to his lips and began to pour. "You are still not being honest, that is not all you did. You killed her in cold blood and then you had your daddy clean up your mess like you always do. Let's be honest, you always complain about your dad, but anytime you do something wrong, you call dear old daddy to fix it for you. This time not only did you screw up, but someone else paid for your sin."

Arthur Landry sat there for a moment and then he began to laugh and he got angry all of sudden. "Do you want me to feel bad for killing that bitch? She was nothing and you are nothing. Who did she think she was to turn her nose up at me, like she was better than me? And who do you think you are, coming into my home and doing this to me? Do you think I am afraid of you? Do you know who I am? I will end you! If anything happens to me, you will never be able to rest again. My father will find you and kill you."

"There he is. There is the real you. I was wondering if I would get to see him or not. You killed her because she didn't want anything to do with you and then your father got some help framing an innocent man."

"He wasn't innocent, he had already killed before that and he even killed after that. So, if you think I am going to feel bad for people thinking he killed her, then you are wrong. He was a murderer and he deserved to die. I wasn't going to die for that monkey or that bitch!"

"Correction, you may not have died for them then, but you will die for them tonight!" As the killer finished his last statement, a beeping sound started. The killer looked at their watch and turned the alarm off. The killer then walked behind Arthur Landry, unlocked the handcuffs, and started walking towards the door. Realizing he was free, Arthur got out of his chair and ran to the killer, but as he was just about to grab him, his chest got tight and it felt as if his throat was closing. He then fell to the ground, and the last thing he saw was the killer walking out the front door.

CHAPTER 19

Nicole had gotten back from the Bahamas late at night and instead of going back to Alan and Patricia's, she decided to stay at a hotel. She couldn't bring herself to go back home and probably would never be able to do so. She had gotten up early so she could come into the office to try to return to some normalcy. Her office was modest in size, though it was still bigger than most offices. She had purposely picked the corner office because she liked the idea of being surrounded by glass and having a magnificent view. Their offices were on the 20th floor and she could see the entire city. To add a sense of privacy, she had installed mirrored window film on the inside to prevent people from seeing what she was doing. The only wall that wasn't glass was the wall leading into her office from the main office.

As Nicole sat her desk, as much as she loved having her own firm and office, it didn't feel like hers right now. As she looked the picture of Marcus on her desk, she started thinking about the day they met. The day they met was by chance. It was one of the nights that she happened to go out while she was working at Wallace & Bennet. Her friends had dragged her out; begrudgingly she went with them to Karaoke. They were always trying to get her to go, but she would always tell them no, but this time they cornered her and she had no choice but to go.

As they walked through the door, they heard what they would later describe as sounding worse than a dying cat. They all begin to laugh as they heard the singing, in fact she almost walked out of the karaoke bar but decided against it. As they all walked in and saw the person on stage, all her friends made jokes about the person's horrible singing, but not her. She remembered being instantly attracted to the person on stage. This was someone who knew he couldn't sing, so she thought, but he didn't care. He just wanted to have a good time and didn't care what others thought. She would later find out that he in fact did think he could sing. She was the type of person who was always reserved and was happy to stay in her shell. Her friends had been trying for the longest to get her to open up more and to sing in front of people, because they would always tell her she had an amazing voice.

Marcus Jones was the first man she ever approached. It was amazing the amount of courage one could get from peer pressure and a couple of glasses of Harlon Estate. It was the best decision she had ever made. Ever since that day they had been inseparable. They were both what each other needed in their lives. They brought a sense of calm and happiness to each other. He was a detective in the police force, which made the dynamics of their relationship complicated, but fun. They both worked long and odd hours, so they could appreciate the time they had together and respected each other because they both were doing something they loved.

Most people thought their relationship was doomed to fail. After all, he arrested bad guys and she set them free. The love and respect they had for each other helped build the trust that each one was doing the right thing in their jobs. They never crossed the line and tried to get the other to talk about things they couldn't. They had too much respect for each other to cross the line and too much respect for themselves to cheat. They would have impassioned discussions; however, they never crossed the line in their discussions. They could always laugh and smile with each other at the end.

People also thought because of their age difference, there relationship wouldn't last. She was a few years older than him, but it neither one cared. In fact, it was something that neither one of them addressed aside from the occasional mom joke here and there. They both loved each other and all the little things didn't matter. They had prided themselves on being able to talk about anything with each other, allowing each other to be themselves, and love each other for it; and they were not going to let age be a deciding factor.

She was startled from her daydream by what she thought was a knock at the door, but ended up being nothing. As she made her way back to her desk, she looked at the documents in front of her. She started going through them, trying to put together all of the information she had learned like the pieces to a puzzle. She had learned from her trip to the Bahamas that both Judge White and Governor Landry had been wiring money to Harry Wallace for over twenty-years, who in turn had been sending money to an unknown account. She knew the key piece to the puzzle was to find out who the unknown account was, but right now she had no way of doing that. She first had to find out why Judge White and Governor Landry were sending money to Harry Wallace in the first place.

While she thought it was somehow connected to the Penny Murder case, she didn't want to focus solely on that and miss a key piece of information. So, she had not only laid out everything she could find out about the case, but also everything she could find that was going on before the deposits were being made. There was not too much public information about the case during the time; most of the information was provided after the fact.

She was able to piece together that Maureen Trudeau, Lauren Johnson, Timothy Donaldson, Bryan Brown, and Jackson Brown had all been victims prior to the first deposit being made. Seeing the names, one of them stuck out to her: Laura Johnson, the daughter-in-law of Judge White. That's it, she thought. Somehow this is connected to Laura Johnson. She didn't know how yet, but she felt this was a good place to start. She was startled by the ringing of her phone. She wondered out loud who would be calling her, as she picked up the phone it was the office manager, Lucas Donaldson.

Instead of hiring secretaries, she and Allen both decided it was best to just hire an office manager. They needed someone to manage everything in the office to make sure everyone was doing what they needed to do. He had made life so much easier for her and Alan. He enabled them to focus on the things that not only they should as managing partners, but he also gave them the ability to still actively practice, without having to worry about things falling by the wayside.

"Good morning, Mrs. Jones. It is nice to have you back."

"Thank you, Lucas, how did you know I was here?"

"It is my job to know that, and besides, your car in is in the parking lot," he responded.

They both laughed at his last statement. As great care as she took to hide her presence, she forgot the most obvious thing. "I am sure you called me for something other than just to say good morning, how can I help you?"

"While I did want to check to see how you are doing, you are right; there is a Detective Howard to see you."

"Is Sgt. Allen with him?"

"No, he is here by himself."

Nicole sat there puzzled for a second. Why would Mike's partner be here to see her, let alone without him. She realized the only way to find out was to speak with Howard. "Send him back to my office."

With that, they both got off the phone. Nicole began moving the paperwork off her desk. She was not ready to share any of the information, let alone with someone she barely knew. As she was finishing putting the paperwork inside her desk, she heard a knock at the door.

"Come in, have a seat" she said as he entered her office.

As Detective Howard came in, he was amazed by the view and the stark contrast between Nicole's office and Garret James's office. Where Garret James went over the top, Nicole opted for subtlety. Everything in her office served a purpose and there was nothing that would be considered the wow factor, except for the two-hundred-and-seventy-degree windows.

"Thank you for taking the time to see me. I apologize for showing up unannounced, but it was really important that I see you."

"Thank you for saying that. But you have to understand I am a bit confused; how did you know I was in the office and why are you here without Mike?"

"I understand your concern on both points. To answer your first question; I must confess I looked into your whereabouts. I know you got back from the Bahamas last night. So, I called your partner to see if you were at his home and he said you were not there and I figured you wouldn't go back home, so this was my next stop. When I saw your car in the parking lot, I knew you were here. I apologize again, but all this was done for a very important reason."

"Forgive me, you must understand my concern; I don't know you and you show up to my office unannounced. And then I found out you were tracking my whereabouts; this is a bit concerning."

"I understand this does not look good, but honestly you are the only person I trust right now. I am not sure who I can trust in the department, and that includes my partner. Ever since I have been assigned this case there have been little things that have not sat right with me. I am not sure what it is, but I am committed to finding out, not only for myself, but for all of the victims. This is for all of the victims, the most recent ones and the ones from the initial killings. Something about that first trial doesn't sit right with me, and if I am being honest, I believe Samuel Johnson was innocent."

Hearing that he didn't trust Mike was a shock to her. This was someone who had been a friend to her family for the past seven years, someone she considered an older brother. Someone who worked with her husband closely and was responsible for making sure he came home every night. While the part about Mike was shocking, she shared his concern about everything else. She too believed there was something at larger at play and she didn't know who to trust in the department. Marcus didn't even trust them, so maybe there was some credence to what he was saying. However, she was not going to tell him this. She knew nothing about him and had no reason to trust him.

"I am sorry, I am going to have to ask you to leave. I cannot and will not entertain this anymore. Mike is family and unlike you, I trust him. I am not sure what you were expecting coming here to see me and telling me this. I have no reason to believe anything you tell me. You come into my office expecting me to help you. I have no idea how I can help you, so unless you want to talk about legal advice, then this conversation is over."

Detective Howard sat there for a second, thinking about his next step. He realized what he had to do. "Thank you for taking the time to meet with me, but before I go, I must show you something," he said as he reached into his bag. As he pulled out a piece of paper he began talking. "I found this when I went back to your home and I believe your husband shared my concerns." As he handed her the piece of paper he continued talking, "also, I found a note about a parking ticket on April 23rd, 1991. This was the same night as Laura Johnson was killed, so I am sure it is connected to her death somehow. I am waiting to hear back about all possible parking tickets in the vicinity of where she was killed and hopefully there will be something that stands out."

As Nicole looked at the piece of paper, she was shocked at what was written on it. At the very bottom of the paper, in Marcus's handwriting, were the words; "Don't Trust Mike, He Was Involved." Nicole sat there in silence for what seemed like forever. She had no idea what it meant, involved in what, why Marcus didn't tell her. She was even more frustrated. As she looked at the rest of the paper and what she saw looked familiar. She reached into her desk and pulled out Harry Wallace's bank statements to make sure her thoughts were correct. As she looked at the numbers for the accounts making deposits into both accounts, they were the same. How was Mike connected to all of this, she thought.

As Detective Howard watched as Nicole pulled the paper out of her desk and began comparing it to the document in front of her, he knew his instincts were right. He knew she knew something; he just had no idea what it was. Now he just hoped he could get her to trust him.

"Now you see why I can't trust Sergeant Allen. If his partner of seven years says don't trust him, what am I supposed to do? The last thing I want to do is bring more stress into your life, but I need to find out if Marcus said anything to you or you found anything." As Detective Howard said that his phone began to ring. As he looked down at his phone and saw who it was, he said, "Excuse me I have to take this," as he got up and walked outside.

As he walked outside the door, Nicole stood up and walked over to the window. As she looked out over the city, she thought to herself, what do I do now? She was in a dilemma; does she trust the person she has known for the past seven years and someone she considered family or does she trust someone she doesn't even know? Even though it appeared Marcus didn't trust him anymore, she still had no idea why. Could have had something to do with Laura Johnson's death or could it be something else. She wasn't sure, but one thing she did know is that whatever it was Mike was involved in, it was connected to Harry Wallace, Judge White, and Governor Landry. "Could Mike know more about Marcus's death that he is not telling me?" she asked herself.

As she sat back down, she knew what she had to do. She was going to have to trust Detective Howard if she wanted to find out what happened to Marcus. It pained on her on some level that she was going to go behind Mike's back, but if there was even the slightest chance that he was involved or might know something about Marcus's death, she had to find out. She started pulling out the all the paperwork that she had, hopefully he was able to make something out of it and provide some answers. She also knew she needed his help, there was only so much information she could get access to. But given his access to the department's databases, he had the ability to access so much more.

As she finished pulling all of the information out of her desk, she heard a knock on the door again. As she said come in, she saw it was Detective Howard returning from whatever phone call he was on.

As he came back in, he said, "Not to rush you, but I need to know your answer. I know this is all a lot to take in, but in order to prevent someone else from dying, I need to know. If you agree to help me, I will share with you everything I have, currently. I will also keep you in the loop on everything I do and find. But if we do this, I need for you to promise this stays between us."

Nicole paused for a second, even though she had already made up her mind, she wanted him to think she still needed to think about it further. After a few moments she said, "I agree, and I will keep this between us. But if I feel you are being dishonest or keeping something from me, the deal is off and I go to Mike myself."

"I can agree to that and in the name of transparency; I just got off the phone with one of my contacts from the Georgia Bureau of Investigations. They are sending me a list of the people who got traffic tickets on April 23rd, near Laura Johnson's home. I was thinking we go through the list together and see if we see any name that catches our attention. We can also compare it with the list I got from the department to see if there was anyone omitted in the department's version. If there is, then we know we have a problem."

She looked at him and said, "Before we do that, I need to tell you what I know. I think it will be beneficial and help focus your efforts on a list of potential suspects." She then began to tell him about the statements she found in Marcus's office belonging to Harry Wallace, and how after she went to the Bahamas she found out that he had been receiving regular deposits from Judge White and Governor Landry. She also told him about the third account and how the deposits started in 1993, shortly after the Penny Murder trial.

Detective Howard sat there intently listening to her tell him everything she had learned. As he watched her talk, he realized all of the things he had heard about her were true, he could see why she was one of the best and why she was so loved and hated. As she spoke more, he realized it wasn't that people hated her, that were just jealous. She was impressive and he was glad she was working with him. As she finished Detective Howard looked at her and said, "I knew it. I could tell when I talked to Governor Landry, something was off and then when we got ready to leave, Allen stayed back and talked to him. He never told me what they talked about. And after the last conversation I had with Judge White's daughter, Trisha, I feel strongly there is something more going on. I may be able to fill in some holes for you and provide you with additional information and I think I know who the third account belongs to. I think it is Garret James. There is something about him that just doesn't sit right with me and the fact he was able to start a law firm so soon after losing a high-profile case, without the financial means to do so, is suspicious."

Now it was his turn to tell her everything he had learned so far. He started first with their interview of Garret James and how it seemed he was a bit to open and how when he went back to get something from his office, he overheard him on the phone telling someone he had did exactly what they wanted him to do and how when he went out with his secretary he found out that he was actually on the phone with Harry Wallace and how over the years, according to her, they had maintained a friendship. He then told her about his conversation with Trisha White and how she didn't trust Sgt. Allen as well and about how she was apparently cheating on her husband with a black man. Also, how Trisha overheard her and her parents arguing about it. He also told her about her trip to Europe during the school year and how odd it was, but it was explained as an opportunity to intern at one of the largest modeling agencies in Paris.

As he finished telling her everything he knew so far, they both realized that together they had a large piece of the puzzle and would be able to get further working together than they had if they were doing this alone. Shortly after he completed his story, his phone rang. Nicole couldn't tell who he was on the phone with, but it seemed urgent. Once he got off the phone, he told her what happened.

"That was Sgt. Allen. They have a warrant for the home of a potential suspect. I have to go. If you start going through the list, I will do the same once I get finished with this, and I will also let you know what happens. I need one more favor, if we are going to do this, I need for you to be safe. If you ever feel unsafe, call me," he said as he handed her his card. "The last thing I want is for something to happen to you because of me."

"I appreciate your concern, but if something happens it won't be your fault. I would be doing this without your help."

With that they said their goodbyes, as he got up to leave. Once he left out the door, she let out a sigh of relief and began going through the lists, trying to identify a name that stood out or that was missing on the department's list.

CHAPTER 20

SGT. ALLEN WAS ABLE to identify the person in the photo through the use of the camera at the Monroe Bank across from Johnny's Quick Stop. They were unable to get a picture of her face. However, they were able to get the license plate of the vehicle she got into, which led them to the home of Tracey Bush. They were unable to find anything of note about her, other than she had only been at the address for a little over a year and prior to that she lived in New Mexico. Sgt. Allen was waiting back to hear from Albuquerque Police Department to see if they had anything on her.

Sgt. Allen and the team had got to the residence at noon and could not see any activity. They had no way of knowing if anyone was home or not, as they they didn't know if the car was in the garage. One thing he knew was they had to go now, and that meant Mike couldn't wait for his partner to get there. Sgt. Allen gave the command

and immediately the team was surrounding the house. He calmly walked to front the door and knocked on the door.

"This is Sergeant Allen with the Monroe Police Department," he said as knocked on the door. He waited for a moment and when no one answered, he repeated the introduction. There was still no answer, so he gave the signal for everyone to get ready, because if there was no response this time, they were going in. He tried knocking one last time, "This is Sgt. Allen with the Monroe Police Department. If you do not answer the door, we are going to knock it down!" He waited a couple of seconds and still no answer, so he called the tactical unit so they could do a forced entry. They readied the battering ram and on the count of three they broke in the door. Sgt. Allen sat back and waited in order for them to go in and clear everything before entering. He could hear officers of the tactical unit yelling, but thankfully no gunshots.

After what seemed like an eternity, Sgt. David of the Tactical Unit came out and told him the house was clear. He motioned for forensics to enter the home as he led the way. There was nothing about the home that seemed out of the ordinary. It seemed like the typical family home. However, as continued looking through the home, he noticed there were no pictures anywhere. This was strange, usually there were at least a few. Instead there were some paintings on the wall, and the home was immaculate; it was as if no one had lived there. He walked around the first floor careful not to get in the way of Forensics. As he made his way up the stairs, the second floor was the same as the first.

Walking through the rooms, he was growing frustrated. There was nothing here; he couldn't buy a break. He had given up hope as he walked down the steps. As he walked down the steps, he heard someone shouting, "we got something out back." Hearing that caused him to pick up the pace as he moved down the steps, so much so that he almost fell. As he made his way through the kitchen and into the backyard, he saw a detached structure in the back. It looked like a mini laboratory. As he walked in, he saw what the commotion was about: there was Tracy Bush lying on the floor. Seeing that, Sgt. Allen's heart sank.

As he looked around, he saw poison dart frogs in cages, with gloves and tools to extract the poison beside them. However, he knew this wasn't the killer. The set-up looked more like someone was doing a research study, as opposed to someone who was using this lab to kill. There was a laptops and handwritten notes, discussing the caring for and the effects of the poison from poison dart frogs. "She's not the killer," he said out loud.

As he was about to look over the site in detail his phone rang. He didn't recognize the number, but seeing it was a caller from Albuquerque, he knew who it was. As he listened intently to Sgt. Thomas from the Albuquerque PD on the other end, he realized his assumption was correct. Tracey Bush had no previous criminal history and Sgt. Thomas had learned she was actually a graduate student. She had moved to the area to study impact of climate change on the coast for her thesis. However, while she was in the area, she had come across the Poison Dart Frog by accident. Since these animals are natural to South America and had never been found in nature in America, with the approval of her professor, she decided to switch topics. She was looking into it further, to see why and how they had survived in the area and what their impact on the natural environment would be. As the Sergeant finished up, Sgt. Allen said thank you, and hung the phone up.

After hearing that he realized the chances of her being involved were slim to none. He found Sgt. Franks and told him what he had learned and how he didn't believe she was connected to the murder, and as a result do not expect to find much. Before he walked away, he remembered the fingerprint from the Miller crime scene.

"Have you found out anything about the print and the bottle from the Miller crime scene?"

Sgt. Franks looked confused for a moment; "Unfortunately the print is not in the system anywhere and the contents of the bottle were in fact poison. However, it was not Batrachotoxin, it was Aconite, more commonly referred to as Wolfsbane. I have already spoken with Adam and he is checking to see if that is what actually killed the Millers. It appears our killer is switching up poisons." He had left a message with Detective Howard yesterday, but he didn't want to cause any problems between the partners, so he omitted that part.

Sgt. Allen said thank you, but he couldn't hide his shock and disappointment. This was the similar path the original killer took the first time around. He originally started using Batrachotoxin, then he moved on to different poisons later. As he walked outside to his car, still disappointed from what had just happened, Detective Howard walked up.

"Sorry I am late, but traffic is still horrible with the protests going on. Judging by the way you are looking; I am guessing you didn't find anything inside."

"Don't worry, it would have just been a waste of your time as well. We didn't find anything inside, and in fact she is not even our killer and more than likely doesn't even know our killer. She's a graduate student, studying climate change. So, we are back to square one. Also, Batrachotoxin was not used to kill the Millers; it was Aconite," a defeated Sgt. Allen said. Everything was starting to take a toll on him, the longer this went on, the worse it was going to get. He started thinking about all the victims, both past and present, his wife, and his partner, and how he couldn't save any of them.

Looking at the look on Sgt. Allen's face, Detective Howard felt sorry for him for a moment and would have believed the look was genuine, but after seeing what Marcus wrote, talking to Trisha, and finding out everything else he didn't buy it. However, he couldn't let him know that. He had to continue to play the part, because he and Nicole agreed it wasn't the time to let him know about the ties between the Harry Wallace, Judge White, Governor Landry, and Garret James. They wanted to wait until they finished looking at the names on the traffic ticket list and then they would see how he would react.

He instead took the comforting approach. "It will be alright, partner. I know it sucks right now, but we will figure this out." Before he could finish his statement, Sgt. Allen's phone rang. It was the Captain. As he answered the phone, the Captain asked if he with Detective Howard and when he replied yes, he told him to put him on speaker phone.

"I need for the two of you to finish up and get to Arthur Landry's house immediately. He was found dead this morning."

Sgt. Allen immediately asked, "Is it our guy?"

"We don't know yet. His mother-in law found his body when she brought the kids home to get some more clothes. Things are about to get even more crazy, so I need for you two to get on it and find out what the hell is going on." With that, the Captain was gone, no goodbye, just a dial tone.

They both decided that Detective Howard would drive, and Sgt. Allen gave his keys to Sgt. Franks and asked him to have one of his officers drive it back to the station. Detective Howard was playing out all of the potential scenarios for everything he learned in his head and Sgt. Allen was too busy thinking about his failures; he imagined himself with a drink right now. As they got closer to Arthur's house, they could see the media had beaten them there. It was a circus; there were news vans everywhere, not to mention the people who were just there to see what was going on. They were barely able to get through the crowd and the media; they both almost punched someone in the process.

As they walked into the house, they saw Adam over the body of Arthur Landry, looking for any potential signs for a cause for death. As Adam looked up, he saw the two officers.

"It appears he has been dead for about twelve hours; I will not know the cause of death until I can get him back to my office and run some tests. It appears he was murdered, you can see the ligature marks on his wrists from him being cuffed and there are cuffs on the chair near the kitchen. It appears the killer let him loose, knowing he would die soon after. There was no note, though, making it unlikely this is the same killer as the others."

Hearing that was a sigh of relief to Sgt. Allen, but it only brought more questions to Detective Howard. He began thinking maybe it had something to do with whatever Harry Wallace, Judge White, and Governor Landry were involved in.

"The family is out back if you want to talk to them. Be forewarned: the Governor is on a war path," he told the two detectives.

They both said thank you and walked out back to find Mrs. Wilson with her two grandkids, the Governor, and his wife.

"We are so sorry for your loss, I think it would be best if we speak over here away from the kids," Sgt. Allen said to Mrs. Wilson.

She was unable to talk at the moment; she could only shake her head as she got up to follow them and she was followed by Governor Landry.

"I understand your concern and the fact it was your son, but I think it would be best if we speak to Mrs. Wilson by herself first," Detective Howard said to him.

"I do not give a damn what you think, I want to know what the hell is going on, everything that happened, and what you are going to do about it," demanded Governor Landry.

Realizing they were not going to get anywhere with him breathing down their necks as they attempted to talk to Mrs. Wilson, Sgt. Allen said; "How about this: Detective Howard will talk to Mrs. Wilson about what she saw and I will tell you everything we know so far and what our plan is?"

While this was a good way to appease the Governor, he only expressed he wanted to hear what she had to say as well. Something about the way he was acting didn't seem right to any of the officers. Sgt. Allen surprisingly didn't relent, shocking Detective Howard.

"We can either do it this way or I will have you escorted off the premises. We have an investigation to do and the more time we spend here arguing with you, the less time we have to devote to finding the killer."

The Governor begrudgingly agreed, only shaking his head and waving his hand off. So, both of the officers went in opposite directions and began speaking to the two of them. Allen began filling him in on what they knew currently, although it didn't appear to be related to the death of his son, because there was no note found. Detective Howard began asking Mrs. Wilson what she saw when she came inside the home.

After a few minutes of talking, Sgt. Allen noticed Governor Landry's demeaner changed, and it almost appeared as if he was afraid about something he was seeing. As he turned around to see what the problem was, he saw Mrs. Wilson pointing in their direction crying. Shortly after that, he saw Detective Howard walking towards them with a purpose.

"Where is it, you son of a bitch?" demanded Detective Howard.

"Whoa, what the hell is going on Detective," responded Allen

"He picked up a note from the crime scene and told her not to say anything about it."

Sgt. Allen looked at Governor Landry and asked, "Is this true?"

Governor Landry regained his stoic look and responded with, "No, that isn't true. I do not know what she is talking about it, I didn't take anything."

"You can either give it to us or I will have an officer come over, put you in cuffs and take it from you myself."

Sgt. Allen was still trying to process what was going, as he saw Detective Howard motion for two officers to come over. "If you have something give it to us, do not make this any worse than it already is. Your grandkids are over there watching, they do not need to see you in cuffs."

A look of defeat came over the Governor's face as he reached inside his pocket and pulled out a note and handed it to Sgt. Allen. As he read the note, a look of disbelief and shock came over his face as he handed it to Detective Howard.

"A Penny For Your Thoughts; What Happens When You Frame Someone For A Murder You Committed."

"I couldn't leave this out for it to become public. I refuse to let my son's name get dragged through the mud for something he didn't do."

If this was any other family, Detective Howard may have believed them, but this wasn't, and he knew he was hiding something. However, what transpired next confirmed his worst fears.

Sgt. Allen put his hand on Governor Landry's shoulder and told him they understood his concerns, but they would make sure no damage was done to his son's reputation. He then took him off to the side and talked to him by themselves. Seeing that made him sick to his stomach and he could only imagine what they were talking about.

While they were talking, Detective Howard's phone rang. He didn't recognize the number, but he answered it anyway. It was Nicole.

"I know you are busy, but I wanted to let you know what I found. You will never believe who got a parking ticket near Laura Johnson's house the night of her murder."

"Arthur Landry," Detective Howard said without a hint of surprise in his voice.

"What, how did you know?"

"I will call you later and let you know what is going on. I have to go now," he said as he hung his phone before they noticed he was on his phone.

"What was that about?" he asked as Sgt. Allen came back from talking to Governor Landry.

"It was nothing, I was just reassuring him everything would be okay; trying to keep him from making this situation any worse. Nothing to worry about."

They both finished up talking to Mrs. Wilson and Governor Landry and on the way out, they stopped to talk to Adam and Sgt. Franks to see if either of them had anything new to add. Neither one had anything at the moment, but would let them know if they found anything.

As they drove away, Detective Howard came to the realization that he was right in his initial thoughts about there being something wrong in the original trial. He had figured out part of the mystery; Arthur Landry had killed Laura Johnson and he was sure Governor Landry used Harry Wallace to help him cover it up, now he just had to figure out how to prove it and how Judge White and Garret James were connected as well.

CHAPTER 21

SGT. ALLEN AND DETECTIVE Howard pulled up to the home of Amber Harris, or Cherry as she was known to her customers. They had found her by going through Arthur Landry's phone records and saw she was the last person he spoke with the night of his death; they were pretty sure she was the last person to see him alive. They rang the doorbell and waited for a few moments, but they got no answer. So, they tried again, just when they had almost given up, they heard someone from behind the door, saying I am coming.

When she opened the door, they were shocked to see the bruises on her face and neck. It looked like someone had beaten her.

"Good morning, Ms. Harris. My name is Sgt. Allen, and this is my partner Detective Howard and we were wondering if we could ask you a few questions."

She looked startled and sounded nervous as she asked what this was about.

Mike calmly asked if they could come in, because this was something that was best if they discussed in private. Amber knew why they were there; she had seen it on the news. Arthur Landry was dead; given their last interaction, she was happy he was dead. She considered the person who did a hero, because they saved her life. After pausing for a moment, she told them it was okay they came in. They followed behind her as she led them to living room. She offered them a seat and asked them did they want anything to drink.

As they sat down, Sgt. Allen began talking: "I know you have probably already seen it on the news, but Arthur Landry was murdered last night, and we believe you were the last one to see him alive."

"You think I killed him," Amber nervously interjected.

Sensing she was nervous and scared, Detective Howard calmly said, "No we do not think you killed him, but we think you may have seen something. Given the bruises on your face, I take it your meeting with him did not go well. I can understand your sense of obligation to protecting the killer, because they killed someone who did you wrong, but this person has killed six other people."

The gravity of the last statement sunk in; she didn't realize that. However, she thought those people must have done something to deserve it, because the killer didn't seem like the type to kill for no reason. "I do not know what you expect from me, I didn't see anything. I take that back, you know what I did see, I saw and felt Arthur's fist hitting my face, I felt his hands around my neck, thinking I was about to die and then…" She stopped there; she didn't want to tell what happened next.

"And then what happened, Ms. Harris? It seems like you were going to say something else, but you stopped." Sgt. Allen asked hoping she could provide more information.

"I have said all I want to say, I think it is time for the two of you to leave."

Just as Sgt. Allen was about to press her some more, Detective Howard interjected. "Thank you for your time Ms. Harris. If you think of anything later, please let us know," he said as he gave her his card.

Sgt. Allen could only look on in shock as Detective Howard motioned for him to get up so they could leave. As they walked out the home and towards the car, Detective Howard could feel the tension from his partner. Once they got in the car, Allen erupted.

"What the hell do you think you were doing? She was the last one to see Arthur alive and could have potentially provided information about who killed him and the other victims."

Detective Howard looked Sgt. Allen and calmly said, "First, never talk to me like that again or else we will have a problem. Secondly, she wasn't going to tell us anything. Did you see her face? If she did see the killer, do you think she was going to say anything, given the killer probably saved her life. What do you propose: we haul her downtown? I can imagine how that plays out in the news: officers harass an innocent victim of domestic violence. And above that headline will be pictures of her bruised face and neck. You do not need to be a rocket scientist to know what happened."

Before they could finish their conversation, Sgt. Allen's phone rang. It was the Captain.

"I just got off the phone with a Blythe Thompson, who says her grandmother Mable Thompson may have some information of importance that may help with the case. I need for you two to go there when you finish at Ms. Harris's. I will be sending the address shortly," he said as hung the phone up.

"Hopefully this works out better than all of our previous leads," Detective Howard said as drove towards Mable Thompson's house."

The car ride to Ms. Thompson's house was another quiet car ride between the two of them. Ms. Thompson lived on the outskirts of town and they both wondered what information she could possibly have that would benefit them. They had no idea, but they were willing to give anything a try at this point. Ms. Thompson lived in a small, older home. As they pulled in the driveway, they could see some people on the porch. As they got out of the car to walk to the porch, Detective Howard got a message. It was from Nicole; he hadn't had a chance to talk to her since yesterday. He put his phone back in his pocket and told himself he would call her once he got back from Ms. Thompson's house.

As they approached the porch, they say Ms. Mable Thompson on the porch with her granddaughter. It appeared Ms. Thompson was in her late seventies or early eighties. She was on the heavier side and she had a walker beside her. As they got closer it appeared, she had some snuff in her mouth.

"Good afternoon, Ms. Thompson. My name is Detective Howard and this is my partner Sgt. Allen. We were told you may have some information for us."

"It is about time, you are only thirty years too late," Ms. Thompson said angrily.

Her granddaughter interjected, "You have to forgive my grandmother, she tried to tell people this information before the first trial, but everyone kept ignoring her."

"Can you please tell me what information and who ignored you," Detective Howard asked.

"Why don't you ask your partner? You don't remember me, do you Sergeant Allen? I may be old, but my memory is still sharp. I tried talking to you before and you blew me off."

Sgt. Allen looked shocked; he didn't know what to say. "I apologize if you feel that way, I had a lot going on at the time and I didn't mean to blow you off."

She looked at him dismissively, she didn't believe him.

Howard jumped in, "I am sorry for your experience Ms. Thompson, I wasn't on the force then, so I do not know what happened or why. But I can promise you whatever you tell me, I will make sure I listen and do what I can to make sure your voice is heard."

This seemed to calm her down. "I like you," she said. "You have honest eyes. I will tell you the Sam that was portrayed at that trial was not the Sam I knew. Sam was a kind-hearted fellow and would give you his last if you needed it. Sam was going to school to try to make a better life for his family."

Detective Howard interrupted, "Are you sure we are talking about the same person? Samuel Johnson didn't have a family."

A slight smile came over her face, as she continued. "You are right, Samuel Johnson didn't have a family, but Samuel Jones did. In order for him to get into that school, he had to change his name. You see he had gotten into some trouble as a kid and he would have never been able to go to law school with a record. It was hard enough to get into law school as a black man and if they would have known he had a record, he would have never gotten in. You see Sam grew up in a small town called Blinton, a couple of hours from here. He had a wife and a daughter there. He told me the stories about how they use to spend time together and how she shared his love of the law. He wanted to show her that you could achieve your dreams."

"Excuse me, did you say Blinton?" a curious. Sgt. Allen asked.

"Yes, I did. Didn't your parents teach you to not interrupt grown people when they are talking?" she said sternly. "He had a wife and daughter back home, who he talked about all the time. But one of Sam's demons was women. I told Sam he better leave those white women alone before he got himself into trouble, but he wouldn't listen. It was a shame those people lied on him and made it seem like he was lying. Two of those women had been in home. Blythe go inside and get that box on grandma's dresser."

"I am sorry to interrupt you Ms. Thompson, but you are telling me that Samuel Johnson was actually Samuel Jones and he did in fact have a relationship with two of the victims?"

"Yes, I am."

As Detective Howard continued to speak, he kept his eyes on Sgt. Allen. "How come none of this came out in trial."

"Ask your partner. I told his partner and I told his lawyer this, but they didn't want to hear me."

Hearing this made Detective Howard grow angrier by the minute. It was his worst fear come true. Samuel Johnson was innocent! Tears had started coming down her checks as she said, "They killed him and he didn't do anything wrong. He hadn't hurt anyone and the worst part about it is his family had no idea what happened to him. I didn't know their names, so I couldn't find them." Just then Blythe came outside with the shoe box and handed it to her grandmother. As she handed the box to her grandmother, she began going through the box, looking for something.

When she had found the one, she was looking for she handed it to Detective Howard. "This is a picture of him and Laura."

Detective Howard looked at the picture and then showed it to Sgt. Allen, who knew instantly that it was in fact Laura Johnson. "I see that is Laura in the picture with him, but who is that other lady in the picture with them?"

"That is April Miller. She and Laura were good friends and she would be with Laura and Sam when they came and visited me sometimes."

"Alright grandma, I think it is time for you to go lay down. I am going to have to ask you gentleman to leave. It is time for her to go lay down and I do not want her to get any more worked up."

"We totally understand. Thank you for taking the time to speak with us," Detective Howard said as they got up to leave.

Before she went inside, she said one last thing that caught both of the officers off guard, "He and Laura had a beautiful baby together! I wonder what happened to him?"

"This was debunked before the trial, which is why it wasn't allowed," an angry Sgt. Allen interjected.

Ms. Thompson looked taken aback, but she calmly said "No, it wasn't. Everyone thought it was Melissa who was pregnant, but it was in fact Laura who was. Why do you think her family sent her away for those months?"

"They said they sent her to intern at a modeling agency in Europe," Detective Howard responded.

"There was no modeling school, that child was pregnant. They sent her away, because they didn't want anyone to find out she was going to have a black baby."

"Okay, that is enough. Grandma it is really time for you to go lay down."

"Thank you both again, you have been really helpful. Take care of yourself Ms. Thompson," Detective Howard said.

"I will, you just make sure you come back by and say hi sometime."

"Yes, ma'am. I will."

As they made their way back to the car, Sgt. Allen was readying himself for the onslaught of questions and accusations from Detective Howard when they got in the car. He was surprised when he got inside the car and they never came. Detective Howard knew that Sgt. Allen expected him to go off when they got into the car, but he couldn't; he was too angry. He couldn't stand the sight of him, let alone being in the same car as him. The drive back to town was a long, silent one. The silence was broken only by Sgt. Allen's phone. It was Sgt. Franks, so he put it on speaker.

"You know that print we found in the Miller's house; well we found a match in Tracey Bush's house on a glass in the sink. So, it is possible, that whoever killed the Millers was close to Tracey Bush. We are going to recheck the house to make sure we didn't miss anything; I will keep you updated."

They both looked at each other in shock after hearing that. However, it didn't change the tone in the car. Neither one still said anything to each other.

Once Sgt. Allen got into his car, he picked up his phone and said, "I think Nicole is Samuel Johnson's daughter. We need to meet!"

CHAPTER 22

THE BOTTLE ON THE table was looking more appealing than ever. Sitting on his couch, Sgt. Allen was thinking about the meeting with Ms. Thompson. He had convinced himself that Samuel Johnson was guilty and now he wasn't so sure anymore. The meeting with her had provided him with information he didn't know at the time, and when taken into account what were now essentially revenge killings, he had more doubt than ever. He was getting sick to his stomach and he wanted something to take the pain away and to help him forget. He could hear his wife's voice telling him not to drink it. But he blacked her voice out and put the bottle up to his lips and began to drink.

After he pulled the bottle away from his lips, there was no feeling of shame or self-hatred as he had expected there would be. Instead there was a feeling of relief and calmness. So, he placed the bottle up to his lips and began to drink more. He sat on the couch and drank until he passed out.

As he began to slowly wake up, he had a massive headache and was having a hard time trying to focus his eyes. There used to be a time, when he didn't have this feeling after drinking. As he went to get up, he couldn't move.

"What the fuck," he thought. He tried again and still couldn't move. If he had been sober, he might have realized he was tied to the chair and he would not be able to move. He kept trying to move, but he couldn't.

"Calm down," he heard an unknown voice say.

"Who is there?"

"The person who is here to make you atone for your sins."

Hearing that he knew who it was. He was wondering if and when they would pay him a visit. He held his head down in defeat for a moment, as he knew what the intruder meant by that.

"Why are you doing this? Why did you kill those other people? Is it some sick game of revenge, killing people who you think violated your sick code of justice?"

"Are you going to try to lecture me on justice. When you and those other victims let an innocent man go to jail and die. Not once did any of you think to do the right thing, even when you knew there were parts of the story that didn't add up. You were too busy thinking of yourselves, how it would make you look or how you could use it to advance your life. You were the worst of them all. You swore an oath to uphold the law and you acted like a criminal the first time you were tested."

Hearing that, Sgt. Allen couldn't respond. He knew that it would eventually come back to bite him. He had a flashback to that night almost twenty years ago. Harry Wallace had invited him out for drinks one night at the Wild Boar, a bar that he had never heard of before on the outskirts of town. It started cordially enough between the two of them, talking about sports and life and then Governor Landry showed up. He was surprised to see the Governor not only show up, but sit at the table with them.

After about fifteen minutes of talking, the real reason for the meeting became apparent. "Detective Wallace tells me that you are one of the up and comers on the police force and sees a lot of potential in you. He also tells me that me that you have fiancée and you need to make some extra money so you can get a her a ring and house. Is this true?"

This caught the young officer off guard. He didn't really know how to respond. He looked over at Detective Wallace and saw him nodding his head yes, he believed in an effort to get him to say it was true. So, he did.

"Good, Good." After responding he called the waitress over and had her bring over a couple more drinks. "I am sure you can agree that sometimes people make mistakes, but people shouldn't be punished for the rest of their life for those mistakes." After he finished that last statement Officer Allen saw him motioning for someone to come over. When they made it to the table, he saw it was Arthur Landry, the Governor's son.

"You know my son Arthur, don't you? Wouldn't you agree, just like you, he has his whole life in front of him? He shouldn't be punished for one mistake, should he? I know you are probably asking why I am telling you all this and why you are here, I will get right to it. I will not waste your time or insult your intelligence any longer. As we all know there is a serial killer running around town killing people and we can all agree this person should be punished." Everyone at the table nodded in agreement, so he continued. "Arthur here, while he can be a bit reckless at time, but what young person isn't, am right. Well young Arthur here, has gotten himself into a bit of a pickle. A young lady died while with him and we need your help to make sure he doesn't pay for an accident."

"You want me to cover up a murder," a surprised Officer Allen asked.

"No, what the Governor is asking is that we help spare him the spectacle of the public, who wouldn't understand this was an accident," interjected Detective Wallace.

"Okay, so what do you want me to do?"

"It has already been done. We have already made put the plan in motion, we just need for you to not raise any red flags during the investigation. She was killed a few years ago, so we just need for you to make sure you go along with your partner in making sure nothing changes as far as the suspect in her death.?"

"Who is it that you accidentally killed, Arthur?" asked Officer Allen. Governor Landry was about to answer, but Allen cut him off, telling him he wanted to hear Arthur say it.

Arthur looked over to his father for permission, his father reluctantly shook his approvingly. "Her name was Laura Johnson and it was an accident; I didn't mean to kill her. I loved her and would do anything to take it back, if I could switch places with her, I would," as he finished the last line he began crying.

"If it was an accident, just explain it to the police, they will understand. But I can't be a part of this," he said as he got up to leave.

"You might want to see this before you leave," the Governor said as he handed him an envelope.

"Where did you get this from, you sick bastard!"

"Like I said it would be a shame for one mistake to ruin someone's life, or in your case multiple people. Why do you think you were put on this case? Do what we are asking you and no one will ever find out, and you will make some money in the process."

Realizing he had no choice he reluctantly agreed.

"Good, we will leave you two to work out the details. Come Arthur, let's leave the two alone."

"Welcome back Sgt. Allen, you left us for a second," the masked intruder said back in the present.

Sgt. Allen remembered where he was and what was going on, after being in a daze.

"What I did was wrong, regardless of the fact I had no choice, but let's be honest, that was not the reason why Samuel Johnson was found guilty. He would have been convicted whether he was accused of killing Laura Johnson or not. I never spent the money, you can have it all," Sgt. Allen said desperately.

Hearing that the killer shook their head. "While that was wrong, that is not the reason you are in this position, I understand why you did what you did. They were going to hurt your family. You are in this position for what you did on May 23rd of this year."

Hearing that date, caused tears to flow down his face.

"Now you remember. You did the very thing, you did over twenty years ago for Arthur Landry. You murdered someone and let someone else take the fall. I assume that was an accident as well? Did you honestly think I don't know who I killed? I just did what you and your conspirators did, made it look like someone else did it."

He was full blown crying at this point. "I am sorry, it was an accident. He was going to ruin me. He found out about Laura Johnson and started saying Samuel Johnson was innocent and I got him killed. I tried to explain it to him, but he wouldn't listen. He kept saying he was going to turn me in. He started saying I killed his father; I had no idea what he was talking about. He would never explain. I didn't want to kill him, but he left me no choice. I didn't want to frame Samuel Johnson, but it was either him or Joanne."

The killer stood there for a second confused as to what he meant by either him or Joanne. "What do you mean either him or Joanne?"

"The Governor had pictures of an accident scene, that my first fiancée was involved in. She had hit and killed someone and left the scene. They had photos of damage to her car, as well as the statement of a witness, who witnessed the entire thing. The case was never solved and the Governor and Harry Wallace said they would keep it that way if I did what they asked. They said if I didn't help them, they would have no choice but to have her arrested. What was I supposed to do? She was the love of my life and he was already going to be convicted."

"So, you saved the life of a murderer and helped lead an innocent man to his death."

"You have to understand I loved her more than anything. I just wanted to protect her and spend the rest of my life with her. So, I did it. The only problem was, the Governor had other ideas. He went to her afterwards, showed her the same evidence and got her to leave town. She left town before our wedding, without saying a word. I never heard from her again."

The killer let out a flippant laugh. "You did all that and they still screwed you over. The worst part about it, is you have continued to protect them since, like a sad little puppy. You are pathetic! Not only did you do that, but you killed your partner and supposed best friend. You were not supposed to kill him. Why did you have to kill him? Why did you have to kill Marcus?" The killer was altering their voice, but Sgt. Allen could tell they were holding back tears.

"Nicole is that you? Why are you doing all of this, is this revenge for the death of your father. I know Samuel Johnson was your father. It was too big of coincidence that you both are from Blinton, you are about the age his daughter would be, both of you grew up wanting to be lawyers, and you moved here. Was this all a set-up, marrying Marcus, getting close to me?"

The intruder looked at him, as the tears in their voice began to disappear and were replaced by a dismissive laugh. "Is that the best you could come up with. You don't remember me?"

The intruder sat down and things got silent for a few moments, as they both sat in silence. The silence was finally broken by Sgt. Allen.

"What do you mean, remember you?"

The intruder slowly removed their mask. When they removed the mask, it was if Sgt. Allen had seen a ghost. "Joe, is that you. I thought...." He was unable to finish his last sentence; his throat tightened, his chest felt like it was about to burst, and then his eyes closed for the last time.

CHAPTER 23

DETECTIVE HOWARD HAD BEEN in Nicole's office early Sunday morning, going over everything he had learned since the last time they spoke. They both agreed this was a good time to meet, because there would not be anyone else in the office. So, they would be able to talk without fear of being interrupted. He started off by saying, "I figured out Arthur Landry had killed Laura Johnson when you called me and told me about the parking ticket. The note found with the body, talked about him framing someone else for a murder that he committed. So, when I put that together with the banking information, it was the logical choice. Also, his father protested to much and tried to hide the note from us."

"He tried to hide the note from you?"

"Yes, he did. He tried to act like he was doing to protect his son's image from a false accusation, but it was obvious that he was trying to protect him from the truth. I am not sure who was all involved in the cover-up, but based off the banking information you found, I would say it is safe to bet Harry Wallace, Governor Landry, and Sgt. Allen were involved. At some point, we are going to have to talk to Mike."

"I know, I want to find out what he knows. He has to have some answers as to why Marcus was killed. I am just not ready to talk to him yet."

"Okay. Initially, we thought we didn't find anything of value at Tracey Bush's house. However, we later learned there was a print at her house that matched a print found at the Millers', so it is likely the killer was close with Tracey Bush. Tracey Bush was found dead in her mini laboratory, but we think her death was accidental."

"Wait did you say Tracey Bush?"

"Yes, I did. Why?"

"I am not sure, that name sounds familiar. I just can't remember where though."

"After we left Ms. Bush's house, we received a phone call from the Captain telling us to go see Ms. Mable Thompson, because she said she had some information that was important. When we got there, she told her she had tried to tell Harry Wallace, Garret James, and on some level Sergeant Allen this information, but none of them were receptive. Get this: she told us how she had known Samuel Johnson for an extended period of time and she had actually met a couple of his friends before, Laura Johnson and April Miller.

She actually had pictures of the three of them together. She then told us that Laura and Samuel had a baby together."

"Wait, are you serious. They had a baby together?"

"I am going to meet with Mrs. White and her daughter later to find out if this in fact true or not. Once I do, I will let you know." He left the part out about him having a family in Blinton, there was something about the way Sgt. Allen reacted when he heard Ms. Thompson mention Blinton. It brought up red flags and he wanted to do some more investigating before mentioning it.

The last part caused Nicole to get quiet and the look on her face changed, which was noticed by Detective Howard. "Is everything okay?" he asked.

"Yes, it is. I am just trying to process all of this. An innocent man was killed and people stood by and let it happen, and one of those people I considered a friend. I let him in my home, he smiled in my face and he was a murderer."

"I understand how you feel, but we don't know if he knew. I am not the biggest fan of Sgt. Allen, but I think we should give him the benefit of the doubt until proven otherwise. We have to figure out the connection between Samuel Johnson and this new killer. I believe this person is killing for revenge, trying to right wrongs." As he finished that statement, he looked at his watch and realized he had somewhere else to be. "I have to go meet with Mrs. White and her daughter, I will call you tomorrow to compare notes," he said as he got up to leave.

Once the door closed behind him, Nicole began typing on her computer. She had heard the name Tracey Bush before; she just couldn't remember where she heard it from. She started by typing the name into social media to see what showed, there was nothing. She then tried typing the name into all of the search engines using "Tracy Bush Graduate Student" as the search terms. When she did that, it pulled up the article about her death and in the article was a picture. She looked at the picture hoping it would jog her memory, but no luck. She still had no idea where she heard the name from. She gave up for now and hoped it would come back to her eventually.

She looked at her watch and realized she had to leave. She was supposed to meet with Zacharia Taylor. He was a detective from the original case, he was involved in the earlier murders, but he ended up retiring before Samuel Johnson was arrested and subsequently convicted. He was a popular detective and Marcus had told her stories about how he was the department's encyclopedia. If there were anything you wanted to know, he was the guy to talk to. Somehow he managed to know about things even after he retired. She was hoping he may be able to provide some information.

Zacharia lived on the west side of town; he had lived in the same house he grew up in as a kid. His parents had died when he was young, so he was responsible for taking care of his six sisters and brothers. He was proud of himself for taking care of them, he viewed them as his kids. He was proud because they had all grown up to be successful. He had kept the house because it kept him close to his parents and he wanted his siblings to always have a place that felt like home.

Sitting in his living room, she could tell he was proud of them; there were pictures and copies of their diplomas everywhere. He noticed her looking at the pictures and said "I know they are my sisters and brothers, but I am so proud of all of them. I watched them grow up and to see them all turn out to be successful with families of their own, it makes me feel good."

"That was very commendable what you did, not too many people would have been able to do a great a job as you did to raise them. They are truly lucky to have you as a big brother."

"Thank you, Mrs. Jones. I must say I was surprised when you called me, I am not sure what I can do for you."

"Marcus always told me if I wanted to know something about a case, you are the person to talk to."

"I always liked Marcus; he would actually come by just to talk to me sometime. It is a shame what happened to him. I am so sorry for your loss. What can I answer for you?"

"Thank you. I know you retired shortly after the original killings started, but I was hoping you could tell me if there was anything that was unusual or that may be connected to new murders."

"If I am being honest, I never liked how they treated that young man. I do not know if he was guilty or not, but I do know one thing, he didn't stand a chance at trial. I wasn't too involved in the original case. I retired after the sixth homicide, George Flowers. It was always strange, because with the exception of three of the victims, Maureen Trudeau, Laura Johnson, and Timothy Brown, Samuel Johnson had no ties to any of the other victims. It is not often you see that in a serial killer: either the victims are all known to them or the victims are all random. Outside of that, I can't tell you anything else19 about the original case. But what I can tell you is that all of the new victims were linked to the old case."

"I know everyone thinks that Melissa Landry was killed because of her connection to the Governor, because her daddy was considered a saint. But that is not the case. Her daddy had his demons. There was talk that he may have helped finesse the evidence that led to the arrest and conviction of Samuel Johnson. There were certain parts about the case that seemed off, but no one had the courage to stand up and say anything. Everyone in town knew where the power was and who ultimately was making the decisions. There was also this little-known fact; up until his death he was pretty close with Harry Wallace, he actually wanted him to marry his daughter. But he was never able to convince his daughter to give Harry a chance.

Also, everyone thought the Millers were this perfect couple, but they had their demons as well. Mrs. Miller's first fiancée died mysteriously, while we could never prove it, there was always the question of if Mr. Miller was behind it. Also, a little-known fact, Mrs. Miller was best friends with Laura Johnson and while she did not testify, she told the police there was no way Laura would be with Mr. Johnson."

Nicole sat there intently listening, absorbing everything he was telling her. Some of the information confirmed the information that Detective Howard told her and there was some information that became another piece of the puzzle, in particular the information about Melissa Landry's father and the Millers.

Zacharia continued, "The only thing I do not know is why Marcus was killed. Everyone else killed was connected to the original killings, with the exception being him. If there is a connection, I do not know it. Do you know anything?"

"Unfortunately, I do not know. Marcus didn't tell me anything. He had to have been working on something I just don't know what it is."

"One more thing, about four months ago, shortly before his death, he came by to see me. He asked me about his partner. He just asked me what I thought of him. It wasn't so much that he asked, it was how he asked. He sounded concerned, like he had a lot on his mind. I asked him why, he just said he was just asking for no particular reason. I knew him long enough to know there was more to it than that, but I didn't push it."

"That is strange that he would ask that." Nicole had an idea why, but she didn't want to share it. Although, he seemed like he was honest, she didn't know him and she didn't want to risk the information she had getting to the wrong people, putting not only her life in danger, but the life of Detective Howard as well.

Just then the front door barged open and she heard the sound of little feet running through the house and little kids screaming Uncle Zac, where are you.

"I think that is my cue to leave. It sounds like you have company."

"Yes, it my nieces and nephews, I am babysitting tonight."

"That is cute. I am not going to take up anymore of your time. Thank you so much for your time, I appreciate it. You have fun tonight." She gave him a hug, just as the kids ran into the room and jumped on him. As she walked out the living room, she could hear them playing and it brought a smile to her face. Just as she was about to walk out the door, she noticed a picture on the wall. It struck her as odd, because one of the kids in the picture looked familiar and it didn't appear to be one of Zacharia's nieces.

As she got in the car and started driving away, she couldn't get the picture of the child out of her head. She finally told herself that she would think about that later, she had to focus on both Mike's and Marcus's secrets first. She was even more convinced Mike knew more about Marcus's death than he was telling, and she was going to do her best to find out what it was. She had to find out not only for herself, but for Marcus as well. So, she turned and went in the opposite direction towards his house.

CHAPTER 24

As he drove to the Whites' house, Detective Howard thought about everything that was going on and how he had gotten himself in the middle of a mess. When he moved to the area almost a year ago, he thought it was for a quieter life. Prior to living in Monroe, he had lived in Pittsburgh, which needless to say was a lot faster-paced than Monroe. However, he had never worked on a case like this before. This was his first serial killer case and his first time dealing with potential law enforcement corruption. This case was made difficult, because he had no idea who he could trust outside of Nicole. He hated involving her, but she was the one person whom he felt he could trust to help him. So far it had worked out, because she had provided him with information that he would have not otherwise gotten. He just hoped she stayed safe.

As he pulled up to the gate to enter the Whites/ house, he remembered the last time he was here. But unlike that time, the home was not was crawling with the media or law enforcement. He pressed the intercom button, "Detective Howard hear to see Mrs. White." After he spoke, there was a slight delay and the gate slowly opened. As he drove through the gate and towards the house, he prepared himself for what he was about to do. "This could go really bad," he thought. Thankfully, Trisha would be there and hopefully she would be able to make things easier.

As he rang the doorbell, he was surprised to see Trisha opened the door. She looked even more beautiful today than she had the first time they had met. Her smile, like a star, was enough to light up the night sky.

"Good morning Ms. White, thank you so much for your help."

"I was surprised when you called me so soon and even more surprised when you said it was urgent that you talk to my mother and that it was about my sister's death."

"I was just as surprised when I found this information out. I must warn you in advance it will not be pleasant, and you may not want to talk to me again."

Hearing that caused a look of shock to come over Trisha's face. But before she could respond she heard her mother in the background saying, "Let him in so we can get this over with."

They left their conversation at that point; Trisha not knowing what he was talking about and Detective Howard dreading what he was about to do. She led him to the living room, where her mother was waiting.

"Good morning Mrs. White, again I am so sorry for your loss and thank you for taking the time to meet with me. I know I didn't make the best impression on you when we first met."

"Don't thank me, thank my daughter. She is the only reason I allowed you in my house again. For some reason she thinks you are a nice person and I should trust you."

After she said that, he looked over at Trisha and caught her shyly smiling. He knew there was no easy way to say what he was about to say, so he was just going to get it out of the way.

"Like I told Trisha on the phone I have found out some additional information about your daughter's death that may be linked to your husband's. I just need to ask you a few questions and I must warn you, some of them may be unpleasant. But I need to ask them so I can figure out what is going on."

Mrs. White just sat there coldly and flippantly responded, "I would appreciate it, if you got to the point. I have things I need to do today and talking to you isn't something I want to spend a lot of time doing."

"I appreciate your honesty and time, so I will get straight to the point. I have reason to believe that your daughter was not killed by Samuel Johnson and that they in fact did know each other," he said as he handed her one of the pictures Ms. Thompson had let him keep.

He paused for a second as she looked at the picture and Trisha got up to look at the picture as well. He wasn't shocked the sight of the picture did not surprise her at all. She just looked at the picture and said, "So what? She is in picture with him, that doesn't mean he didn't kill her."

"I understand that, but at the time everyone said that it was impossible that she would have associated with him; including you, your husband, and Mrs. Miller, who is also in that picture. After seeing your response to the picture, I think you knew this at the time, but you denied it anyway."

He could sense she was getting angry and he was at risk of losing her and any chance at getting to the truth. "I am not here to bring up the past or try to embarrass your family, I am just trying to find out what happened, because I believe your husband was killed because of something that happened during that original trial. So far all of the victims have been connected to original trial somehow and I know your husband was the Judge on the case. I know your daughter was not killed by Samuel Johnson, but she was in fact killed by Arthur Landry."

Trisha let out a gasp, but Mrs. White did not look surprised at all. "I am sorry but what does this have to do with the death of my husband."

Detective Howard realized she knew. "You knew that he killed her, didn't you?"

Mrs. White grew quiet as tears began to flow down her face.

"Mom, say it isn't true."

"You have to understand it was a different time back then. I didn't find out until later on. I heard your father on the phone with Governor Landry. You have to believe me; I didn't know when it happened. I am so sorry." She said as she looked at her daughter, both of them crying. "After I found out, what could I have done; your father wouldn't let me. Abraham said the guy had killed eleven other people, so it wasn't like he was innocent. I had no proof, so I had to just swallow it and deal with it."

"I understand, Mrs. White and believe you when you say you didn't know when it happened and there was nothing you could do afterward." He didn't want to tell her that he believed he was in fact innocent of the eleven other murders; he thought that would have killed her emotionally. "Mrs. White, I apologize, but I have to ask you one more question. Did Laura have a baby with Samuel Johnson?"

Mrs. White looked as if a thousand-pound weight had been lifted off her shoulder as she sighed. She didn't answer immediately as she tried to gather herself emotionally. Trisha looked confused as she looked at both Detective Howard and her mother. Mrs. White got up and walked over to the window, looking out of it as she spoke.

"I always knew this day would come. I am sorry you had to find out this way, Trisha. Yes, there was, but it wasn't one; she had twins. They were born on June 20th, 1989. They were beautiful babies, but when Abraham and her husband Michael saw them, they both said she had to get rid of them. Abraham said there was no way he was going to have black grandkids and Michael said there was no way people were going to find out his wife had slept with a black man. Trisha was heartbroken, she loved those kids and didn't want to give them up. I tried talking to Abraham, but he didn't want to hear it. He was dead-set on those kids getting out of the house. So, one night I took the kids out of the house."

She could barely finish the last sentence as she burst into tears. Trisha got up and walked over to her mother and gave her a hug, as they both were crying. Detective Howard sat there in silence, not knowing what to do.

After a few moments, Trisha began wiping the tears from her mother's eyes.

She looked at her daughter, saying thank you to her daughter and apologizing again, as she continued, "One night I took the kids out of the house, because I knew if I didn't Abraham would kill them. So, I took them to Mable Thompson."

Hearing that name shocked Detective Howard. Ms. Thompson never mentioned being given the kids. How could she leave that part out, he thought. He didn't know, but he was going to find out as soon as he left here.

"I knew my daughter knew her and my daughter loved her. She had told me as much. Mable Thompson was an old friend of mine. We knew each other as kids, in fact she knew Laura as a child." She started crying again. "I had treated her so badly, but when I needed her, she was there for me without hesitation. I asked her not to tell Laura or anyone else where she had gotten the babies from, or else they would be in danger. When I came back that night, I told everyone I had killed the babies and buried them where the roses are planted near the docks. It killed me to see the look of pain in Laura's eyes, but I had to, in order to protect them. Abraham only smiled and acted like nothing ever happened. That was the day I started to hate him."

"That is why Laura would go sit out there by them every day. She would come over every day just to sit out there, sometimes for hours," Trisha said.

Her mother couldn't speak anymore, she was engulfed in tears. He realized that both mother and daughter needed to talk alone, and he also needed to go back and see Ms. Thompson. So, he said, "I will leave the two of you alone, so you can talk. I am so sorry for bringing up the past. But thank you for being honest with me, Mrs. White."

The last image of them he had was him walking out the door and seeing them hugging each other. He could feel their pain and felt bad for not only them, but Laura as well. They all had to suffer because of the actions of others.

He shook his head and said a prayer for them as he walked
out the door.

CHAPTER 25

NICOLE WAS TRYING TO think how she should approach Mike. She had run through a number of scenarios in her head of what she would say and how he would respond. None of the scenarios ended well in her head. As she turned down the street to his house, she still had no idea what she would say to him. As she got closer, she realized she was just going to be up front and go from there, they were friends after all, at least that is what she thought. As she pulled into the driveway, she saw his car and was happy to see it. She didn't call, because she didn't know if she would be able to keep herself from exploding at the sound of his voice.

As she walked up the steps, she readied herself for what was about to happen. She rang the doorbell and got no response, which was strange, because Mike usually responded immediately. She tried again and still got no response. She was starting to get nervous; this definitely wasn't like him. She decided she would try to call, maybe someone had given him a ride. As the phone began to ring, her heart sank to the floor, because she heard his phone ringing in the house.

She began frantically to knock on the door while screaming Mike's name; she still got no answer. She tried the door, it was locked, she then went to the windows, trying to look through to see if she could see anything, still no luck. Then she remembered she had a spare key in her car; she ran to get it. After what seemed like forever, she was finally able to find it. She ran to the door opening, terrified about what she was about to find. Her voice shaking with fear and concern, as she screamed for Mike multiple times. As she made it to his study in the back of the house, her heart sank: there was Mike, lying on the floor. She knew he was dead before she got to the body.

She just lost it; she broke down crying. She hated herself in that moment for all those terrible thoughts she had about him. She realized none of that matter to her anymore. She wished she could take those feelings back. She wished he wasn't lying right here in front of her dead, but she couldn't change that. Then she saw something on shiny on the table on top of a piece of paper. She got up to see what it was. When she looked, she saw it was a penny and under it was a note that read; Penny For Your Thoughts: What Happens When You Kill To Protect Your Secrets.

After she read those words she fell to the ground. What the hell does that mean, she thought? She had no idea what was going on, she was more confused than anything. Was Mike a killer, who did he kill? She was now more confused than anything. All she knew was she just lost someone else close to her. In that moment she felt the pain she felt when she lost her father and then her best friend. She felt the walls closing in on her, she was having a hard time breathing. She had to get out of the house, she needed some air.

As she ran out the house, she didn't even notice the lights. She didn't realize the cops were outside until she heard someone yell, "Freeze, put your hands up!" She froze instantly when she heard those words; she had no idea what was going on. She instantly put her hands up, she felt someone come behind her and start putting cuffs on her.

She then heard the officer say, "follow me to my car." Once they got to the car, he heard one of the officer's yell, "we have a body inside here!" Once she heard that, she began crying all over again, she couldn't stop.

"Miss, I need for you to calm down and tell me who you are and what happened."

She heard the words, but she couldn't get anything out; it hurt too bad to remember what had happened, let alone say it. She just stood there, looking into nothing, her eyes glazed over.

"Miss, miss, are you okay," the officer said with concern in his voice.

She still couldn't speak, she just continued to stand there.

The other officer walked up and whispered something to the officer standing near her.

"Ma'am, I am going to need you to calm down and tell me what happened." The officer said again, his level of frustration starting to grow. The other officer was on the radio, and she could hear him say they had a dead officer at 243 Orange St.

In that moment she realized she had to say something or else it would be a repeat of what happened the night Marcus died. She finally gathered enough strength to talk. "My name is Nicole Jones and the person in the house is Sgt. Mike Allen. When I came here, I found him like that."

"Look who can finally talk. I am going to need for you to have a seat in the car until we get this figured out," the officer said as he opened the door and pushed her inside.

Sitting in the back of the police car in handcuffs took her back to the night of Marcus's death. She tried to figure out how she got to this moment. Six months ago, her life was perfect, and now she didn't know what it was. She was in the back of the car for what seemed like forever. She watched multiple other police cars pull up, she saw the first officers on the scene talking to other officers and pointing at her. She finally saw a face she recognized; the Captain had shown up. He didn't look her way; he immediately went into the house. After about ten minutes he came back out and went over and talked to the officers that put her in the back of the police care.

She saw him look over in her direction as the officer pointed at her. Once they made eye contact, he looked back at the officer and appeared to be yelling at him, but she wasn't sure. She saw him walking to the car with a purpose, once he got there, he opened the door and helped her get out. He then had her turn around so he could remove the cuffs.

The Captain's eyes were bloodshot, she could tell he had been crying. Even when he spoke to her, it was if he was fighting back tears. "I am so sorry you had to go through this again. I can only imagine what you are going through right now. I need for you to tell me what happened. The neighbors called 911 and reported they heard screams coming from Mike's house."

She paused for a moment, before she finally began to speak. "I came over to talk to Mike, just to say hi and see how he was doing. I rang the doorbell, multiple times and he didn't answer, which is not like him at all; especially considering his car was in the driveway. When that didn't work, I called his cell phone, thinking he may have been with someone else. However, I could hear it ringing from inside his house. That is when I got nervous. I started banging on the door and screaming his name, trying to get his attention."

"Did you see or hear anything out of the ordinary while you were outside? Please, nothing is too small."

"I am sorry I wish there was more I could provide, but outside of that I do not know anything." As she said those words, she could see the hope fade from his eyes, which made it harder for her to ask the next question. "Did you see the note?"

"Yes, I did. But don't worry, we believe there is nothing to it. We believe this killer is just targeting anyone who was involved in the original case, not because Samuel Johnson was guilty, but because they were obsessed with him and looked up to him, because he was a serial killer."

As he said those words, she knew them to not be true. This wasn't some obsessed fan; this was someone who was close to killer, and they were killing for revenge.

All of sudden they could hear someone yelling in the background; neither could make out what was being said and who was saying it. They both turned around and saw someone forcing himself through the crowd. As he got closer, they could make out who it was and what he was saying.

It was Harry Wallace approaching them shouting, "Arrest her now." They both looked on in shock, he was now standing in front of them. "I said arrest her, first Detective Jones and now Sgt. Allen. I told you one day I would get you," he said looking at her.

"We can't arrest her; we do not have any evidence that she was involved. We have witnesses that confirm her story. She didn't show up until this evening and he was already dead by then. Witnesses saw her banging on the door and screaming for Sgt. Allen to open the door."

"That doesn't mean anything. She could have come earlier."

Nicole just stood there looking at him. She would not give him the satisfaction of showing him any emotion. She looked at the Captain and asked, "Can I leave now?"

"Yes, you can. Just make sure you have your phone, just in case we have any more questions and if you think of anything else please call me." Once he finished his statement, he gave her a hug and walked away."

Now it was just the two of them. Harry Wallace looked over at her and said, "You may have everyone else fooled, but not me. Sgt. Allen called me and told me who you were. I will make sure everyone knows and bring you down."

She didn't acknowledge him or what she said as she walked away. As she walked away her grief for Mike was slowly disappearing, as she whispered, "That motherfucker!"

CHAPTER 26

DETECTIVE HOWARD FINALLY MADE it to the home of Mrs. Thompson for the second time. He had to find out why she didn't mention the kids as well as what happened to them. Maybe they could provide some information about this new killer. He knew this was a long shot, but he had to be optimistic; they were running out of leads. He looked at his watch to check the time; It was five o'clock, he was hoping she was still awake. He hated showing up unannounced like this, but he hoped she would understand. He began to knock on the door, he got no answer. He knocked again, but he still got no answer. He even tried calling her name and when that didn't work, he walked around the house to see if he could see or hear anything. He had no luck.

He decided he would just come back another day and this time he would call before he came over. As he was getting back into his car, another car pulled into the driveway.

"Finally, some good luck," he thought. As they got out of the car, he saw it was Blythe, her granddaughter.

"Good evening Ms. Thompson. I am sorry for showing up unannounced like this, but I really need to speak with your grandmother."

As she got closer, Howard realized she had been crying.

"I am sorry, is everything okay?"

"No, it isn't. I just left the hospital," she paused after saying that trying to gather herself. "My grandmother died," she finally said, with tears flowing down her eyes.

"I am so sorry to hear that. I cannot imagine the pain you must be in. I am sorry I will leave."

"Please don't. I don't want to be alone right now, and my grandmother knew you would be back and wanted me to show you something when you did. Please follow me to the house."

He was shocked and heartbroken. He only met her that one time, but Ms. Mable Thompson seemed like an amazing woman who reminded him of his grandmother. His feelings of sadness were also tied to the fact that he may never know what happened to the kids now that she was gone. He followed her to the house, not really knowing what to expect; what could she have possibly wanted him to know. He followed her inside, not knowing what to expect next.

As they walked into the house, it smelled like a combination of moth balls and scented candles. Once they got into the living room, he said, "May I ask what happened?"

"She had been sick for a long time and she just stopped fighting."

"I am sorry for your loss again. She seemed liked an amazing woman."

"Thank you," she said with a slight smile on her face.

"Forgive me, but I am not sure what your grandmother would want you to tell me."

Once she turned on the lights in the living room, there were pictures everywhere. He went over and looked at the pictures, and there were some in particular that caught his eye. There were some in particular that caught his eye, there were pictures of young black man that bore a striking resemblance to Marcus. He had never met him, but he remembered what he looked like from pictures he had seen working the case. "Are those pictures of Marcus Jones?"

"Yes, they are."

"Why does she have these pictures?"

Blythe stood their quiet for a moment. He realized with everything she had been through that night; he was coming off a bit oblivious. He caught himself, "I am so sorry, you have had a major loss in your life, and I am putting you through this."

"It's okay, I have to do it for my Big Mama, or I am sure she will find a way to come and get me from the heavens.

Grandma always said she took care of him when his parents died. She said they were distant cousins. Everyone always had their doubts, but no one ever questioned her about it."

"Did she ever say anything about another child or any other children?"

"No, she didn't."

"Did she ever meet Nicole?"

"No, she didn't. She told the both of them it wouldn't be wise if they ever brought their families to see her. I think part of it was out fear, that someone would find out who they were. She didn't tell them who their mother was or the circumstances that led to them coming into their life. So, whenever they came to visit, they would do so by themselves. While she never met Nicole, she knew all about her. While she never met her, Marcus told her all about her and she would save any articles about the both of them. Give me a few minutes, I am going to go get what grandma left for you. She left me very specific instructions to give this to you. She said she wanted you to know the truth."

Sitting there alone he tried to process what this all possibly meant; could Detective Jones be the son of Samuel Johnson, and if Marcus were his child, what happened to the other one? He was stuck; he had no way of finding out. He couldn't go back to Nicole with this information, because what did he truly know? He only had possibilities and nothing concrete. That wouldn't be fair to her or the memory of her husband. He owed it to both of them to get answers before bringing this to her.

He sat there trying to come up with ways to find out. He realized the person who he should talk to was his partner. While he wasn't sure of his involvement in the Samuel Johnson trial, he knew that Mike cared for his dead partner and his wife. So, he could put his issues to the side and consult with his partner to find the answers he was looking for.

After a few minutes Blythe came back in holding an envelope in her hands. "Here you go, my grandmother wanted me to give this to you. She said she doesn't know what is in it, but Marcus had wanted her to keep it for him."

As he took the box from her, he said "Thank you for this and thank you for taking time to speak with me, I understand this is a difficult time for you. For you to do this, I really appreciate it."

Once he got to the car, he put the envelope on his lap and was about to open it, until he saw that his phone was flashing, he had a voicemail. He played the voicemail and it was the Captain telling him to call him immediately, and he could tell from the sound of his voice it was urgent.

When the Captain answered the phone, he tried explaining what had happened, but the Captain cut him off.

"I have something I need to tell you; it's about Sergeant Allen." The Captain paused and Detective Howard felt himself trying to rush him along to tell him what had happened and what he heard next, caused his heart to sank.

"He is dead. They found his body in his home, the copycat killed him."

After hearing those words, he didn't know what to say and even if he had, he wouldn't have been able to speak. They had their disagreements, but this is the last thing he wanted. He put the box in the backseat and drove to Sgt. Allen's home, like his life depended on it. Once he got there, the number of people there had dwindled. He found a young officer on scene, who told him everyone else had left already and they had already moved the body. When he asked the officer what happened, he was even more surprised. He found out that Nicole was the one who found the body. He figured she must have gone there to confront him about everything she had found out, even though they promised they would make the decision together. He wasn't mad; given that it involved the death of her husband she had every right to do so without consulting him.

After speaking with the officer and finding out everything he could, he left and, on the way, home he tried calling Nicole, but he only got her voicemail. Knowing what she had been through that night he understood. He figured he would try again tomorrow. He decided he would head to the station and find out what other information was available; in particular he had to find out what the note said. He had his ideas, but he couldn't be sure.

Once he got to the precinct, he immediately made his way inside, heading straight for the Captain's office. He looked at his watch. He knew it was late, but he was hoping the Captain was still in the office. When he walked inside there was only a skeleton crew there, but he could see the Captain's light on in his office. Finally, some good luck he thought. Once he got to the door, he saw the Captain was still inside. The Captain had a look of defeat on his face, it looked like he had been to hell and was still trapped there. Detective Howard could only imagine what he was going through; two officers killed by the same serial killer.

"Captain, what do we know so far? I went by his house, but there was only a couple of people still there. I was able to find out Nicole Jones found the body. Do we know anything else?"

"So far, we do not know much, we are still waiting on the cause of death from Adam. We assume it is the same as everyone else, some sort of poison and there was a note. So, it was in fact our killer."

"Captain, can I see the note?"

As the Captain handed him the note, he held his hand and said, "this doesn't mean anything. The killer is just saying things now to get under our skin and to make Mike looked bad to discredit him. It isn't true."

When he saw what the note said, he understood why the Captain prefaced his last statement. He couldn't believe it, as much as they had their disagreements and he felt he was hiding something; he couldn't believe this. He just sat there in shock, with the words from the note, replaying constantly in his head.

Penny For Your Thoughts; What Happens When You Kill To Protect Your Secrets.

Whom did he kill and what secrets was he protecting? Mike thought.

CHAPTER 27

As Joe lay in the bed, the events from the previous night weighed heavily on their mind. Joe always knew they were going to have to do it, but it didn't make it that much easier. But he had to pay for what he did, they all had to pay, and there was still some left who had to pay for the part they played over twenty years ago. None of them could understand the level of pain their actions and inactions caused. They had killed an innocent man, taking him away from his family. They had made a mockery of the justice system. A bunch of rich, white men bent the law to fit their needs, everyone else be damned. They couldn't stand by and let them get away with it any longer. They all had to pay and they all would.

Joe wanted to stay in bed, but they had to get up, there was more work to be done. Joe walked down the steps and went straight to the basement. The basement served as their lab and office space. On one side was their garden and pets and the other side was their computer and paperwork. Over the past year, they had spent the majority of their time in the basement. They ate, slept, and worked there most days. They sat down at the desk and began going through the documents on the desk, looking for two in particular. When Joe found the documents, they began typing.

Once Joe finished and were happy with what was written, they printed it. Joe grabbed the documents, placed them in a bag and headed out of the house. It was a bit chilly outside; it had just turned to winter. While the Georgia winters did not get as cold as most places, it was still cold enough. Once Joe got into the car, they had to wait a moment for the car to defrost. They tried to play everything out in their head, they had a lot of driving to do today and had to make sure they stuck to schedule; there couldn't be any delays.

Driving into Monroe brought back memories, as it always had, even more so over the last six months. When Joe first came up with this plan, they didn't know if they would have what it took to see it through, to do everything that needed to be done. However, they had almost accomplished what they sat out to accomplish. This trip would be a quick one, just like all the other ones over the last few years. There were no more happy memories of this place. Growing up here they use to love it, but that all changed when they learned the truth.

Joe grew up thinking it was different and the city was one big family, but those thoughts were shattered when they learned the truth. Their happy life was torn apart. Joe tried for a couple of years after they learned the truth to make it work, but they couldn't take it anymore. They could no longer look at people the same way, not just those involved, but also all of those who turned a blind eye or were so blinded by anger they couldn't see the truth. It shook Joe to their core so much, they just left, without saying goodbye to anyone, friend or family. It felt as if they couldn't breathe, they felt as if they were suffocating, and the longer they stayed, the worse it got for them.

They had finally reached their destination. They found a parking spot and were there to meet with Stacey Davis. She was not just an investigative journalist with Channel 11, she was the best in the area. She was going to help Joe execute the next phase in her plan. Joe had reached out to her and told her they had come across some information about corruption in the city and thought it was important the town knew about it. The meeting between the two was brief. Joe handed her the documents and told her everything she needed to know was in them and left immediately after, not staying long enough to answer any questions. Joe didn't have time to talk, they had somewhere else to be and the information had to be covered in tonight's news.

Over the past year, Joe had learned that Garret James came to Monroe once every couple of months to meet with Harry Wallace. Tonight, Garret would be back in town for their meeting and he would be staying at the Blue Dragon, same as always. Joe had called the hotel and verified that is where he would be staying again. Joe had gone inside the lobby to wait for him to come downstairs. Joe waited in the lobby for what seemed like an eternity. Every time the elevator would ding, they would look up to see if it was him. Each time they were disappointed.

Just when Joe thought he wasn't coming down; they heard a familiar voice. Joe turned around to see Harry Wallace and Garret James walking towards the bar. Joe waited until they had walked in and taken a seat at the bar before going in. Joe took a seat at the bar as well, it was crowded, everyone was inside watching Sunday Night Football, the Falcons were playing the Seahawks. Joe was able to blend into the crowd; they had never met Garret James before, but they did know Harry Wallace. While they had changed their appearance, they didn't want to take any chances of being recognized. After about an hour the moment Joe was waiting for arrived.

Just as the Falcons were moving down the field, the game was interrupted with a Breaking News bulletin. Everyone in the bar, erupted with anger, some even throwing peanuts at the screen. There was Stacey on the screen, as she began speaking, the bar got quieter.

"This is Stacey Davis, Channel 11, with breaking news. Channel 11 has discovered evidence that Samuel Johnson, the convicted Penny Murderer, who was convicted for his crimes, was in fact innocent. He was a victim of Harry

Wallace, a power-hungry detective who would later use the trial to start his legal career; former Governor Landry, who used his influence to frame Samuel Johnson for a murder his son created; and Garret James, who was supposed to defend him, but instead took money to let his client be found guilty, so he could further his career. Stay tuned for the news after the game for more details."

The bar remained in absolute silence even after the news returned to the game. Everyone was in shock about what they just heard. There were those who called it bullshit and said she was just making it up, because they were there, and they know what he did. This led to arguments and some minor scuffles occurred. This allowed both Harry Wallace and Garret James to get out of the bar unnoticed. Joe could see them talking off in the corner; it looked like Harry Wallace was yelling at Garret. Joe couldn't get closer to hear what they were saying. It was okay, they had something they needed to take care of, and besides, Joe could imagine what they were saying.

Harry Wallace walked into his room still trying to figure out who found out and leaked the information. He didn't have time to think about that right now, he had to get the hell out of there. He grabbed his bag and started putting his stuff in it. He was so focused he didn't notice the person behind him, as they stuck him with the needle. He turned around in shock trying to figure out what happened. He saw the person, but he couldn't do anything, he felt dizzy and the room started spinning before he fell to the ground.

Garret awoke to find himself tied to the chair in the room, still not understanding what was going on. Then he heard someone open the door, he couldn't see who it was because he was facing the window. He then felt someone place their hands on his shoulders as they sat in front of him. Joe placed their fingers on their lips, motioning for him to be quiet, as they removed the gag from his mouth.

"You scream, you die, are we understood?" Joe said as they finished removing it. "How does it feel?"

Garret looked confused. He had no idea what they were talking about.

"How does it feel to have your life ruined? To know that your life is in the hands of someone else, to know that despite what you say or do in this moment you are no longer in control of your life. That is how Samuel Johnson felt when you led him to his death. You were supposed to represent him, to help him. But instead you looked out for yourself and you let him die. You built your success off his death. Tell me do you ever think about him, what you did to him?"

Garret sat there with tears streaming down his eyes, his voice trembling, "I am so sorry, I didn't have a choice, they made me do it. I can give you names and details if you let me go."

Joe laughed, "I always figured you were the weakest, but didn't really think you were this dumb. Do you think I need names and details; I know everyone who was involved. Didn't you see the news? You have nothing to offer me."

"That is where you are wrong. I know something that no one else knows. I know who the real killer was. No one else knows who it is, and I will tell you if you let me live."

Joe stood there for a second, just looking at him. Then a sly smile came on their face as they bent down and whispered in his ear; "I already know who it was," as he felt a sharp pinch in the back of his neck.

A look of surprise and fear came over his face. He had no idea what to respond to; how did she know and what did she just do to the back of his neck. He started to feel himself getting lightheaded. "What did you do to me?'

"Don't worry, it will be over soon," Joe said as they got up and started walking towards the door.

After a few moments he knew what that meant. His skin started burning, he could barely breath. His breathing started to get shallower by the second. His chest started burning, but he couldn't grab it, because his hands were still tied behind his back. His body started convulsing so badly, he fell to the floor. Foam started coming from his mouth and then it ended.

Before Joe left out of the room, they removed their mask. As they Joe got on the elevator, a smile came across their face, one more down, they thought, as the elevator closed.

CHAPTER 28

SITTING AT HIS DESK, Detective Howard was trying to process everything that had happened over the last 48 hours, including the death of Sgt. Allen and the bombshell that dropped last night. While it was shock to most people, it served as confirmation for him. Part of him was happy the truth was out, but he also knew his job had just gotten a little harder. The office had turned into a mad house over the past couple of days. They were getting calls from people saying they had additional information about the original murders, some saying they knew who did it, there were people calling to say how much they hated the police, and then there were those who called to say they were the copycat.

The protests outside had only grown, but thankfully so far there had not been any violence. Detective Howard started trying to get his notes together because Harry Wallace was coming in for questions. He released a statement late last night denying everything and even said he would be going into the police department tomorrow to answer questions because he had nothing to hide. He refused to let this these salacious rumors tarnish his reputation. No one had heard from Governor Landry since the news broke. Howard had called Jacksonville to alert them about Garret James and to see if they could keep an eye out, just in case he tried to flee the area. He also called Elizabeth to ask how she was dealing with the news; they had continued to talk since their last date.

Harry Wallace walked through the door surrounded by lawyers, walking with a purpose. He walked directly to the Captain's office, and a few minutes later, the Captain came out and got Detective Howard. As Detective Howard walked into his office, he found Harry Wallace there, sitting at the table flanked, by his lawyers.

"This is how this is going to go; I am not going to answer any of your questions."

Detective Howard looked confused, "Then why did you come in?"

"I came in to let you know that I will not sit here and let this you or anyone else from this department dredge up the past. It is obvious what is going on here. Someone is trying to garner sympathy for both of these killers, by painting myself, Governor Landry, and Garret James in a negative light. When I find out who that person is, I will make sure they pay. From now on, nothing about this investigation gets out to public and I will be kept in the loop at all times and I want you to find out who released this information to the news. I have already spoken to the mayor, consider yourselves my employees until I this case is solved."

Once he finished his statement, he got up, along with his lawyers and left the building, leaving a stunned Captain Brown and Detective Howard.

"What the hell was that," asked Detective Howard.

"I have no idea, but I don't give a damn what he says. I do not work for him. I need for you to go check with Channel 11 and see what you can find out about the source. I know it is a long shot, but we have to start somewhere."

"Can you have someone else go to Channel 11? I need to go to Blinton."

The Captain looked surprised. "What the hell is a Blinton and where is it?"

"Honestly, I am not even sure. All I know is this is where Samuel Johnson was from and I may be able to gather some information about him and anyone who was close to him. The killer has to have a personal connection to him somehow."

"Okay, keep me posted. I will go by Channel 11 myself; I have a good relationship with some of the people working there, in particular Mrs. Monroe."

The two-hour drive to Blinton was a drive through the some of the smallest towns in Georgia, filled with old buildings and lots of trees. But it gave him a chance to think and reflect on things. This case kept getting crazier and crazier and he didn't know where it would take him next. Driving into Blinton was like going back in time. It was a small town and it looked as if it had been overlooked by modernity. He saw the General Shop and some people standing outside, he figured this was as good a place as any to start. So, he parked his car and started walking towards the group.

As he got close to the group, he spoke, but no one said anything, everyone looked at him as if he was an alien. He started again, "My name is Detective Howard," as he reached into his pocket to pull out his badge. Before he could get his badge out, most of the group dispersed. There were only two people left; both of them looked like they were the two oldest in the group. He didn't mind, because for what he needed help with, they would probably be the best source of information.

One of the gentlemen looked at him and said, "I guess you are here about Sam. It only took you twenty-four years to find the town." Seeing the surprised look on the Detective's face he added, "We do get the news out here."

Detective Howard, understood his frustration and he realized this was going to be harder than he thought. "Yes, I am here about Sam. I understand your frustration about how what happened to him."

"Say it, he was murdered, and we are more than frustrated with what happened. We are pissed. You all killed that man and didn't have the decency to tell his family that you killed him," the other gentlemen interjected angrily.

"I am sorry, I do not know how to respond to that. I share your anger with what happened to him. I was a kid when it happened so I couldn't do anything then, but I can do something now. But in order to do that I need your help. I am not here to bring any trouble or make things difficult for you or anyone else in this town, I am here to find the truth, so I can figure out what happened."

The younger of the two was about to speak again, but the older gentlemen cut him off. "What are you going to do with this truth?'

"I am going to clear Samuel Johnson, excuse me Samuel Jones's name and then I am going to arrest two killers, the first one in the 90s and the one active now."

"Why would we help you catch this new killer, they are only punishing those who got Sam killed," the younger gentlemen responded.

"I understand this new killer's frustration, but they can't just go around killing people. If they kill everyone involved, then it will make it even harder to clear Mr. Jones's name. Believe there is a part of me that would love to join them, but I can't. The way they are going about this is wrong."

The two gentlemen looked at each other, as they pondered what Detective Howard said. They took a few minutes to think about, then finally the older of the two spoke. "Follow me, I know someone who can help, but you will have to convince her to talk to you. My name is Marcus and this is John. My car is over there; you can follow me."

"Nice to meet, the both of you. Who are you taking me to meet?"

"His mother," Marcus said as he walked to his car.

Detective Howard stood there frozen for a moment, trying to grasp what he just heard and who he was about to meet.

CHAPTER 29

DETECTIVE HOWARD FOLLOWED THE gentlemen as they drove through the town. They ended up driving through the town and turned down a dirt road. As they drove down the road, Detective Howard saw some cows and what appeared to be abandoned farms. After a few miles of driving, they got to the end of the road and to the left was an older white home.

"This is Ms. Mary Lee James's home. Good afternoon ma'am, how are you doing? I brought a cop, he wants to ask you a few questions," Marcus said to a lady sitting on the porch.

She didn't say anything, she didn't even look up to acknowledge his presence. She just kept doing what she was doing. Once they got closer to the porch, without looking up, she said to Marcus, "there is some dinner in the kitchen if you want it."

Marcus and John gladly went into the house to get something to eat. When it was just the two of them out there, Detective Howard was about to speak, but before he could she said, "Let's go inside, it is hot as the dickens out here." She slowly got up and led him inside to the living room. Walking into her home was like walking into his grandmother's home. He could smell the food in the kitchen and all of sudden he got hungry. Once they sat down, Ms. Mary Lee asked, "How may I help you, young man."

"My name is Detective Howard and I am with the Monroe Police Department and I was hoping I could ask you a few questions."

"If you are from Monroe, then I guess you are here to ask me about Sam."

"Yes ma'am, I am. Anything you can tell me I would really appreciate it. I know it has been a long time and I showed up here unannounced, but I could really use your help."

Ms. Mary Lee paused for a few moments, as it looked like she was off in the distance thinking about a painful memory. Then finally she said that it would be okay if he asked her some questions.

"Thank you so much for taking the time to speak with me. What can you tell me about Samuel ……. Jones's wife?" pausing to correct himself, as he almost said Johnson.

"Sweet lady, she was very caring, both her and Sam loved each other dearly. I know that may be hard to believe, given everything he did while he was in Monroe. But Sam was battling his own demons that he could never get rid of. Sam had a rough childhood, meeting Tiffany saved his life, she was able to help him get focused. Then when they had their daughter, Denise, it made him want to become even better."

"Denise loved her father and was always with him. No matter where he went, she always wanted to go with him. She was his little shadow. She was the sweetest little girl; she was always trying to help people. Both her and her father shared the dream of becoming a lawyer. He would tell her all about what he was going to when he became a big-time lawyer and how when she was old enough, they would start their own firm together." She had to pause to catch herself, as tears began streaming down her eyes.

Detective Howard looked at her and seeing her emotions changed, he started to get concerned. "Are you okay, do you need to take a moment?"

She waved her hand, telling him no she didn't want to stop, as she continued. "He had tried to get into law school before, but he had been denied because of his past criminal history. So, he decided to change his name, not because he wanted to break the law, but so he could provide a better life for his family and to fulfill a promise he made to his daughter. The day he left to go to school was a happy and sad day, but he and Tiffany were determined to make it work. He would come home at least once a month on weekends to see his family, sometimes more. But I could tell he was struggling. The weight of everything was wearing on him and he started going out more and meeting other people."

"What happened to his family while he was gone?"

"They both struggled in the beginning, but over time, they both started handling it better. They both started returning to their normal selves. Denise started back becoming that energetic young lady, who would help anyone. Then they just stopped hearing from him, and he stopped coming home. No one had heard from him; Marcus went into Monroe a couple of times to look for him, but he never found him. Eventually, everyone just said he had moved on and found him another family. This tore Tiffany and Denise up, they both struggled with it. And then…."

She started crying as she couldn't even finish her last statement. Detective Howard sat there paralyzed with emotion. He felt sorry for her and could tell she was in a lot of pain. He got up and walked over to her and put his hands on her shoulder, trying to comfort her, she reached up and placed her hand on his, whispering thank you.

After a few minutes she continued, and Detective Howard returned to his seat. "And then Marcus came back from a trip there with a newspaper and a sad look on his face. All he could say was they killed him, as he handed me the newspaper. It was an article about the Penny Murderer finally being put to death, and there was a picture of Sam."

She held her head down, she was visibly shaken, as she tried wiping the tears from her eyes. "They killed my baby."

That last statement seemed odd to him, but he didn't want to interrupt her, because he feared if she stopped talking again, she wouldn't finish. "That tore Tiffany and Denise apart. They had no idea how to deal with it. Not only was he dead, but he was convicted of murder and they didn't know. They both felt bad, they couldn't even get the body to give him a proper burial, they cremated him and put his ashes in the trash."

Detective Howard, just sat there, not really sure what to say. He felt bad for her, he felt bad for the family. That was a lot for any family to deal with, given the death of his parents, he felt bad for Denise, especially. "Where can I find them?"

She got quiet, tears still falling down her face, her voice shaking even more as she said, "they both are dead. They were unable to cope with everything that happened. Denise stopped coming out. Her friend would try to help her, but she was unable to and one day she never came out of her room and Nicole found her lying on her bed, with the bottle beside her. Her mother died soon after."

Detective Howard was fixated on the name Nicole in the story. It couldn't be, he had to make sure one way or the other. He reached into his phone and found a picture and showed it to her. "Is this Nicole?"

A smile came over her face. "Yes, that is Nicole. She and Denise were like sisters and when she died, it hurt her bad. She still comes in her to check on me sometimes and she calls too. She loved Denise so much she wanted to honor her and Sam's memory, so much so that she became a lawyer, like they wanted to. She even has a big firm, she called me to tell me that she had did it and to honor their memory she included their name in the name of the firm. Given what happened to her parents, it is a miracle she made it out of here."

Detective Howard sat their stunned, hearing her say that made it all make sense. He never questioned why their two Jones's in the name of the firm. He was also curious what happened to her parents. "What happened to her parents?"

"Her mother killed her father in front of her. No one knows why, but it is nothing but God, that she is where she is today, given everything that happened to her."

Hearing that almost floored Detective Howard; he was amazed that after everything she had been through, she was able to accomplish everything she had. He had so many more questions he wanted to ask her, but he couldn't put her through any more. She had been through enough and he couldn't stand to remind her about the past any more than he already had. She looked exhausted. He thought briefly about asking her if had she heard anything about Sam having kids outside of his marriage, but he realized that would have been cruel and a line he wasn't ready to cross.

Before he could say anything, she called for Marcus. Once he was in the room, she asked him to walk Detective Howard to his car; she was going to lay down. Detective Howard thanked her for taking the time to speak with and apologized for everything again, as she got up to go lay down.

"Ma'am, I am sorry one last question: Has anyone else come by and talked to you about Sam?"

She paused for a moment and without turning around said, "There was one other person. A girl named Mary stopped by. She was very pretty. She said she was a writer and was working on a story about Sam and wanted to learn about where he came from. She was sweet lady."

That was strange, he thought. He had not heard the name before, so it didn't ring a bell. He decided he would make a note of the name just in case. It was 50/50 if the name meant anything.

CHAPTER 30

NICOLE WAS LAYING ON the bed with old photos spread out across the bed. She had been reminiscing about good times and remembering everyone she had lost. Everything that she had been through had finally gotten to her. She didn't know if she could or even if she wanted to go anymore. The feeling took her back to when her mother killed her father, then when she found Denise's body, when she found Marcus's body, and lastly when she found Mike's body. It was too much she thought, why me. Everyone says God does everything for a reason, butr she just needed to know that reason.

What did she do to deserve this? She just felt like closing her eyes and never opening them again. That would be the easiest thing and she would no longer feel any pain. Her dedication to work was partly a defense mechanism, because since the death of her father and Denise, she had been afraid to form emotional connections with people, for fear something would happen to them. Now here she is, having lost two of the closest people in her life, and she was back to feeling that way again. The news about Mr. Jones being innocent didn't help. It made her angry, not only should he not have died, but neither should her friend. She began to feel anger and resentment at everyone involved. She thought if Mike was involved, then he deserved to die as well.

The more she thought about the new developments in the case, she grew more and more angry at all of those involved. Her rage was growing to the level of hate. She felt an even higher level of hate for this new killer. Why kill Marcus? He had nothing to do with what happened to Mr. Jones. She didn't know why, but she told herself she was going to find out who the killer was and make them tell her why. She wasn't ready to die just yet; she had found her renewed sense of purpose.

Nicole sat up on the bed and realized there was one person she could talk to and get some answers. She decided she was going to talk to Harry Wallace. She figured the best place to get the answers she needed was to go straight to the source. She was done tip-toeing around, trying to get answers. She was going to tear things down with a sledge-hammer now. So, she got up, got dressed, and headed out to go see him.

The protests today were even worse than they had been the previous week. The report from last night had only intensified them. There was an increase in the number of people protesting the police and the city government, as well as an increase in the number of those individuals voicing their support. As Nicole looked out the window, she saw people she recognized on both sides of the protests. While she had always had the utmost respect for law enforcement and the government, after everything that had happened, she felt differently today, and for those who were counter-protesting, she said screw them.

As she pulled into the parking garage for City Hall, she gathered herself and walked into the building like a woman on a mission. She made it through the metal detectors and the person at the front tried to get her attention and ask her who was she here to see, but she ignored him. She knew where she was going, she didn't need directions and she didn't want to give him any warning.

As she walked off the elevator on the 18th floor, she walked through the doors to the main office of the District Attorney's office, bypassing his secretary, whom she could her behind her saying she couldn't go back there. She didn't care, nothing was going to stop her.

She barged into his office, startling Harry Wallace. "What the hell are you doing in here in here, Nicole?"

"I am sorry sir, I tried to stop her," the secretary said apologetically.

"It is okay, you can leave us. Nicole, I must say I am surprised to see you in here. But I am actually happy to see you. We have some things we need to talk about."

Nicole sat down and looked at him coldly. "I always knew you were a dirty son of a bitch, but this I would never have expected this. You didn't just stand by and watch an innocent man get killed, you led the charge. How do you live you with yourself?"

"You have no idea what you are talking about and I sleep pretty well. What about you and your secret? I know who you are and more importantly I know who your daddy is, or should I say was. Your friend Mike Allen told me he found out who your daddy was," he said with a sly smile on his face. He could see the part about Allen really upset her. "It's a shame, you actually believed he was your friend."

"That doesn't bother me, he was just as guilty as you and besides neither one of you know anything about me! But I know everything about you. You are a small man who framed an innocent man, who will pay for his crimes. I know about the payments over the years from Governor Landry and Judge White to you over the years and the ones to Garret James. Not only do I know about it, I can prove it. It is only a matter of time before you go to jail."

"You have no idea what you are talking about. You have no proof of anything and even if you did have records, they don't tell anything, they are just showing I was giving some money, which can easily be explained. But you on the other hand, it will be pretty easy to make a case against you as the copycat. You got upset that your daddy was killed and you started killing people you felt were responsible for his death, including your husband and his partner."

Nicole laughed at his last statement. "You are even more clueless than I thought. If that is all you have, please have me arrested now, so I can embarrass you like I always do in court. You bring your truth and I will bring mine and let's see who comes out on top."

"As much as I am enjoying this, I have a meeting, so I am going to need you to get out of my office!"

It didn't bother her that he was kicking her out; she had accomplished what she set out to do. But before she walked out the door, she turned around and said, "How does it feel to have to look over your shoulder and wonder if you are next?"

Once she walked out of the office, Harry picked up the phone and told the person on the other end, "We have a problem, she knows."

CHAPTER 31

A PENNY FOR YOUR Thoughts; What Happens When You Help To Convict The Person You Are Supposed To Represent. For the first time, Detective Howard knew exactly what one of the notes was talking about. Housekeeping had found the body of Garret James in room when they came to clean this morning. So far news of his death had not gotten out, but Howard knew that was only a matter of time. He had not been given a new partner yet and he was thankful for it. He was hoping the process would drag out for an extended period of time.

He walked over to Adam, who had finished up his initial look at the body. "What do you know so far?"

"Same as the other victims, it was likely poison, the point of entry is the back of the neck. Time of death is around 11pm last night, but I will know more when I get the body back to my office. Other than that, I have nothing else."

"Just keep me updated on whatever you find."

He didn't expect to find much, and given the location, he didn't expect forensics to find anything of value either. Whatever they did find could easily be explained away by someone as them having been in the room at some point prior to the night of the murder. He still needed to speak with Nicole about what he had learned on his trip to Blinton. His plan was to go this morning, but he got called to come to this homicide. So, he had to work it, before he could do anything else.

He went downstairs to talk to the housekeeper who found the body. When he spoke to her, he got the answer he was expecting: she didn't see or hear anything. He spoke to some of the other hotel staff and the people in rooms near the victim and none of them had seen anything either. As he was just about to give up hope, he looked up and saw the video cameras in the lobby.

He walked over to the receptionist and said he needed to speak to the manager. "I need to get access to the camera feed, in particular from last night."

"I am sorry Detective, I can't give it to you without a warrant, corporate policy. But what I can do is go ahead and save the data for the time period you need, so when you come back with the warrant, it will be waiting for you."

Detective Howard said thank you and found Detective Johnson and asked him if he could work on the search warrant, because he needed to go take care of something else.

Johnson was confused as to what Howard had to do that was more important than this, but he agreed to do it none the less. There was nothing more he could do here, and he didn't believe in wasting time when he could be doing other things. He was going to see Nicole; he had to find out what else she was hiding.

He walked into her office building the same time as her, meeting her in the lobby.

"Well this is good luck, my meeting you here. I was just about to come up to your office. I need to speak with you about something, if you have time."

Nicole was taken aback that he was there, she didn't feel like or have the time to talk to him. She had other things on her mind and some things she needed to take care of that she needed to get done immediately. But she knew if she told him no, that would only create more questions and she didn't have time to deal with those at the time. So, she agreed to it.

Once they made it to her office and were alone he began. "First, how are you doing? I know that you and Allen were pretty close, even though the relationship was going through its challenges currently. Finding the body had to make it worse."

She appreciated his concern, but honestly his death, while initially traumatic, the more time she had to process everything, she felt less and less about it. But she didn't want to tell him that. She had to act as if it still bothered her. "Thank you for concern, it was a shock that not only he died, but to find the body made it even more traumatic." She said while acting as if she was holding back tears.

"I am sorry to hear that and if I can do anything please let me know. I should tell you, because I know you will find out soon, but Garret James is dead. He was found in his room at the Blue Dragon."

Nicole was shocked, but not surprised to hear that he was dead. The killer had made it a point to target those people who were involved and Garret James, out of everyone, was the worst. A sense of happiness overcame her with hearing the news that he was dead. She thought it was well-deserved for the pain that he had caused her and Mr. Jones's family. He was the reason Denise's entire family was dead; his inaction led to their deaths. He got what he deserved, as far as she was concerned. "Wow, that is shocking to hear. I guess it shouldn't be that big of a surprise, given he was Samuel Johnson's attorney and he let him get convicted for a crime he didn't commit. Especially given the killer has made it a point to target people who they felt were responsible for Samuel Johnson's death."

As she was talking, he realized she was a good actor. If he hadn't have learned who she really was, then he would have believed she was truly sad about Sgt. Allen's death and shocked about Garret James's death. He figured she was probably celebrating both of their deaths as he was sitting there talking to her. He felt it was strange that she seemed pretty sure the copycat had killed him. She didn't ask or phrase the question in a manner that made it seem as if she was unsure; she was definitive in her response. Maybe this wasn't the right time to tell her that he knew her truth, he thought. He decided he would wait and do some more investigating, because maybe she wasn't as innocent as everyone thought.

He decided to make an audible to his original plans. "What can you tell me about Marcus's family? Where are his parents, does he have any siblings?"

She paused for a second, not sure why he would be asking about Marcus's family. "His parents died when he was young, he was raised by his grandmother, who died after he graduated high school. He has no siblings and no other family. Why do you ask?"

She seemed sincere in her answer, like she didn't know the truth about him. While he had some doubts, he couldn't tell her the truth about Marcus's parents and his sister, yet. If he was wrong and she wasn't involved, hearing the truth about him would push her closer to the brink and he wasn't ready to do that.

"I realized I never asked before. I figured Sergeant Allen knew and if there was anything of note, he would tell me. But with him being gone now, I just had to ask for my own education." He looked at his watch as a way to cover his immediate exit. "I didn't realize the time; I need to get back to the precinct and talk to the Captain about Garret James' death.

Nicole was taken aback by his abrupt exit. There was something about his visit and the way he acted that was strange. She couldn't figure out what it was. She didn't have time to try to figure it out right now, she had other things that she needed to do. She started debating whether she should have told him she was at the Blue Dragon last night. She eventually decided she was right not to tell him. She started typing on her computer, she had to figure out where she knew the name Tracey Bush from, it had been driving her crazy, the name sounded so familiar, she just couldn't remember where she heard it. While she was sitting there typing, her phone rang, it was Ms. Mary Lee.

"Hi Grandma, how are you doing?"

"I am doing good, honey."

"I will be by to see you soon; I am just busy at work. Do you need me to bring you anything when I come?" She knew the answer before she asked, but liked to ask anyway.

"No honey, just your smiling face."

"This isn't like you to call me during the day like this. Is everything okay?"

"Yes, it is, I just wanted to tell you that an officer from there came by and saw me yesterday, asking about Sam, Tiffany, Denise, and you."

Nicole's heart sank when she heard that; that is why Detective Howard came by. He found out the truth, but why did he not say anything?

"What did you tell him?"

"I told him everything, except what you were looking for. Is that okay?"

"Yes ma'am, that is okay. I have to get back to work, but I will call you this afternoon to check on you, okay?"

After she got off the phone, her heart was racing, she knew if he told anyone the truth, then she would be arrested immediately. She knew how it would look, she would be painted as a revenge seeking family friend, and it didn't help that she found the bodies of two of the victims. She had to get out of the office, because she knew this would be the first place, they looked for her. She told Lucas she was stepping out and she would be back tomorrow.

CHAPTER 32

DETECTIVE HOWARD SAT AT his desk trying to decide what he should do. Each decision had overarching consequences. He could tell someone the truth about Nicole and if he did, he knew the information would get back to Harry Wallace and he would push for her immediate arrest. That was something he didn't want to put her through if he was wrong. But he also knew he couldn't do this on his own anymore, he needed help. He wasn't from the area, so he didn't know everything about the old case and how the town actually operated. He realized that even though he and Allen had their disagreements, Mike was right about one thing: he had no idea of how this town operated and the people in it. He was stuck and he had no idea who he could trust.

As he was sitting there, Detective Johnson came up to his desk. "We got the warrant; you want to ride with me?"

Detective Howard gladly grabbed his stuff and followed him out the door. The car ride with Detective Johnson was drastically different from the ones with Sgt. Allen. They actually used the time to talk. Detective Johnson actually listened and actually asked for his thoughts, which caught him off-guard. It was something he had not been used to in the time he had been there. But he appreciated it. They both had shared their doubts about the original trial, but each from a different perspective. Detective Johnson grew up in the area and after his football career ended, he moved back to the area. The fact he grew up in the area brought a different perspective to the table.

They were unable to finish their conversation because they had pulled up to the hotel. They walked inside and up to the check-in counter and asked to speak with the manager. The receptionist picked up the phone and called him, shortly after she came from behind the door.

"Detective, welcome back! Do you have the warrant?"

"Yes, I do," Detective Howard said as he pulled it out and showed it to her.

"Everything seems in order, follow me please."

They followed her to her office, where she pulled out a DVD with the recorded time frame. "Here you go as promised, I hope you find what you are looking for."

"Thank you! I have one more favor to ask, would it be okay if we watch it here?"

She thought about it for a second. "Yes, that will be fine, there is a computer in the office, that no one is using right now. You both can watch it there. She led them to another office and logged onto the computer. "Here you go, and if you want you can broadcast it to the tv, if you want to see it bigger."

"Thank you again, this is a really big help."

As she walked out the door, they both sat down and began watching the footage. The footage started at 4 pm, which was shortly before Garret James checked in at 4:10pm. She is a life-savior, Detective Howard thought. She actually took the time to figure out when he checked in and to start the video accordingly. They saw him walk in at 4:05 and he walked over to the counter to check in and waited in line. After he checked in, he immediately went upstairs. About fifteen minutes later he came back down to the lobby and left.

"This is going to be painful. Did you want to watch in shifts to make it easier?"

Detective Howard thought about it for a moment. "That is a good idea, but I think we should both watch it, just in case one of us doesn't see something, the other may catch it in real time."

Detective Johnson didn't have any objections, so they continued watching. In order to speed up the process, they decided to fast forward. Whenever someone would come in, they would stop the video so they could get a look at the people who came in. So far, they had not seen anyone unusual. Only five people came in and they all checked in; two of them were an elderly couple and the other three were all part of the same family. Sunday afternoons were generally slow, and that Sunday was no different. He finally showed back up at 5:30pm and went up to his room. From 5:30 pm to 7:30 pm eight other people came in. They saw nothing out of the ordinary. Three of the people checked in together, two of them sat down in the lobby, both were wearing Falcons jerseys, and the other three went inside the bar.

Just as they were about to give up hope, they saw Garret James come back downstairs and walked towards the bar. Then they saw someone come in. They both looked at each other, "Doesn't that look like Harry Wallace?" Detective Howard asked.

"I think you are right, but what is he doing there?"

They got their answer as he walked over to Garret James and they both walked into the bar together. "Didn't he say the last time he saw him was at the original trial?" After the bombshell report, Harry Wallace's statement denied everything and in particular, he said he didn't have a relationship with Garret James then and he didn't now.

"Well it sure as hell looks like he has a pretty good one according to this."

They continued watching the video and at 8:45 pm, they saw the both of them come out of the bar and it appeared Harry Wallace was yelling at Garret James. This was around the time the news about their suspected crimes and subsequent cover-up about the Samuel Johnson trial. They stood there talking for about five minutes, then Harry Wallace left, and Garret James went back up the elevator. They kept watching the video and about five minutes after Garret James went up the elevator one of the people who had come in wearing a Falcons' Jersey went to the elevator, which they both thought was strange. They rewound it to try to get a look at the person's face. The person had their face painted, but you could still make out some facial definition.

They kept watching to see when they would come back down. They knew Garret James was murdered around 11 pm, so if the person came down before then, they knew they were not the killer, but if they didn't, then they had a suspect. They waited patiently for to see if the person came back downstairs. They at looked at the time and it was 11:01 pm. Just as they thought, they had identified a suspect, the person wearing the jersey walked off the elevator.

Their heart sank when they saw the individual come off the elevator. They were just about to give up hope when Detective Howard saw something. He looked at the time and saw it was 11:30pm; Garret James was already dead. He saw Nicole getting off the elevator and casually walking out the front door. He sat there in silence for a few moments.

Detective Johnson beat him to it. "Wasn't that Nicole that walked off the elevator.

"We need to get back to the precinct, I need to talk to the Captain."

CHAPTER 33

DETECTIVE HOWARD SAT IN the Captain's office with Detective Johnson. "Captain as much as I hate to do this, I think we should look at Nicole as a suspect or at the very least a person of interest in these murders."

The Captain and Sgt. Johnson both looked him in surprise. They both had known her for an extended period of time and neither one could believe that she would be involved in something like this.

"You are going to have to explain this to us. We both know her and there is no way in hell she would do this."

He wasn't ready to tell them about Marcus yet, because he still had not been able to confirm any of that information. So, he just told them about the information he learned about Nicole. "I understand your hesitation. I am still having a hard time believing it myself, but there are just too many coincidences are there is something else. She has been keeping a major secret from everyone." Hearing that caused both of them to sit up in their chairs, as they were waiting to hear what this secret was.

"She was best friends with Samuel Johnson's daughter, and she is the one who found her body when she committed suicide. She saw first-hand the impact his death had on his family. Not only did she find the daughter's body, but she saw the damage both her daughter's suicide and the death of her husband did to his wife, as well as seeing how it impacted his mother. She still keeps in contact with his mother today. Taking that into account along with the fact she found two of the victim's bodies and we know she was at a third crime scene; it is just too much to ignore."

They both sat there in silence, neither one could believe what they just heard. Detective Johnson broke the silence: "Are we sure we want to go down this road with what little we have? Especially in light of everything that is going on? There are a large number of people who believe an innocent man was convicted, who was later killed in prison, and if we arrest the person who found his daughter's body, we are only going to make things worse. There are already people who are sympathize with the killer and you can't get any more sympathetic than that."

"I understand your concern, Detective, but we have to do something. We have the chance right now to get ahead of this and make sure this is done with the utmost level of compassion and discretion. If we wait and don't act now, we run the risk of the DA finding out and making this an even worse situation. I know Nicole and hope there is a good explanation for her not disclosing her past. The only way to find out is to bring her in. Bring her in, but do so with discretion, I do not want this on the news."

Later that day, Nicole was sitting at her desk, when Lucas came in followed by both Detective Howard and Detective Johnson. "I am sorry, I told them you were busy, but they just barged in any way."

"It's okay Lucas, how may I help you two?"

"We are going to need you to come with us."

"What's wrong? Is everything okay?"

"Yes, everything is okay, we just need to ask you some questions down at the station."

Nicole didn't like where this was going. She had seen this too many times before not to know what this was. While she was not going to be arrested, it was going to be strongly suggested she come with them or she would be arrested. While she knew she didn't do anything wrong, she didn't want to go through the embarrassment of being arrested. "Is it okay if I drive my own car, I have had enough of being in the back of a police car?"

Detective Howard understood her concern, but it was something they couldn't do. "Unfortunately, we are going to have to insist you ride with us. I drove my car, so you will not be in the back of a police car."

The drive to the precinct was a quiet one. Each person was thinking about the current situation. Detective

Johnson felt bad that Nicole had to go through this, she had already been through so much and there they were putting her through even more for what, he thought. Detective Howard was trying to convince himself he was doing the right thing and Nicole was thinking how much they all were going to pay for putting her through this.

It was a relatively short drive to get to the precinct, the protests had died down, so they didn't have to deal with the congestion they brought. As they pulled into the precinct parking lot, there weren't too many cars in there. They parked in the back, where no one could see them bringing Nicole in; they were trying to make it as inconspicuous as possible. Once they got in the building, they took her to interview room 1 immediately, so no one would see her in the building. The last thing they wanted was for someone to see her. They decided Detective Howard would go in alone at first.

"Why am I here?" Nicole asked as soon as they all sat down. She wanted to get straight to the point and not waste any time getting to the point.

"We just have a few questions to ask you. We have come across some new information and we need you to shed some light on some of the information we learned."

Nicole immediately realized what this was about; Detective Howard was going to use the information he learned on his trip to Blinton to try to tie her to the murders. She always knew someone may find out about her past, she just never thought it would be under these circumstances. She figured she would beat them to it, why prolong the inevitable she thought. "Let me guess, you think because I was friends with the daughter of Samuel Jones, I killed all those people."

"Now that you mention that, how come you didn't tell anyone that, especially given everything that has transpired?"

"I didn't tell anyone because it was no one's business, honestly. I didn't see the need to tell anyone. If I would have told anyone then I would have been in this seat earlier, not because of any evidence, but because of my connections to Samuel Johnson. I didn't want to deal with that and the memories it would have brought."

"Actually Mrs. Jones, that is not the only reason you are in here. You are here because we can tie you to three of the crime scenes; Detective Marcus Jones, Sergeant Mike Allen, and Garret James."

"So, you think I killed them all? Why would I do that?"

"Because you wanted revenge for what they did to your friend's father."

"Good theory, but it doesn't explain why I would kill Marcus."

"Maybe you killed him because he found out what you were planning. But we can come back to that. Why didn't you tell me you were at the Blue Dragon at the time of Garret James's murder? We have you on video coming down the elevator shortly after he was killed. Why were you so certain he was a victim of the copycat. I never told you how he died, and you never asked?"

"You know what I am not under arrest and you can't hold me here. I am done answering your questions. I am leaving."

Immediately after she said that Harry Wallace barged through the door. "Correction, you are under arrest for murder. We got you, we found your prints at two of the crime scenes and at the home of Tracey Bush. How long were you two working together?" He held out a picture of her and Tracey Bush together, along with several other people.

She was shocked, the only places they could have found her prints were at her home and Mike's home, but those would be obvious and not enough to arrest her for and as far as the picture she remembered that picture, it was at Mike's wedding, but she didn't know Tracey Bush. "I would like to speak with my lawyer," she said stoically.

"As is your right, I am going to enjoy taking you down. Get her out of here and take her to a cell."

Detective Howard was confused, and he needed answers so he went to the Captain's office to figure out what the hell happened. "Captain, what the hell is going on?"

"We just got a match to the prints we found at the Millers', Tracey Bush's, and Garret James's hotel room. They belong to Nicole. We have proof she was at those addresses.

It hurts me more than anyone, but we had to do it. It wasn't based off Harry's personal feelings."

Detective Howard stood there in silence; he didn't know what to say. As he looked out of the Captain's office, he saw Nicole walking in handcuffs as she was led to the holding cell.

CHAPTER 34

NICOLE SAT IN THE interview room, waiting for Alan to show up. She had spent the night in jail, and she couldn't believe it had come to this. She was sitting there in an orange jumpsuit with her hands cuffed to the table, like she was a criminal. She tried to play it out in her head, how she got to this moment. It sucked and she didn't know what to do. She was stuck in a jail cell for something someone else did and she couldn't do anything about it. The only good thing that came out of all of this, was she remembered why the name Tracey Bush sounded so familiar, she was a friend of Mike's wife. The only time she met her was at their wedding, but she had heard about her.

She heard the door open, thankfully it was Alan. "Are you okay, Nicole?"

"Yes, I am okay. Thank you for coming."

"Are you sure you are okay, no one did anything to you did they?"

"I am sure."

"Good, now what the hell Nicole? I won't worry about it now, but in the future, we will talk about why you didn't tell me about your past. I don't care where you come from or who you knew. I know you and I know that you could not have done any of this. There has to be a logical explanation for all of this."

"There is, but I can't tell you."

"Nicole, I understand there were some things that you wanted to keep to yourself, for your own reasons. I am okay with that, but now is not the time for this. I am working on getting you bail, but I need to know everything. I can't be left in the dark. Imagine yourself in my shoes right now and you had a client who wouldn't tell you anything. What would you, what *have* you told them before? You know how this works, I can't help you unless you tell me and if you want to get bail, you can't defend yourself."

Nicole sat there for a moment, thinking about what he just said. She knew he was right, but she had a hard time bringing herself to open up and tell anyone anything about her past, let alone him. This was something that she couldn't even tell Marcus. It was all part of her painful past and one of her biggest fears was what happened if she got stuck in that place emotionally again; she wasn't sure she would be able to get herself out of it.

"I understand what you are saying, this is hard for me. It is nothing against you, I trust you, I really do. It is just hard for me to talk about not just the past, but to explain everything that has happened since."

"You have to trust me that not only do I have your best interest at heart, but you do not have to go through this alone. Me, Patricia, and Lindsey are here for you. You do not have to go through this alone anymore."

Tears began to flow down her eyes. It meant a lot to hear him say that. "Okay, I will tell you everything. You already know that I was close to Samuel Johnson, or as I knew him Samuel Jones, and his family. But what you don't know is I found out a couple years ago that it was possible he may have had a child with a woman here, so I have been trying to find out if that was true and if so, who are they. This is why my prints were found at the Millers' and in the hotel room of Garret James. I went to see them to ask them what they knew about it. Needless to say, neither one told me anything. They both told me I had no idea what I was talking about and there was no baby. When I left, they were all alive, I didn't kill them. I had no reason to kill them."

"Why did you go see the Millers'? What made you think they would know?"

"I remember reading about the trial and Mr. Jones said that he had an affair with both Laura Johnson and Melissa Landry, so I figured out who were friends with each one and I went to each one and asked them if it was true. It didn't work, because everyone said it wasn't true. I didn't just speak to the Millers; I spoke to a couple other people as well."

"What about Tracey Bush? How did your prints get in her house and how do you know her?"

"That's the thing; I have no idea how my prints got into her house. I only met her the once, at Mike's wedding. I didn't remember until they showed me the picture. I had no idea where she stayed."

"This helps. I need a list of all of the people you talked to about this; I need their names, dates, and where they live. I will try to contact them to get proof of what you just told me. This will eliminate the narrative that you went to them to get revenge. Your arraignment is scheduled for this afternoon, at which point I will be asking for bail. It will more than likely be a substantial amount, but I am confident you will get bail."

"Let's be honest, the chances of me getting bail are slim to none, there is no way in hell I will be granted bail. I appreciate your optimism, but I will be here for the foreseeable future."

He couldn't look her in the eye after her last statement. He knew it was true, he was trying to get her to be hopeful, he didn't want her fallen into even greater depression. But he realized they did in fact need to face the reality she was not going to get bail. People were going to use this as an opportunity to exact revenge for the embarrassment she caused for the DA and some of the judges. His being her lawyer was not going to help things, because people viewed him in the same light. While they were loved by those they defended, it came with a price they both were willing to pay. Neither one was concerned about offending anyone if it meant keeping innocent people in jail or getting them out.

"It is a long shot, but we will still give it a shot. We can't be negative."

She wanted to say that is easy for you to say, you aren't the one wearing this orange jumpsuit and these chains. But she agreed with him instead. They spent the rest of the time going over strategy and what to expect at the arraignment. As the time for the arraignment drew near, Alan left so he could get to the courthouse and she had to be moved so she could take the jail's transportation.

The ride to the courthouse was only ten minutes. She spent the time just looking out the window, not thinking about anything. She decided that was her problem. She had spent too much time thinking. She just wanted to let her mind go and maybe something would come to her that would help. Pulling up to the courthouse, she saw a crowd of people and multiple news vans. All defendants are usually taken through the back entrance for not only safety reasons, but to also avoid the crowds. She wasn't surprised at the sight of the crowd or the fact she was being brought through the front door. She figured Harry would make sure there was a large crowd in an effort to further embarrass her.

As she got out of the van, she could hear everyone trying to get her attention and some shouting questions at her. She kept her head up and straight, acting as if no one was there. As the officers led her up the stairs, there were even more people near the doors. The officers had to fight through the crowd to get her through. There were people shouting and pulling on her. They were finally able to get her through after what seemed like forever.

She let out a sigh of relief as she finally made it to the courtroom. The courtroom usually felt like home for her, but not today. It felt foreign. She was used to being the one greeting the defendant as they came in. This time it was Alan greeting her, with her in cuffs. He asked if she was okay when she came in. They both sat down and began going over some last-minute things before it started. Shortly after she sat down, Harry came in. He looked over at the two of them and gave a sly smile.

"Look at him, I can't wait to take that silly smile off his face. I am going to so enjoy it when he is the one in cuffs," she said as she looked over at Alan.

"We both are!"

A short time later the bailiff shouted, "All rise, the Honorable Judge Philip Harris."

Nicole heard Alan curse under his breath; she felt the same way. Judge Harris was a protégé of Judge White. They both were really close; in fact, it was Judge White that instrumental in Judge Harris becoming a judge. They both knew that whatever chances for bail she had pretty much went out the window when he came through the door.

"Good Afternoon Mr. Wallace," Judge Harris said as he looked at the District Attorney. "Mr. Keyes, is your client ready for the reading of the charges?"

"My client would like to waive the reading of the charges and enter a plea of not guilty."

"Is this correct Mrs. Jones?"

Nicole looked at him confidently and said; "Yes!"

"What do you say about bail, Mr. Wallace?"

"The prosecution requests the defendant be remanded. She is charged with the murder of seven people, to include two police officers and a Judge."

"I am inclined to agree with you, these charges are pretty serious. Do you have anything you would like to add, Mr. Keyes?"

"Yes, your honor. The defense would like to request ROR. Mrs. Jones has been a pillar of this community for years. She has extensive ties to the community and doesn't pose a flight risk. She wants to clear her name."

"Your honor, the prosecution strongly objects to ROR!"

"I am sure you do. Bail will be set at five million dollars, the defendant will surrender her passport, and will wear an ankle monitoring device."

This shocked not only Harry, but Alan and Nicole as well. None of them expected this outcome. Harry attempted to get Judge Harris's attention to reconsider, but Judge Harris cut him off before he could say anything.

"Get with my clerk to schedule the preliminary hearing!"

That was it, as the bailiff shouted, "All rise," and the Judge got up and left the room, leaving everyone in shock. Alan hugged Nicole and told her he would get her bailed out as soon as possible. Finally, a victory she thought. After the past forty-eight hours she had, she was happy she wasn't going to be spending another night in jail.

CHAPTER 35

DETECTIVE HOWARD SAT AT his desk going through paperwork, trying to see if he had overlooked anything. The more time he had to think, the worse he felt about telling everyone what he found out about Nicole. He never wanted it to get to this point. He felt bad for her; not only did she lose her friend, because her father was wrongly convicted of a crime and subsequently killed in prison, but now she was arrested possibly for a crime that she didn't commit. He cursed himself and told himself he would do everything he could do to make sure that he found all of the evidence that either exonerated her or proved she was guilty. He couldn't leave room for any doubt, not in this situation, he had to be one hundred percent sure or else he would make sure she didn't go to trial.

As he was sitting at his desk, he heard someone call his name. It was Sgt. Mary Wagner and she was there with Amber Harris.

"Good morning Detective Howard, Amber Harris wanted to see you. She said she had something to tell you and it was really important."

Sgt. Wagner left them alone as she went back to the front of the building.

"How may I help you, Ms. Harris? Did you remember something?"

"Is there somewhere else we can go talk alone?"

She seemed shaken as she asked him that question. "Sure," he said as he took her to one of the interview rooms. "Don't worry the cameras are off, no one can see or hear us in here. What is it that you would like to tell me?"

Ms. Harris sat there for a few moments, like she was trying to convince herself to tell what she knew. Detective Howard didn't want to do anything to scare her and cause her to go into a shell, so he just sat there patiently, waiting for her to get comfortable enough to talk. Then after a few moments, she finally began to speak. He could tell she was still nervous, as she barely spoke above a whisper.

"You were right about what happened that night. I was there with Arthur. We were having a good time, then all of sudden he changed. He got this look in his eye and it was like he was entirely different person, he snapped. He started hitting and choking me, calling me Laura. He was saying all kinds of crazy things." She stopped talking as she had to regain her composure. He could tell it was really traumatic for her.

"Can you tell me what he was saying?"

She looked up at the ceiling for a moment, like she was waiting for an answer to fall from the heavens. "I don't remember exactly, but it was something along the lines of why did you do this to me, I loved you. He just kept saying it over and over again as he hit me." She broke down crying.

He reached into his jacket and gave her handkerchief, as he asked her if she was okay. She nodded her head and continued.

"I thought I was going to die. I thought he was going to kill me. He was going to kill until…." She stopped talking as she held her head down.

"I know this his hard Ms. Harris, but I need for you to tell me what happened next."

She gathered herself some more and continued. "And then they showed up. I had my eyes closed getting beat, then it stopped immediately, and I didn't hear anything. When I opened my eyes there, they were in front of me. I thought they were going to kill me, but they gave me my things and told me to get out of there, they would take care of everything. So that is what I did. I left and didn't look back. I didn't know they were going to kill him."

"Is there anything you can tell me about the person that would help me identify them?"

"They had a mask on, and their voice was altered, but there was one thing, which is the reason why I am here."

Finally, some good news he thought. He sat up in his chair waiting to hear what she was about to tell him.

"I saw their eyes, they were blue. That is why I am here. Honestly, I hope you don't catch the person, because as far as I am concerned Arthur got what he deserved. But I couldn't sit here and let an innocent person pay for something they didn't do. Just to make sure I looked at a picture of Mrs. Jones's eyes and they are not blue, they are brown. She wasn't the person who saved me that night. I couldn't live with myself if I sat back and allowed an innocent person go to jail and I could have stopped it."

"Are you sure you are remembering this correctly, and who knows, this person could have been wearing contacts to change their eye color?"

"I know what I saw. If you don't believe me, that is on you, but it wasn't Nicole Jones that killed Arthur. It was someone else, someone with blue eyes. Do not contact me again, because I will forget everything I told you." She got up and left as she finished her statement.

Detective Howard sat there thinking about everything that Ms. Harris had just told him. Honestly, he didn't know if he should believe her, and if he did, how was he going to get others to believe her. It seemed like everyone was so sure that Nicole did it, it would be even harder to get them to believe him and if he was somehow able to get someone in the department to believe him, there was one other large problem, Harry Wallace. There was no way he was going to believe her. Then he realized there was no her to believe, because she wasn't going to talk anymore and that would only make it worse. He had to figure something out.

After sitting there for ten minutes, he got up and went to the Captain's office. "Captain, I think we made a mistake. I am not sure she actually did it. Amber Harris just came in." Seeing the Captain was confused as to who she was he added more information about her. "Cherry, she was with Arthur Landry the night he was killed."

"Oh, okay!"

"Well she just came in and confirmed that Arthur beat her. She thought he was going to kill her, she said he just snapped. Get this, he started calling her Laura and asking why did she do it to him, and that he loved her."

The detectives had already told the Captain they believed Arthur had beat her, so that isn't what surprised him, it was the part about calling her Laura.

"I think it is safe to assume that he killed Laura Johnson, especially when combining it with all of the other evidence."

"True, but I am not seeing how this helps Nicole."

"This last part will. She said she saw the person's eyes and they were blue. She said they were not the same eyes as the killer. She was pretty sure about it and she said it wasn't Nicole."

"Get her back in here then!"

"She said she will not repeat what she just told me. So, we are stuck. We have this information, but we can't do anything with it, because we have no witness."

"We could get a material witness warrant!"

"I don't think that would be a good idea. If we did that, she definitely won't say anything, which will only make things worse. There is something else I need to tell you as well." He decided it was time to tell someone else about Marcus.

"What is it?" The Captain could sense it was something bad, that he was about to hear.

Realizing what he was about to say was likely to illicit an animated response from the Captain, he tried to lessen the blow the before-hand.

"I apologize for not saying anything sooner, but I wasn't sure. I still am not sure, but I think it is time that I tell someone. When I talked to Trisha White and her mother, I found out that Lauraand Samuel Johnson did have a baby, twins in fact. On the night of their birth, Mrs. White told her daughter, her husband, and son-in-law that she had killed them, when in fact she had taken them to Ms. Mable Thompson."

The Captain sat there in shock and he listened to what his detective was telling him. He didn't know whether to be happy or grateful at that point.

"I was never able to confirm this, because unfortunately Ms. Thompson died before I could ask her about it. However, on the night I went back to her home to talk to her, it was the same night as Mike's death. I met her granddaughter and we went inside her home and there were pictures of Marcus."

"Wait are you telling me that Marcus is the son of Samuel Johnson?"

"I am telling you that I am not sure. The story that she gave her family about where Marcus came from didn't add up. It could be that he wasn't one of the children, because no one knows what happened to the second. So, it could be that she gave away both babies and Marcus was in fact her cousin's son. This is why I didn't say anything sooner, because honestly, I do not know. I just have more questions."

The Captain sat there in silence trying to absorb everything that he had just heard. It was a lot and he was still having a hard time trying to wrap his head around everything. This case was getting crazier by the minute. "Who all have you told about this?'

"I haven't told anyone else; you are the only one."

"Okay, let's keep this between me and you and right now. We have to figure out how to find out if this true or not. Do you know what day they were born?"

"They were born on June 20th, 1989."

"This may not mean anything, but Marcus's birthday was in September. We need to check adoption and group home records for all of the kids born around that time to see if we can find any additional leads. It may take some time, but it is a start and we have to start somewhere. We have to make sure we are working quick, because if Nicole is in fact innocent, we need to find the real killer immediately. She has been through enough already and we have put her through enough already. Take Detective Johnson with you, I trust him."

The Captain immediately called Detective Johnson and told him to come to his office. The Captain began telling him everything Detective Howard had just told him, including what Ms. Harris had told him. Just like Captain Brown, Detective Johnson was there, surprised at what he heard. "Detective Howard will fill you in on what needs to happen next. I do not need to stress how important this to each of you. This stays between us until we can prove this one way or another."

They both sat down at their desks and began the tedious task of trying to identify any children who were born on June 20th, 1989 and figure out where they were now. After three hours, they had identified three possible children, but when they contacted them, they found out two of them had moved out of the state years ago and had not been back since and the other one was dead. Detective Howard's frustration was growing; the pressure he had put on himself was making him crazy. "This is pointless, I need a break." Detective Howard got out and walked outside to his car.

If he had one, he would have taken a drink. He couldn't focus straight he was so angry. He hoped the fresh air and sun light would help him, because he was sure he was going to blow in a couple of minutes if he didn't go outside.

"What am I doing? Think, think," he told himself as he beat himself in the head. As he was standing outside, it began to rain. "Great," he thought. It was raining and the sun was out; only in Georgia would this happen. He realized his umbrella was in the backseat, so he opened the door to get it. He wasn't ready to go back inside and he didn't want to sit in his car, he didn't want to feel confined. As he opened the door and reached to get his umbrella, he saw an envelope.

It was the envelope Ms. Thompson had left for him; he had forgotten all about it. He got inside his car and closed the door behind him as he opened it. Inside, he saw there were some pictures and some documents. He looked at the documents and it was copies of two birth certificates. One was for Marcus Jones and the other was for a Mary Jo Jones. He thought it was strange at first, then he looked at the birthdays and they both were the same, the time of birth separated by ten minutes.

The name for mother was listed as Laura Johnson and the father was listed as Samuel Jones, but his signature was missing. He looked at the signature for Laura Johnson and realized she must have found out about the children somehow. "But how," he thought. He realized the only people that could probably answer that question were Ms. Thompson and Laura Johnson, but both of them were deceased. Looking at the birth certificate confirmed what he suspected: Marcus Jones was the son of Samuel Jones and he had a twin sister named Mary Jo Jones. He then looked at the pictures; it appeared to be Marcus and Mary as babies together. The other pictures were one of Marcus and the other was a picture of an unknown woman with Ms. Thompson. He suspected the older woman was likely Mary.

Detective Howard put the items back in the envelope and went inside. Detective Howard sat at his desk looking at the birth certificates and the pictures trying to make sense of what it all meant. He finally had definitive proof that Marcus was in fact the child of Samuel Johnson and he had a sister who was apparently named Mary Jo Jones. He was at his desk looking at the pictures, still trying to process the two were not just brother and sister, but were twins. They couldn't be even further from each other; one was a large black man and the other was a white woman. As he was studying the pictures, Sgt. Wagner walked up behind him.

"What are you doing with pictures of Marcus and Sgt. Allen's ex-wife?"

Detective Howard was shocked. "What did you say? Are you sure this is Sgt. Allen's wife?"

"Yes, that is Mary. The hair is different, but that is definitely her."

As Sgt. Wagner walked away, his heart sank. He remembered from the stories they told each other that Sgt. Allen's wife had died in an accidental fire. "Every time I take a step forward, something happens, and I end up taking two steps back," he thought. He wanted to throw the information in the trash can, but then he remembered something. Ms. James said someone named Mary had come to see her. He knew it was a long shot, but he had to find out to satisfy his sense of curiosity. He walked over to Detective Johnson's desk.

"You want to take a road trip with me? I will fill you on the way."

Detective Johnson got up and said "Yes."

CHAPTER 36

JO SAT IN HER basement; she could hear the children upstairs running around. She usually tried to stay out of the
basement when they were home and awake, but she had to
finish up the last batch. She was almost finished and wanted
to make sure everything was going to go according to plan
and she planned for every contingency. She had seen the
news and what had happened to Nicole Jones. She felt bad;
Nicole had been arrested for something she did, but she
couldn't think about that right now, she needed to finish.
She had a short time frame to do what she needed to do tonight, so there couldn't be any issues and if there happened
to be any, it couldn't be any she didn't plan for.

She walked up the steps and it was like the kids had a
sixth sense she was in the kitchen; they both ran to see her.
When she asked them what that noise was while she was
downstairs, they both looked at each other and got quiet.
She laughed and gave each one a kiss, as she told them the

babysitter would be there shortly and to be on their best behavior. She looked at them and was happy they had each other. While she may have not been perfect and the way she raised them may have been outside the norm, according to a lot of people, she always did her best to make sure they were happy and to make sure they always looked out for each other.

She started thinking about her childhood. Both her parents did the best they could, but she always felt like something was missing. Like there was a part of her somewhere else and she could never figure out what it was. She finally figured out what it was when she was twenty-six, after she was married and had her own kids. She got into a bad car accident when she was fifteen, almost losing her life. She was in the hospital for a month, with broken bones, severe burns on thirty percent of her body. She found out later that she needed a blood transfusion and her parents always told her that it was her father who donated blood to her. However, when she looked at her medical records, she saw something different.

Under the section for blood transfusion, the donor section was marked unknown. She thought that was strange, so she went to her parents and asked them about it. The look on their faces said it all, she didn't even need to hear what they said next. They told her she was adopted and they apologized for never telling her, but she was their daughter and they loved her. She was hurt by the betrayal. As much as she wanted to forgive them and get past it, it was hard for her to do so. She hadn't spoken to her parents in years.

The one thing she needed from them though, they couldn't provide. She wanted to know who her birth parents were, but they couldn't tell her. All they could tell her was the adoption agency they got her through. She was able to use that information to track down the person who was working the day she was brought in. It was Mrs. Georgia Faulkner. She was able to find out where she lived and went to talk to her.

She was surprised to see her, but she remembered Jo. When she spoke with her, she found out that she was not brought in by one of her birth parents, but by Mable Thompson. Mrs. Faulkner didn't know where she got her from, only that Ms. Thompson couldn't take care of her and wanted to make sure she got a better chance to grow up and be successful. Mrs. Faulkner told her that even though she brought Jo there, she cared for her deeply. In fact, she would come visit every few days to visit her. She would sit with her for hours, holding her, feeding her, making sure she was okay, up until the day she was adopted.

After she found this out, she found where Ms. Thompson lived and would drive by her house, but at first, she never went to the door; she was too afraid. She would just sit down the street and look at her house. Ms. Thompson was usually outside so she would see her often and she would always see her family stop by. Then finally one day she mustered up enough strength and walked to the front door. When Ms. Thompson opened the door, she recognized her immediately, tears started falling down her face and she gave her a big hug. She brought Jo into the house and told her how happy she was to see her, and she had never stopped thinking about her.

After a few moments of talking, Jo finally mustered up the courage to ask her who her parents were and why she took her to the home. Ms. Thompson hesitated at first, but Jo finally convinced her to tell her everything. Ms. Thompson told her about her birth parents and how both of them had been brought to her. She was shocked and didn't know what to say, after all these years she now realized why she felt like a part of her was missing. She had a brother; she was excited and sad. She wondered what he was like and what life would have been like growing up with him.

She asked her where her brother was and Ms. Thompson's response nearly put her into shock. It was Marcus Jones, someone she didn't just know, but someone who she considered family. It took her a moment to process everything and understand everything that she had just learned. She had a brother and she wondered if he would be as happy as she was. She was excited, but nervous, because she knew she had to tell him.

When she asked Ms. Thompson about her father, her joy went away. Ms. Thompson told her about how he was going to school to better himself, by becoming a lawyer and also about his family. The part about having a family shocked her, she couldn't believe it, somewhere out there she had a sister. Not only couldn't she believe that, but both her mother and father were cheating together. That was almost too much to process, she didn't know what to do or say.

Just when she thought things couldn't get any more shocking. Ms. Thompson told her about her father being arrested and convicted for being the Penny Murderer. Ms. Thompson tried convincing her that her father was innocent and would never hurt anyone, but it didn't work. She felt sick to her stomach. She remembered reading about the stories in the paper and how the evidence was pretty overwhelming. Her father was a serial killer! She didn't know what to say or do. She wondered what did that make her.

She couldn't stand to hear about her father anymore, so she changed the subject. She asked her something that was almost as painful as learning about her father. She asked her why she didn't keep them both. She wondered was she not good enough, what was it about her that made her want to give her away.

She remembered the tears in Ms. Thompson's eyes as she tried to explain it to her. She wanted to keep her, but she knew she wouldn't be able to, because it would cause questions and possibly put both of them in danger. She knew people would wonder how she suddenly had two babies, the same age, and one appeared to be white. She knew talk would spread and there would be the chance her grand-father and Victor White would find out. She couldn't take that chance, because she was afraid of what they would do to the both of them.

She told her the reason she kept Marcus and not her, was because she looked like little white girl. It was easier for her to explain keeping Marcus than it was for her to keep Jo. She told her had she known her skin would have dark-ened she may have done things differently. She did what she thought was best at the time. She then told her something that she didn't know. Ms. Thompson told her that she had actually met with four families, before finally deciding on the Davis's. Ms. Thompson told Jo that she wanted to make sure she was with a family that loved her. Ms. Thompson fought with the director to be involved in the adoption pro-cess until he finally agreed.

She could see the pain in Ms. Thompson's eye; she instantly felt sorry for her. She could not imagine what it must have been like for her to be given two kids and expect-ed to take care of them and try to keep it a secret. It hurt like hell, but she understood it. She sat there with her for a few moments in silence, then she left. But not before telling her she would keep this between them; she would not tell Marcus anything she found out today, yet. But before she got up to leave, she had to ask one more question. "Did our father ever meet us?"

Ms. Thompson paused for a second and appeared to smile briefly. She told Jo that Samuel never got to meet her, because when she was born, he was back home in Blinton for the summer. By the time he came back for the summer she had already been given up for adoption. Ms. Thompson told her that he did however meet Marcus, but he had no idea he was his son. Laura had never told him about the kids, in fact they never spoke again after she had the babies. He knew she was pregnant, but she told him she was pregnant by her husband. Ms. Thompson told her that up until Samuel was arrested, he treated Marcus like his own. She had told him that he belonged to one of her kids and they had given him to her for her to take care of. Ms. Thompson let her know that he had told her he would always be there to help the both of them, because he knew Marcus needed a male figure in his life and he knew she needed help.

It was something about that last statement that made her start seeing her father in a different light. He had his faults and there were many, but he had some good in him as well. He was helping an old woman take care of a kid that wasn't his. She left the conversation thanking Ms. Thompson for her time and she promised she would not say anything to Marcus about what she had learned. She let her know before she did, she would talk to her first so she could have the opportunity to explain everything to him at the same time.

So, anytime she saw Marcus, she would try to act normal and not let him know anything was different. It only got harder with each passing day. She tried to continue living her life, but that two was hard. She couldn't tell her husband anything, so she just kept everything to herself. She started looking into the Penny Murder case and the more she looked into it, the more she found out that her father may have actually been innocent. She started seeing things that didn't seem right and a system that didn't treat her father fair. As she was going through the stories, one of the names that popped up in the investigation was Mike Allen, her husband. This shocked her and was the day she started making her plan.

She awoke from her daydream with the sound of the doorbell; it was the babysitter. There was no need to give any last-minute instructions, she had been using the same babysitter for the past two years, so it was like she was family. She knew the kids and how to handle them. As she walked out the door, Chris, her youngest, ran up to her and handed her small piece of paper with a drawing on it. She looked at it, and told him thank you and gave him a hug. Before she got in her car, she looked back at the house and whispered, "It's almost over."

CHAPTER 37

GOVERNOR LANDRY SAT AT his desk, looking out the window. He loved coming out to his lake house. It always relaxed him and the best thing about it, no one knew where it was. It was purchased as a gift from a donor through a series of shell corporations. He had owned the lake house for a number of years and only a select few had ever been there. His own family had never even been there. He had been at the house since the story about his involvement in the alleged cover up during the Penny murder trial. He had no idea who leaked the information or how they got it, but he had people finding out. He was going to make sure they paid and it was going to be long, slow, and painful.

He was upset. Not only did he have to deal with the leak, but someone killed his son. He and his son had their differences and while he viewed him as a disappointment at times, he still loved him. The Governor was going to make that person pay as well, as soon as he figured out who it was. He knew that he was a target of this killer, but he felt relatively safe because they wouldn't be able to find him. He started thinking about the night his son came to him and told him he had killed Laura Johnson. Part of him wanted to tell him to go to hell and deal with it, but he knew it would have killed his mother. He reached out to Harry Wallace immediately for his help and it was him who came up with the plan to make it look like she was a victim of the Penny Murderer.

Now because of the both of them, he was in danger of losing everything, including his legacy; the most important thing to him. He wanted not only him, but his family to be remembered with regard. Now he was being called a racist and a murderer. While he could be called a lot of things and he had views that were not considered appropriate, he was not racist. He didn't do what he did because Samuel Johnson was black, he did it to protect his son.

Family was everything to him. Even though he was demanding of Arthur, he loved him and only wanted what was best for him. While the fear of embarrassment played a part in how he treated him, the biggest motivation was the love he had for him. He would do anything for him and had. His father treated him the same way he treated Arthur, so he thought it was how he should be. But now he started thinking maybe he should have done things differently; he realized it was too late for these thoughts or a change of heart. His son was gone and never coming back.

Now not only him, but his family was in danger of losing everything; money, legacy, and power were just a few. He didn't know how to fix it and it was driving him crazy. He was a fixer, he knew how to fix things, but this was one thing he didn't have the answer to. He promised himself if he could get out of this he would be better towards his grandchildren. He was interrupted by the doorbell. He was expecting his attorney; they were going to go over some options just in case.

When he opened the door, no one was there. He thought that was strange, as there was no one else within miles of here. He immediately ran inside and went to grab his phone. As he picked up the phone to start dialing the room went dark and he fell to the floor.

After about thirty minutes he slowly started to regain consciousness. He was still a disoriented as he tried to remember where he was and what happened. He was finally able to focus his eyes and remember where he was; he still had no idea what happened. He went to move but he couldn't, he started to get nervous. He began asking himself, did I have a stroke? He couldn't move any part of his body.

He realized he was lying in the bed, but he had no idea how he got there. The last thing he remembered was that he checked his door and there had been no one there. He was trying to look around to get an idea of what was going on, but he couldn't move his head, he could only move his eyes. The only thing he could see was the ceiling.

Jo was sitting at the foot of the bed, just watching him, not saying anything. She was enjoying watching him suffer and trying to figure out what was going on. She figured this is what her dad must have felt like when he was convicted and sentenced to death for a crime he didn't commit, unlike Governor Landry. She rubbed the needle against his leg, but he didn't notice, and she knew he wouldn't. She had given him enough rocuronium bromide to keep him from moving for the rest of the day.

After a few moments she got up, Governor Landry saw a shadow on the ceiling as if someone were walking in front of a light.

"Who is there? Who is there?" He asked repeatedly, his voice trembling with fear. He didn't know who was there or what they wanted; all he knew was he was scared. Then he thought it might be the killer and he began to panic, he tried to move again. Still no luck, he shouted out "who is there," again. Still nothing, his level of panic increased with each passing second.

Jo was begging to question herself. Is it okay, that I am enjoying this so much? She quickly dismissed the thought, after what he had done to her family, it was more than okay that she was enjoying this. After a few more moments of silence and watching him, she finally decided to announce herself.

"Good morning, Governor Landry, I hope you are enjoying the accommodations."

"Who is there, who are you?"

Jo walked over to the head of the bed and propped his head and shoulders up on pillows so he could see her. She didn't bother to wear a mask or alter her voice this time. She wanted him to see her face, the face of the person he took so much from. "Are you comfortable?" she asked.

"Who are you to do this to me? Why are you doing this? Do you know who I am?" he demanded.

She wanted to laugh, he had seen her numerous times over the past two years, but he still didn't know who she was. "Just like him to not recognize the help," she thought. "I know who you are, and you are here because of crimes you have committed. You are here because you were a part of the conspiracy that took my parents from me. You are the reason you are in this position. Your actions lead you to this moment."

Governor Landry looked confused; he had no idea what she was talking about. She could be talking about a number of people, after all as the Governor he oversaw multiple executions and even when he left office, he was involved in what some would call shady business dealings, that led to the death of some people. It didn't dawn on him that he was about to fall victim to the so-called copycat. "Tell me who you are: we can work something out. I can make you a very rich and powerful woman."

"I am not here for money; I am here for revenge. You honestly do not know why you are here?"

Governor Landry didn't know what to say. He was at a loss for words. He just looked at her with a blank look on his face. He did the only thing he could think of to hopefully get out of this. "My chest," he said as he tried to contort his face to give the impression he was in pain and having a heart attack. He figured the only way out of this was to try anything possible.

Jo just looked at him and laughed. "You can quit the act. We both know you are not having a heart attack. Stop it, you are embarrassing yourself."

"I recognize you. You work in the D.A's office. What the hell is going on? What are you doing here? Why are you doing this?"

Jo looked at him, almost feeling sorry for him. "Don't worry I will explain everything to you. I will explain everything to you, so you will know the reason why you die today."

Governor Landry's eyes got big and he started sweating.

"Don't worry you will die the same way as you let so many die while you were Governor. According to you and all your friends it is safe and painless. You want to know why you are here; you are here because your son killed my mother and you let my father die and you helped to cover both up. See, you are not innocent at all. You are the worst, you think just because of who you are, it means you and your family don't have to follow the rules. You can do whatever you want and get away with it."

Governor Landry got quiet; he didn't know what to say. He thought by coming out to his lake house, he would be able to hide from the killer. He had feared this moment. "How did you know where I was?"

"People should be really careful about what they say on the phone."

He was confused, he hadn't told anyone anything over the phone. He had always been careful about not disclosing the location of this place. He hadn't told anyone anything. "What are you talking about; I didn't tell anyone anything on the phone?"

"Not you, your lawyer. He has a pretty big mouth, and this is why we are where we are right now. Do you have any last words?"

Governor Landry didn't say anything or even acknowledge her last question. He told himself if he was going to die, he was going to die with dignity. He refused to give her the satisfaction of seeing him beg or show weakness.

She grabbed the needle and looked for a site on his arm. Governor Landry couldn't feel anything but he assumed she was looking for a vein to inject him with whatever she had in the needle. Once Jo found the vein, she slowly pierced the needle into his skin, injecting the mixture into his veins. Governor Landry could feel the poison coursing through his veins. Then all of sudden he began convulsing, he could feel his chest tighten, his skin felt like it was burning, he was in extreme pain, he wanted to call out to God, but he couldn't speak, and then everything went dark.

Jo watched him until he stopped moving, then she checked his pulse to make sure he was dead. She checked and there was nothing. She made sure she got everything that could have tied her to being there out of the home; she couldn't have a repeat of the Millers. Once she got to the main road, she pulled the phone out of her purse and called 911; "I need someone to come to 425 Hickory Lane, I just heard a man scream, I think someone is attacking him, please send help." She hung up the phone and threw it out the window into the woods and then drove away.

CHAPTER 38

NICOLE SAT ON THE bed looking at the ankle monitor, thinking to herself, how has it come to this? She had tried to remain strong through everything that had happened to her and those close to her, but she couldn't anymore. The severity and weight of everything had finally gotten to be to much. She tried to remain strong, but she was falling further into depression with each passing moment. Alan, Patricia, and Lindsay had all tried to get her to come out of the room, but she wouldn't, she couldn't. She had almost given up hope; she couldn't take one more surprise. Not only were her husband and friend dead, but she was arrested for their murders and would have to stand trial for them.

She had not eaten for the past couple of days, and she had barely drunk anything. Alan and Patricia were worried about her; they felt bad. They knew she was in pain, but there was nothing they could do to help her. They wanted to give her space, but they also didn't want to give her too much, because they knew she was in a dark place and the longer it lasted the worse it could get. Alan had been working at home, Patricia had taken some time off, and even Lindsay volunteered not to go to school so she could be there for her. They all at least wanted to be available just in case she needed someone to talk to.

Nicole turned on the TV in an effort to find something to take her mind off. She instantly regretted her decision. There on the TV was Harry Wallace talking about her and the case. She could tell he was loving this.

"I would say good afternoon, but it is anything but that. As you all have heard, Nicole Jones has been arrested and charged with the murders of Detective Marcus Jones, Melissa Landry, Judge Abraham White, Patrick and April Miller, Arthur Landry, and Sergeant Mike Allen. We plan on proving that she committed these crimes because of a long-held grudge against these individuals. That is all I can say for now. While that is a significant, that is not the reason I am with you here today. I want to talk to you about what the report from a week ago. I know some of you do not trust me and believe the things you saw on TV and my releasing a statement or even coming out here and denying it will do nothing to change that. But what I can do is through my actions show you I am committed to being as transparent as possible. So, to show you how committed I am to transparency, I am appointing a special prosecutor to go back and look at the original Penny Murder trial.

"This prosecutor will not report to me, they will work independent of the DA's office. If they find any hint of wrongdoing by me or anyone else, they have the ability to arrest that individual without getting approval from me. Ms. Ingrid Smith will be the special prosecutor. She has been with the DA's office for the past two years and has proven herself to be beyond reproach.

"I understand this doesn't solve all the problems, but hopefully it shows you all that I have nothing to hide and the investigation was conducted with no bias against Mr. Johnson. The evidence, just like over twenty years ago, will show beyond a shadow of doubt that he committed those murders." As he finished his last sentence, he stepped away so Ingrid could walk up to the podium.

Ingrid walked up to the podium and looked out at everyone. "I will keep this quick; I will not let you, the citizens of Monroe, down. I am here to make sure you get the answers you deserve. I do not work for the DA or the city; I work for you." With that she stepped away from the podium without taking any questions.

Nicole was in shock watching the press conference. She couldn't believe what she had just seen. Her initial reaction was that this was just like Harry to put on a show in order to give everyone the impression that he was stepping aside and letting someone look into the actions of individuals from the original trial. This was likely just for show. There was no way he was going to be hands-off, he could trot out this black woman to try to appease people, but she knew it was all for show. She actually felt sorry for her that she was being used this way. But then something caught her eye as she studied the individual closer. She looked and sounded familiar. She couldn't quite place it at first.

Her face was a little different, she was wearing glasses, and possibly colored contacts to hide her blue eyes. She knew who that was, but she couldn't believe it. "Jo," she whispered in shock. She paused the TV, looking at her, trying to find something, anything to show her that she was being paranoid. It couldn't be her; she was dead. She died with her kids in the fire; but what was she doing with her kids on TV? She paused the TV and went through her photos until she found one of Jo. She compared the photo with the picture on the TV. There were some differences, but she was sure it was her.

What the fuck, she thought. She just sat there trying to process everything again. She started thinking about everything that happened and how everyone felt when she died. It was a sad time, everyone that knew her loved her and her kids. Her death almost killed Mike. Everyone talked about their age difference, but it was obvious that she loved him. She saw something in him that made her want to spend the rest of her life with him. While her time knowing her was not as long as they would had liked, she still had built up a relationship with her. They had started to hang out together and do these things as friends.

Nicole grew up an only child, and after what happened to Denise, she never embraced the thought of getting close enough with someone for them to be like sisters. She had friends, but she was never as close to them as they thought. She was always afraid and then the one time she let her guard down, it happened again. While the circumstances of her death were different, she died.

She got up out of bed and took a shower and got dressed; she had to find out if she was right, and if so, why. Once she opened the door, and made it to living room, there was Patricia and Alan sitting down watching tv together. She had hoped they would be somewhere else, so she could sneak out.

They both sat up quickly when they saw her, Alan speaking first. "Good morning, it is nice to see you out of bed. Would you like to come join us?'

"I appreciate it, but I was about to run out for a second. There is something I need to take care of."

Both Alan and Patricia looked surprised. They both were wondering the same thing; what could she possibly need to take care of with everything that was going on.

"You know we love you and want to give you, your space. But neither of us think it is good for you to go out alone right now. Especially since as a requirement for your bail, you are not supposed to leave the house except for specific reasons. Given the fact you are wearing an ankle monitor, we do not want you to take any chances. We have no idea of what you are going through, but the last thing we want is for something else to happen to you. If there is somewhere you need to go, let me go with you," Patricia said with a look of concern on her face.

In her shock and need to find out what was going on, she had forgotten about the conditions of her bail. It was probably not a good idea to show up to the D.A.'s office demanding to see someone whom there was no record of her meeting and who was just appointed a special prosecutor. She realized she was going to have to take another approach to getting answers.

"You're right, it is probably not a good idea to go out by myself. I was just going to go by the house and make sure I had gotten everything out. With the upcoming sale, I just want to make sure I didn't leave anything there that I forgot about. I am sorry."

She said this in an effort to not arouse any suspicion. She had sold her house. Considering Marcus had been killed there and her need to sell it immediately, she took a loss, but she didn't care; she was never going back. She had gotten everything out that she wanted, but she figured it was good excuse to come up with that wouldn't arouse any suspicion.

"You don't have to apologize; we just don't want anything to happen to you. I know I am being a mama bear that you do not need right now, but if anything, else happens to you I am going to hurt someone. You are family and we love you."

"I love you guys too. Yes, you are being a bit of mama bear, but it is okay. I know you are only doing it to help me. I would be happy if you went with me."

She would have to figure out another way to meet with Jo, Ingrid, or whatever she was calling herself these days.

CHAPTER 39

As THEY DROVE UP the lake house, both Detective Howard and Johnson admired the scenery. They were unable to make it to Blinton because they got a call from dispatch telling them they needed to get to Lake Tindal. Lake Tindal was the most exclusive part of the city, it was mostly vacation homes for the wealthy. The homes in the area were spread out, separated by trees. So, it gave the impression to whoever lived out there, they were they are alone. Each home had its own private road that lead to it. The area was home to mostly people who were not originally from the area, including some famous people. Only a few of the people who had homes there were actually from Monroe.

As they pulled up to the home, they saw multiple police cars and the coroner's van. They were surprised to see the Captain standing outside. They knew instantly when they saw him, this had to be big. They figured it must have been someone famous, because they knew of no one from Monroe or associated with their case who lived in the area.

"We appreciate the call to come out Captain, but we are not sure why you called us out here? As much as I would love to see someone famous, I am not a big fan of seeing a dead one or working that case and the copycat."

The Captain got a serious look on his face. Both Detectives could tell what he was about to say was serious. "This call isn't about some famous person. Governor Landry is inside dead. He is another victim of the copycat."

They both looked at each other in shock. No one had seen or heard from the Governor since the bombshell report. Detective Howard had been trying to find him, but no one knew where he was. He had tried every place he could find that he was listed as an owner. He had given up hope and assumed he had left the country. But it turns out he was here the whole time.

"I know none of us really thought too much about him, but this just changed everything about this case. This case just got elevated to national attention and is going to attract everything that comes along with that. Also, you are partners now. I need for you two to get on this and find out what the hell is going on. I do not need any excuses; I need for you to find this son of bitch or we all are going to be looking for new jobs." The Captain didn't give them a chance to respond, he walked away and started talking to another one of the officers.

Detective Johnson looking at him now, "Are you ready to do this, partner?"

"Let's go, partner."

They walked inside the house and saw Sgt. Franks and while it was still early, they walked over to him to see if he had found anything yet.

"So far we only have this," Sgt. Franks said holding out the note and penny in an evidence bag. "It looks like our killer got the next person on their list. I thought we were watching him?"

Detective Howard paused while looking at the note; "We tried, but we didn't know where he was. He went into hiding right after the news report came out identifying him as playing a part in helping to convict Samuel Johnson."

"I guess he didn't do a good enough job of hiding."

"I guess not."

The note read: A Penny For Your Thoughts; What Happens When You Execute An Innocent Man?

They all looked at each other and knew what the note meant. Detective Howard had grown visibly frustrated. It was obvious what the killer was doing and who they were going after, but they still couldn't stop them. They still had no idea who the killer was. It was like they were running around in circles chasing their tails. He feared the killer would run out of victims before they were able to stop them. He wondered how many more potential targets there were; the only one he could think of was Harry Wallace, but there could be more. He had no way of knowing one way or another, he just knew he had to figure something out

Detective Howard asked Detective Johnson if he could stay out and finish talking to Sgt. Franks while he went to go talk to Adam, and then they would swap notes. Sgt. Franks told him he was in the back of the house, third door on the left. Detective Howard left the two of them there to continue to talk. As he walked to the bedroom where the body was, he looked at the pictures on the wall and noticing the furniture in the room, he whispered to himself with a laugh, "I am in the wrong line of work."

Detective Howard found Adam in the bedroom, looking at Governor Landry's body. "Good afternoon! What do you have so far?"

"It appears he was injected with something in his arm," as he pointed to the needle still in his arm. "I am going to have to get it to the lab so they can run tests, as well as do a toxicology test to see what is in his system. With the exception of the needle still being in his arm, everything else matches the other victims. However, it appears his death was more violent than that of the previous victims. It appears his neck is snapped, likely from convulsions from whatever he was injected with. It is unlikely the killer broke his neck and then poisoned him. I could be wrong, but that is what I believe. It looks like he was killed sometime this morning, I will be able to give you a more definitive time after I get him back."

"Is it okay if I look at the body?"

"Sure, go ahead, just be careful to not touch anything as usual."

Detective Howard walked over to the body, looking at it closely trying to see if he could see any potential clues. In the process he bent down and whispered in his ear, "You finally got what you deserve, you evil son of a bitch!" He continued looking over the body to see if there was anything, but he had no luck. So, he decided to look over the rest of the room to see if there was anything that could potentially help. He was just about to give up hope, until he thought he saw something at the foot of the bed. Half of it was hanging out from underneath.

When he picked it up, it appeared to be a drawing by a kid. He looked at it and thought it was odd that it was here. He didn't view Governor Landry as the sentimental type; in fact there was nothing in the home that indicated he had family. If he didn't know any better, he would have assumed he didn't have a family. Taking all of that into account, he believed the drawing belong to someone else, more than likely the killer, he thought. He grabbed an evidence bag from his pocket and placed the drawing inside. He figured it may come in handy later.

As he walked back up front, he saw Detective Johnson and Sgt. Franks still talking to each other. When he walked over, he heard them talking about some of the older details about the case. He walked over to them and handed the drawing to Detective Johnson.

"I found this in the bedroom, I don't think it belonged to Governor Landry. I think the killer may have left it in the bedroom. I am not sure what, if any value it has, but I think we should keep it just in case."

Detective Howard handed the evidence to Sgt. Franks so he could log it into evidence with any other item they found. He didn't expect them to find much of anything. After that, both he and Detective Johnson decided they would leave and head back to the precinct to talk with the Captain to see what leadership was saying and to discuss their next steps. The drive back to the precinct was a quiet one, neither man said much. They were both thinking about what lie ahead and what everything that had happened meant. They both knew they were about to walk into a mad house and experience stress like neither of them had ever of experienced.

As they got closer to the precinct, protests were still going on, but they were still pretty tame compared to how they had been when they first started. They still had not seen any violence that occurred during or after the protests ended each day. They both were thankful for that, because they knew the city was like a powder keg and one thing could cause it to explode.

As they walked inside the precinct, the secretary walked up to Detective Howard and handed him an envelope. When he asked what it was, she told him she didn't know, a courier had dropped it off for him. He took the envelope and they continued on their way to the Captain's office. They passed him as they were walking through the office and he told them to go ahead and wait in his office, he would be there in a few minutes.

Both of the detectives sat down and Detective Howard decided to open the envelope to see what was inside. As he looked at the first document, his eyes got big and his mouth dropped. The more documents he looked at, the more his shock grew. He couldn't believe what he was seeing. He must have been talking out loud and didn't realize it, because he heard Detective Johnson ask, "what is it?"

He didn't know what to tell him, so he handed him the documents he had already looked at. Detective Johnson was just as shocked as he was as he read the documents. They couldn't believe what they were looking at. Neither one of them would have thought this would have fallen into their lap. When the Captain came in, Detective Howard got up and handed them to him.

"You have got to see this!"

"What is this," the Captain asked as he started looking over the documents as well. He was just as shocked as the two Detectives were as he read them. "Where did this come from?"

"I am not sure; it was delivered here by a courier for me."

"Do we think this is legit?"

"It sure looks that way and it corroborates a lot of information we already know and it fills in the blanks for some of the information we do not know."

"Before we do anything with this information, I need for you two to verify as much as you can with this information, I am going to reach out to the D.A. and see what they say. This stays between us, until we can verify this information and the D.A. makes a decision about what to do."

CHAPTER 40

HARRY WALLACE SAT AT his table reading the various head-lines that had appeared over the past few days. He had decided to take a couple of days off. He was admiring himself; a lot of the news written about him was positive. He told himself only he could have turned a negative into a positive. There were some negative articles, but for the most part it was positive. His decision to appoint a special prosecutor to look into what transpired with the original Penny Murder trial was received well. There was nothing to find, and if by some miracle something was found, there was nothing that could be done. Someone was already tried and convicted for the crime and no judge would dare do anything that would undermine that verdict. Samuel Johnson got a fair trial and he was found guilty and no one was going to change that.

He was not worried about the investigation itself. He and Ingrid had already discussed any information she found she would share with him first and they would discuss what to do. She was a good, young prosecutor; someone he could mold and, even better, manipulate. She looked up to him and was so eager to learn, she would do whatever he wanted her to do. He figured if things took a turn for the worse, he could always blame her and make her the scapegoat somehow. She had no idea and for him that made it so much better.

He started thinking back to the events so long ago that led to all of this. He had gotten away with everything for so long, he figured no one would ever find out what had really happened. Somehow all of the information had gotten out. He had no idea who was responsible for the information, he figured it had to have been Garret James. He was always weak; he was weak when they were kids growing up. Him and his friends only allowed Garret to hang out with them because he would pay for everything and do whatever they asked, because he wanted to be a part of the group so bad. Things didn't change when they got older, Garret still would do anything to be his friend. He was able to use his connections to get Garret assigned as the defense attorney for Samuel Johnson and from there he basically told him what to do.

He smiled at the thought the way he manipulated the whole thing at the time. It was a work of genius, but now it had fallen apart. Thankfully, him and Ingrid were on the same page, but if that somehow changed, he was prepared to leave the country. He had home villa Positano, a small town on the coast in Italy no one knew about. He was ready to go at a moment's notice, he had money and there was nothing anyone could do to stop him. But there was no need for that, because he was so much smarter than everyone else.

While he should have felt bad for his former partner, Mike Allen, he didn't. He couldn't believe he was that stupid to fall for everything. The photos for his fiancée's so-called hit and run were actually staged. The Governor had come up with the plan and they were able to get Joanne to go along with the plan, all it took was money to get her to go along with the plan. "I should give her a call," he thought to himself. They had remained in contact over the years, she was in California living her life. He wanted to tell Mike he knew where she was and he was actually seeing her, just to make him feel worse. But he realized that would cause the plan to fall apart. He couldn't understand Mike, it was obvious he was not going to advance in the department, but he still stayed for all those years. He was pretty sure he knew both him and Governor Landry were the reason he never advanced beyond Sergeant.

He felt bad for Governor Landry, he didn't deserve to die in the manner that he did. He had heard his death was painful, but he thought, better him than me. The other downside to his death, was that he was going to have to drop the charges against Nicole. That was the worst part about it. He had relished her arrest and her being dragged through the headlines in a negative manner. She was getting what she deserved, and he didn't want it to end. He could have dropped the charges when Governor Landry died a couple of days ago, but he wanted to make her sit and think about everything for a few more days and to give himself time to write a speech that would deflect any blowback from his office, to the police department.

Wallace had just decided it was time to write his speech. As he was about to start typing, there was a knock at the door. He was wondering who it was that would be bothering him this early in the morning. He ignored it, because he figured they would go away. No one he knew would be bothering him and everyone knew that if you were going to come see him, you better call first or you would not be getting into his home. He heard the knock again, he tried to ignore it, but he heard it again. He was frustrated and angry at this point, so he decided to get up and go see who was at the door and give them a piece of his mind.

When he opened the door, he was surprised it to see Detective Howard and Detective Johnson. "Good morning, gentlemen. I am not sure why you are here bothering me at my home. I am off today, but will be back in my office tomorrow if you need to talk to me." He didn't wait for them to respond, as he began to close the door. However, the door stopped suddenly. When he looked on the other side of the door, he saw Detective Howard had put stopped the door with his hand.

"What the hell, Detective? I am going to need for you to step away from my door and leave my house."

"I am sorry but that is not going to happen. You are going to have to come with us."

"What the hell are you talking about?"

"Harry Wallace, you are under arrest for the murder of Maureen Trudeau, Isaiah Forester, Daniel Morehouse, Diane Sullivan, Eric Washington, Danny White, Cynthia Brown, Jimbo Baker, Luara Johnson, Elizabeth Turner, Jennifer Thomas, Natalie Baker, and Samuel Johnson." Detective Howard didn't need to say all of their names, but he wanted Harry Wallace to know why he was being arrested. He wanted him to hear the names of all his victims, to include Samuel Johnson.

"What the hell are you talking about? You can't arrest me, let alone for something someone has already been convicted of."

"I don't know anything about all of that, but all I know is I have a signed arrest warrant, so you are under arrest. You can either come peacefully or we will use force. Honestly, I am hoping you resist."

"You will be sorry for this! You have no idea who you are messing with. I will be out by the end of the day and you both will be looking for new jobs when I do."

Detective Howard began reading him his Miranda Rights as Detective Johnson put the cuffs on him. Just as they were about to walk out the door for the building,

Detective Howard looked at him and whispered, "Say hello to the public."

Once they walked out the door, there were numerous reporters and citizens out front, as if they had been waiting for him to come out. Harry just held his head down, ignoring the reporters shouting questions at him and the sounds of others saying lock him up. Both Detective Howard and Johnson slowed down purposefully, in order for reporters to get as many pictures as possible and to prolong Harry's time in the spotlight.

"You two are slick, just wait, you both will pay for this," he said once they got in the car.

Neither detective acknowledge him, and they both enjoyed the ride to the precinct. The sounds of Harry Wallace complaining only made it that much better.

Nicole was at the station, as she had officially had the charges against her dropped and had gotten that god-awful ankle monitor taken off. She was sitting in the Captain's office, as he apologized repeatedly for everything that she had been through. He didn't try to make any excuses. He put it all on him and wasn't going to pass the blame. Nicole appreciated it, but she understood he was under pressure and even though he tried to deny it, she knew who ultimately made the decision to have her arrested.

As they were sitting there talking, Nicole looked outside of his office and saw Detective Howard and Johnson bringing Harry Wallace through the building. Nicole got up and started walking towards them. The Captain called her name, but she kept walking, she didn't hear him. She was on them to hear anything they said. She kept walking until she had made her way to them and she was face to face with Harry Wallace.

"What do you want? Are you here to gloat? If you are, go ahead, but don't get to comfortable, because this is only temporary. I will be out by the end of the day. They don't have anything on me."

Nicole looked at him and simply said, "I'll pray for you," and she walked away with a smile on her face.

Detective Howard and Johnson led him into the interview room, but before they could sit him down, he immediately said, "I want to speak with my lawyer, I have nothing to say to the two of you."

After waiting what felt like an eternity his lawyer finally showed up. His lawyer's name was Paul Southernland. He grew up in the area and was considered one of the top defense attorneys, not just in the city, but in the region.

"What the hell took you so long to get here?"

"I went by the D.A.'s office to try to find out what the hell is going on. No one would talk to me."

"What do you mean no one would talk to you? What about Ingrid?"

"She was the one who told them not to talk to me. I am not sure what they have, but whatever it is, it has to be damning."

"Hold up, what do you mean she told them not to talk to you. Who does she think she is?"

"She is the one with all of the power in this case, since you made her the special prosecutor and since you are in jail, she is the one that has all of the power in this situation and no one else can do anything about it."

"Get me the hell out of here and I will deal with her."

"Unfortunately, you can't do anything or even talk to her about this case when you get out. You more than anyone should know that you will not be getting out of here today. You will have to wait until your arraignment tomorrow at the earliest; the way you wanted the system to work here. After I leave here, I am going to continue to see what I can do to find out what information they have and prepare to have these charges dropped tomorrow, because someone has been tried and convicted for these crimes already. I know it sucks, but I need for you to deal with this tonight and I will take care of everything tomorrow."

Harry didn't say anything, he simply waved him off. He realized he was stuck here for tonight, but he was going to make sure that everyone that was involved in this would pay for what they had done to him.

Both Detective Howard and Johnson waited at their desk talking about everything that had transpired. Finally arresting the person responsible for the crimes that Samuel Johnson was convicted for was a big step. While he was now dead, at least they would be able to clear his name. This would probably do little to console his family or those who were impacted by his conviction; in fact, it would probably only create more pain and angst for them. There would be a period of time during which things would get bad in the city and if for some reason Harry Wallace was acquitted or didn't face trial for what he did, then things would explode.

While all those things were important, they had something more important to focus on. They still had to find out who the copycat was and how and if they were connected to Mary Jo Jones, before someone else was killed. All of that was easier said than done, but they knew where they could start. They both realized Nicole knew her and may be able to provide them information that may be helpful.

They knew getting Nicole to not only talk to them, but to trust them was going to be hard. But they both knew they had to find a way to make it happen. They had to do something, they couldn't just sit there, because they had no idea what this new killer had planned next. All they knew was this person had killed two of their own and they were not going to let them get away with it. They were going to do all they could to find this killer and bring them to justice.

As they were getting ready to finish up for the day, Hercules's phone rang. As he was on the phone talking, Detective Howard noticed the change in not only his voice, but his face as well. Something was going on and he could tell it wasn't good. Thoughts began racing to his head as to what could be going on and one of them were good. He decided to try to focus on paperwork to keep himself from going crazy trying to figure out who was talking to and what they were talking about.

Once Hercules got off the phone it took him a moment to process what he had just heard and he still couldn't believe it. He was so lost in the moment it took him a while to process what he had just heard. He was getting frustrated with not just what he had been told, but with everything else that had happened as well.

After a few moments he was able to compose himself. He saw his new partner working on paperwork and got his attention. "Hey partner, that was the Captain; they found Adam's body in his home. He is dead!" Sensing he was about to get asked more questions, he said, "we do not know any more information, at this time, we have to go out to his home to find out what is going on.

They both looked at each other in silence and just stood there, paralyzed in the moment. They realized things were only going to get worse if they didn't find out what was going on. Walking out the door, Detective Howard couldn't help but let more lingering doubt about everything that had occurred creep back in. "What the hell is going on," he thought to himself.

CHAPTER 41

Jo woke up that morning refreshed. It was the best night's sleep she had had in a long time. She sat at the table, looking at her kids and enjoying the moment. She had done it; she had gotten revenge for the murder of her father. She still had a long way to go, but she wanted to enjoy the moment. She was able to accomplish everything she had set out to do so far. Now it was time for the hard part. She could have killed Harry, but she wanted to make him suffer. She wanted to expose him for what he did not only to her father, but all the other victims as well.

When she first came up with this plan, she wanted to make his suffering slow, but to also punish everyone else. She hated Mike Allen, Mellissa Landry, April Miller, Arthur Landry, Governor Landry, Abraham White, and Garret James. She didn't feel the least bit upset or sad for anything she had done. They all deserved to die, she thought. She believed death was to nice of a fate for Harry Wallace, she wanted him to be exposed and for everyone to see him for the monster he was. She decided the best way to this, was by forcing him to stand trial for his actions. She knew it was not going to get any easier, but she was ready for the next steps, she had to see it through.

She knew the longer this lasted, the greater the risk of someone finding out about her. It was a risk she was willing to take because she had to see it through and she had to be the person. She had spent the past seven years working to this moment. After she faked her death, she went to law school under her new identity. One of the good things about being married to a cop: she was able to get access to his files and she found someone to help her get a new identity. She took every precaution to make sure she couldn't be traced back to him. She had convinced him that it was best for him to leave the area, because the police knew about him and it was only a matter of time before he was arrested.

The hardest part was setting the fire and burning the bodies of the mother and two children inside. They were already dead, she had a friend who was able to help her not only find the bodies, but to make it appear that it was actually her and her kids. Even though they were dead, she still thought about them to this day. She hated that she had done it, one thing that made it somewhat easier was they didn't have any family, so they weren't missed, which on some level made it even sadder.

While her father and mother may not have been proud of everything she had done, they would at least be able to appreciate this next part. She was going to make the person pay who was responsible for the death of her father and covered up the murder of her mother by using the system that had failed them. Getting a job at the DA's office and gaining the trust of Harry was easier than she thought. She had started working there a year prior and was able to move up through the office, quickly gaining Harry's trust.

Not only was she a talented litigator, but she stroked his ego as well. She took the same position as him on everything, even when she didn't agree with it. It was all a part of her plan. It had worked, they both were working side by side and she was able to convince him to let her be the special prosecutor. She was able to convince him that she would keep him informed and no matter what she found; she would clear him of any wrongdoing. Working with him every day for the past couple of years was hard, and every day she felt like she needed to take five baths when she got home.

She hated what she put through her kids through. Luckily, they were both young so they didn't remember anything. She had told them their father had died in an accident. She knew it was cruel, but she couldn't tell them the truth. She could no longer continue living her old life like everything was perfect. She wanted to cause Mike as much pain as he caused her family. She loved him more than anything when they first met and didn't mind the age difference or the fact, he was white. She loved him for the person she thought he was. But when she learned the truth it almost broke her. She remembered being in a trance for days, trying to process everything she had learned.

The one regret she had, was not telling Marcus they were brother and sister. She had went to tell him the night of his death. She thought it was strange that Mike came out of the house, looking suspicious. She didn't think anything of it at the time. She rang the doorbell, but there was no answer. But when she tried the door, it was unlocked. As she went in the house calling his name, she didn't get a response. When she went up to the bedroom, she found him dead lying in bed. She kneeled beside the beside the bed, looking at him, crying uncontrollably. Her brother was dead and then she realized Mike had killed him. In that moment she decided it was time to start her plan. She hated making it appear that Marcus was killed by someone else other than Mike, but she knew he would eventually be punished. But she also knew that it would confuse him as well, because he would know something was not right, because he killed him, or so he thought.

She looked at her watch and realized it was time to go; she had to get the kids to school and she had to get to the courthouse for the arraignment. She told the kids it was time to go and as usual they both acted like they didn't want to. She was finally able to get them up and to grab their things. As she watched them walk out the door, she realized they could never find out about any of this. They couldn't know who their grandfather was, his family, or the things she had done to get justice for him. She also realized she couldn't get caught, because it would crush them. She knew what it was like to have a parent who was a convicted murderer. She had taken so much from them as well through this process. She had killed their father, the man who at one point she loved more than anyone. She still couldn't believe that he killed Marcus.

After she dropped the kids off at school, it didn't take her long to get to the courthouse. The courthouse was only ten minutes form their school. As she walked up the steps to go inside the building, she readied herself for what was about to happen. She had to be on her game or else this would end before it even got started. She looked forward to the moment when she looked over at Harry and he saw her as the person who was going to be responsible for him going to jail and his life being ruined. She smiled at the thought.

As she walked into Courtroom Number 9, Harry and his attorneys were already there. They both made eye contact as she went to her table. He gave her a look like he was cursing her for what she was doing, but she rather enjoyed it and had to turn her head to keep from showing the smile on her face. She sat down and began pulling out the paperwork she needed for this morning's proceedings, making sure everything was organized properly.

After a few moments the bailiff shouted, "All rise, the Honorable Judge Dianne Lewis."

She had never met Judge Lewis before, but she had heard she was fair.

"You may be seated," she said as she took her seat. "Good morning everyone, we have before us the case of The People vs. Harry Wallace for the murders of Maureen Trudeau, Isaiah Forester, Daniel Morehouse, Diane Sullivan, Eric Washington, Danny White, Cynthia Brown, Jimbo Baker, Luara Johnson, Elizabeth Turner, Jennifer Thomas, Natalie Baker, and Samuel Johnson. How does the defendant plead?"

"Your honor before the defendant pleads, he should not be arrested for these crimes. Someone has already been tried and convicted for these crimes already. As we all know you can't convict two people for the same crimes."

"Normally, I would say this isn't the appropriate time for this argument, this is a unique circumstance. I must say Ms. Smith, I find these charges a bit troubling giving someone, as the defense says, has already been tried and convicted for these crimes."

Jo expected this, but plans had already been put into motion to eliminate this argument. "I understand your concerns, but the process for vacating the conviction of Mr. Samuel Johnson, after which his conviction will be expunged from his records, has begun. The prosecution has already signed off on it and Judge David Blair has already signed off on it. So, by the end of the day, Mr. Johnson's record will show he was never convicted of these murders."

Harry didn't give her chance to continue with her statement as he stood up and interrupted. "Who signed off on this? I am still the DA and this needs to be approved by me and I assure I would have not signed off on this, because he was guilty."

"Mr. Southernland can you get your client under control. He is not to speak during these proceedings unless he is asked a question." Judge Lewis said as she looked at Harry sternly. "Please continue, Ms. Smith."

"Thank you, Your Honor. I would like to point out to the defense that in regard to this manner I have the final approval, which he knowingly gave to me when he made me the Special Prosecutor. So, in line with my appointed duties, it became apparent through evidence we will present during trial that Mr. Johnson was the victim of a justice system that purposely fabricated evidence and violated his rights. Some of those violations were committed by the defendant in an effort to cover up that he was in fact the one to commit the crimes. As you can see from these documents, the process to have his sentence vacated is already in motion, as I stated, and will be complete today." Jo held out the paperwork for the bailiff, who grabbed them and handed them to the judge."

"Everything looks in order, so it appears Mr. Southernland your client will be the only person charged with these crimes. So, I ask you again; how does your client plead?"

A look of dejection came over Mr. Southernland's face and one of anger came over Harry's face. Harry couldn't believe what was happening, this was actually moving forward and all of the work he did was being undone by this ungrateful bitch.

"My client pleads not guilty and waves the reading of the charges, your honor."

"What is the people's position on bail?"

"Given the severity of the crimes committed by the defendant, the steps he took to cover the crime up, including framing an innocent man who was convicted of the crimes, the fact he has the ability to flee the country, and at the time of these crimes he had sworn an oath to protect and defend. He has access to a substantial amount of money in offshore accounts, as well as homes in countries with non-extradition treaties that we know about and there are probably some we do not know about. As a result of all this, the prosecution is asking this defendant not be granted bail."

"Your honor, that is preposterous. My client has been an upstanding member of this community his entire life and will stay here to fight these bogus charges so he can clear his name."

"Bail denied! I cannot in good conscience give the defendant bail when taking all of this into consideration. Your client, more than anyone, knows that anyone charged with the crimes that he is charged with should not and would not get bail if he were the prosecutor. Get with my clerk to set up a date for the preliminary hearing. That will conclude these proceedings, everyone have a great day."

"All rise."

With that, Jo walked out of the courtroom. She could hear Harry yelling at her, but she refused to turn around and acknowledge him. She kept walking out of the courtroom as if she didn't hear anything. As she walked outside the courtroom, she saw James Carter on the steps of the courtroom, with the Johnson family, her family. He was giving a press conference talking about the injustice the family had experienced and how the system failed Samuel Johnson. She wanted so much to go over to them and tell them, everything would be okay, she would make sure of it. But she couldn't and would never be able to tell them.

Seeing them on the steps put a damper on the excitement she was feeling from earlier. She needed to see her kids. She wanted to hold them and just spend time with them after everything that had happened. When she went and picked them up, neither was as excited as she thought they would be to be getting out of school early, but she told them they were going to have a party, make all their favorite foods, and play games, their demeanor changed. They had to stop by the store to grab some supplies before they went home.

When they finally made it home, she told them to take their things upstairs and prepare for the party. They both ran upstairs excited about their upcoming party. While they were doing that, she started bringing the groceries and supplies inside. Seeing the number of items, she purchased she had had no intention of buying, she told herself she should have probably gone to the store before picking the kids up.

She paused for a moment as she was in the kitchen putting things away and getting things ready for the party. She started to prep herself for what lay ahead. She was about to go to war with Harry Wallace and she couldn't lose. She decided she wanted to turn the T.V on and see what was being said about everything. When she turned to the news, she was shocked. On the screen was the face of Adam Anderson, as the news anchor said "We have breaking news, Adam Anderson the City Coroner was found dead today. Stay tuned with us for more updates."

She stood there paralyzed in the moment. She didn't even know what to say or do. She didn't hear the doorbell ring and subsequently her daughter walking up behind her.

"Mommy," her daughter said.

Jo tried to regain her composure before she turned around to see what it was her daughter wanted. "Yes," she said as she began to turn around.

As she turned around, her daughter said, "Mommy, she says she is a friend of yours." When she turned around, she was shocked at who was standing in front of her.

"Hi, Jo!" said Nicole.

ABOUT THE AUTHOR

JAMES SMITH GREW UP in a small town in Georgia with a love for creative writing and always dreamed of writing a book. He retired after twenty years in the US Army, where he received two Bronze Stars and countless other awards and decorations. He also got both his BA in Criminal Justice and MS in Performance Improvement while serving in the military. When he retired in 2018, he revived his dream of being an author. This is his debut novel. His goal was to create not only a great story, but a series that engages the reader, introducing them to characters they can love, hate, and sometimes both.

James is married with two daughters, and they currently live in Georgia.

CPSIA information can be obtained
at www.ICGtesting.com
Printed in the USA
LVHW051134160321
681669LV00021B/883

9 781649 907035